ONE SUITOR WAS DISMALLY DULL

Celina had never imagined that a gentleman could be as thoroughly worthy and as completely uninteresting as Mr. Lawrence Coleraine, the aristocratic clergyman who persisted in promising her unending wedded bliss.

THE OTHER WAS DANGEROUSLY ATTRACTIVE

Celina could not imagine what the lordly Marquess of Wroxton could see in her—when she was exercising all her wits to turn his eyes and affections in a more suitable direction.

Celina was torn between a marriage that would consign her to a life of perfectly proper boredom and a marriage that would ruin the lives of those she was pledged to help as she desperately tried to make up her mind and not listen to her heart. . . .

The Accessible Aunt

The Accessible Aunt

by

Vanessa Gray

NAL BOOKS ARE AVAILABLE AT QUANTITY DISCOUNTS WHEN USED TO PROMOTE PRODUCTS OR SERVICES. FOR INFORMATION PLEASE WRITE TO PREMIUM MARKETING DIVISION, THE NEW AMERICAN LIBRARY, INC., 1633 *BROADWAY, NEW YORK, NEW YORK* 10019.

SIGNET, SIGNET CLASSIC, MENTOR, PLUME, MERIDIAN AND NAL *BOOKS*
are published by The New American Library, Inc.,
1633 Broadway, New York, New York 10019

First Printing, January, 1984

1 2 3 4 5 6 7 8 9

PRINTED IN THE UNITED STATES OF AMERICA

Chapter I

Celina Forsyth, the tenant of the Dower House on the estate of her brother, stood in the doorway of the front bedroom upstairs, watching its present occupant with an expression of some sadness, mingled with affection and a touch of resignation on her clear-cut features.

"One would think, Mary, you were planning to be gone for a year. Surely two trunks are somewhat excessive for only a month's absence."

Mary Remington, a distant cousin and presently companion to Celina, laughed. "It is so kind of Edmund to lend me a carriage for the journey. It would seem a waste if I did not avail myself of the opportunity to take my trunks. If it were left to my own family, I should have to travel by the mail coach."

"Nonsense!" said Celina stoutly. "I should not have allowed any such ramshackle arrangement. If my brother had not come through, you would have traveled in my own carriage."

Mary took a last look around. "I think I have forgotten something. I shall probably remember what it is just past Bartonville."

With a rush of affection for her friend, Celina slipped her hand through Mary's arm and pulled her gently toward the stairs. "Come down and have some tea. Elkins will cord your trunks, and I am persuaded Polly is already standing on the doorstep lest the coach depart without her."

Celina was not in the current fashion of beauty. Her fair hair had a regrettable tendency to curl in the most common manner, and her features were not quite regular. Her only real asset was a pair of magnificent eyes. Their dark-gray color was unusual, but even more rare was the hint of amusement that lurked in them. After two uneventful Seasons she had returned home with a realistic appraisal of her probable future, and now, at the age of twenty-six, she had gained if not resignation at least acceptance of her unmarried state.

Mary Remington had been easily persuaded to come to the Dower House as her companion. Now Mary was to spend a month with her own scattered family on the occasion of the wedding of one of them, and Celina did not look forward to her absence.

Mrs. Elkins brought tea into the small parlor. "They sent word," she announced, "that the coach would be here in half an hour. The land knows, Miss Remington, when you'll get a chance to eat again. I thought you'd best have a cup of real tea to hold you through the day. That slop they serve in inns, begging your pardon Miss Forsyth, ain't fit for a cat."

After the cook had left, Mary said, "What will you do while I'm gone, Celina? Not that you won't find entertainment enough, but I confess I am curious."

"I'll have my family," Celina said stoutly.

"That almost makes me change my mind about going," said Mary dryly. "You'll be up at the Manor three times a day, embroiled in their stews—"

"But they are the only family I have," Celina said softly. Mary recognized Celina's state of mind. She had more than once tried to protect Celina from her relations, but it would take a miracle—or a disaster—to show her the true state of affairs.

Celina's life since she had moved to the Dower House on her return from London had fallen into a deep rut. Her family called her, and she came. It mattered little that her sister-in-law, Eleanor, was a selfish, jealous woman and that her eldest niece, Lydia, just home from her first Season in London, clung to Celina like a drowning man to a lifeboat. Nor did it matter much to Celina that her second niece, Nelly, approached life like a whirlwind, sweeping all before her, nor—

Such thoughts were futile and lowered Celina's spirits past enduring. Summoning the lively sense of humor that lay just below the surface, Celina laughed. "I may get married. I had expected to spend my days unwed—and therefore unperturbed, for you must know that I see very little advantage in the married state."

"Doth the lady protest too much?" murmured Mary, biting into a macaroon.

"But now," Celina swept on, ignoring Mary's remark, "with such an estimable gentleman on our doorstep, I wonder if I should reconsider my conclusions."

Mary's bright eyes danced. "The curate, Celina? Pray do not cry the banns until I return!"

Celina affected to brood over her answer. "N-no, I think not, Mary. I must first strive to achieve sufficient patience to suffer his sermons."

"One wouldn't have to go to church, would one?"

"Or listen, if it came to that. Not that he is a catch to be disdained, you know. The Honorable Lawrence Coleraine—the name has a nice ring to it."

"Celina, will you ever be serious? Your sense of humor will lead you into trouble, I warrant you."

"You think so? I know my sister-in-law, Eleanor, says as much quite often, but then she has no humor of her own, and I must conclude that she is envious."

"No doubt, but nonetheless, Celina, your lively spirits will lead you astray."

Celina, perhaps to keep at bay the real loneliness that would invade her the moment that her brother's coach, bearing Mary and her maid, Polly, disappeared down the driveway, clung to her wispy fancy. "Very well, then, I shall seriously consider the Honorable Lawrence. You must know that only five people stand between him and the earldom. And truly, I have little ambition. I shall be well content to dream of being Countess of Rommillies at five removes."

Mary, tolerant to her bones, nevertheless felt anger rising in her. "Celina, you are abominable. You really are not considering him. It is quite beyond decorum that you make such fun of him."

Celina, unabashed, yet had one more arrow in her quiver. "Too bad, for I so enjoy watching Edmund's face when Mr. Coleraine begins one of his sermons about his precious sheep. My brother thinks of course that the subject has four legs—"

Celina did not know quite why she had pursued the stupid fancy to its death. She was as a rule calm, even serene, and her lively intelligence leaped in her speaking eyes. But there was no time to wonder. She glanced sidelong at Mary. Proffering an olive twig, she said, "Pray do not be gone more than a month, Mary, for I confess I shall be desolate enough to do anything in your absence. Even, heaven forbid, give way to more foolish raillery and disgust everyone around me."

Mary smiled sunnily. "Believe me, I shall not worry about you. My dear sensible friend—you could not lose your head. We all depend on your steadiness. Your family does, and of course I do."

Celina was saved from answering by a rap on the dolphin knocker, clearly heard in the parlor.

"Surely that cannot be Edmund so soon?" cried Mary. "Where is my cloak? Polly! That girl is never around when I need her."

"I did not hear carriage wheels," Celina pointed out, but Mary had already left the room.

It was indeed not Edmund. The visitor burst through

the door to the parlor, and suddenly the room seemed overfull.

"Aunt Celina," cried Nelly, "you must help me!"

Mary's recent remarks still lingering in her ears, Celina was startled. *You must help me!* Her treacherous memory, rather than soothing her, maliciously pointed out that she had heard these very words more times than she could count. And, said Memory, have you ever heard the reverse?

Celina banished Memory. Edmund's children were in truth the only family she had, and why should she not help them? She gathered her shattered calm together and presented her serene countenance to her troubled niece.

"What is it, Nelly? I gather that some disaster has struck the family."

"How can you be so calm, Aunt? Disaster's the proper word." She rescued her shawl, which was slipping from her shoulders, and cried out, "Henry's leave is over!"

"Is that all?" Celina clutched at her common sense, as though at an anchor. "But you knew that he must return to his regiment. I believe you yourself informed me."

"Of course I knew it. Henry has no secrets from me. But don't you see? I expected to be married by now. Henry's got the most darling little cottage, a good ten miles from his parents. A good thing, too, for you know I cannot abide them."

Nor can they be ecstatic over the thought of their only son marrying Nelly, thought Celina. But she held her tongue.

"Surely you cannot be serious. Your mother would never let you be married in such haste. And do sit down, Nelly. Your pacing to and fro like that gives me the headache."

"Headache? What is that when my life is ruined?"

Nevertheless, Nelly sat down, sitting on the edge of the chair as though the slightest notion would bring her to her feet again.

"Ruined, Nelly?" said Celina soothingly. "Surely not. You must expect to marry Henry sometime in the future."

Please God, thought Celina, that Henry had not been

revolted by Nelly's constant histrionics. It was beyond question that she would not be a peaceable wife. But there had been no suggestion, she reminded herself, that Henry wanted a peaceable wife. It was all very tiring.

"Future!"

"I do wish, Nelly, you would not echo my every word. Since you have not married him in the past, then it must be the future."

"Mama won't even let us be engaged!" Nelly said tragically.

"I do believe," said Celina pacifically, "that I have heard this news before."

"Not this, Aunt. I may not be betrothed to Henry until—" She broke off. "The injustice of it all! What has she to do with me, I should like to know!"

Celina's head began to ache in earnest. She closed her eyes. Nelly peered at her. "You are not listening! Nobody cares. Even you, Aunt Celina. I was persuaded you would take my part."

"I do not wish to oppose your mother—" said Celina quietly.

"Wait till you hear what a maggot my mother's got in her head now!"

"Nelly, such want of proper respect toward your parent I shall not allow."

"Oh, all right. But listen to me please, dear Aunt. My mother will not allow me even to be betrothed to Henry until Lydia is *wed*!"

Celina, startled, opened her eyes. "Surely not," she said before she thought.

"You see," said Nelly in triumph. "It is totally beyond everything. Lydia will never wed. She had a whole Season in London, and"—Nelly lowered her voice dramatically—"she didn't take!"

"Now, Nelly, that's not true."

"She did not have *one single offer*!" stated Nelly, emphasizing each word so that Celina could not mistake the depth of the disaster. "Not one! And what shall I ever do?"

Celina's sense of humor came to her rescue. Not for a minute did Nelly bemoan her elder sister's unhappy fate. Nor did she spare a moment for her mother's undoubtedly real concern that Lydia's chances would be spoiled if her younger sister was married first. Surely even Nelly must see that questions might arise were she to marry, especially as she was clearly not prepared to wait for a decent interval between betrothal and vows.

Celina mulled over several choices of retort and dismissed them all. Nelly's sensibilities were sufficiently exacerbated as it was. "Well," she said tentatively, "I can see it is very distressing—"

"It's disastrous! Dear Aunt, will you help me?"

"Help you?" said Celina helplessly.

"You're my last resort." Nelly, calmer now, summoned up all her powers of persuasion. "No one else cares, Aunt Celina. I've never come to you yet but that you straightened it all out—" She stopped short, thinking it might be better not to remind her aunt of previous demands made on her, of which there had been a great deal too many. She fell diplomatically silent.

"I don't see what I can do," Celina pointed out. "After all, I cannot wave a wand and provide a husband for Lydia."

"Of course not," said Nelly quickly. It was clear that whether or not Lydia remained a spinster for the rest of her natural life had no claim on Nelly's sisterly feelings or even on her attention. The help she demanded was entirely on her own account.

"Talk to my mother. I am persuaded she will listen to you."

"But really, Nelly, your mother would consider me quite forward, and rightly so, if I were to point out that she was wrong."

Her reply was unfortunately phrased. Nelly pounced.

"Then you do think it gigantically unfair! I knew you would! And I know you can persuade—"

Whatever she was about to say was forever lost. The sound of carriage wheels turning into the gravel drive to the Dower House came clearly through the windows, open to the early September breeze.

A swift glance was sufficient for Nelly. "It's Papa! He won't half be pleased to find me here. He doesn't want Lydia to marry, you know. She's his favorite, and he wants her at home. Dear Aunt," she said quickly, picking up her shawl, "you are the only one who understands. I knew you'd help me!"

With the quick smile that must have charmed Celina once more if it hadn't seemed so calculated, Nelly vanished through the inner door of the parlor, on her way out through Mrs. Elkins's kitchen.

Celina leaned back in her chair, feeling much as she imagined a piece of flotsam might feel as the last wave tossed it on the beach. Edmund had come with his carriage to see Mary off on her journey. She could hear his firm step on the porch. She opened her eyes and saw Mary standing in the doorway through which Nelly had just vanished.

"A Cheltenham tragedy?" said Mary, lifting her eyebrows.

Celina shook her head slightly. "A temporary upset," she said, hoping she spoke the truth but aware of a strong doubt.

Edmund was a most satisfactory brother, she decided, watching him say everything that was civil to Mary. He handed her up into the coach and saw that Polly was comfortable and possessed of her mistress's bandbox, which she would keep with her inside the vehicle. He had lent Mary not only his coach and coachman but also a groom and a footman for the two days' journey.

Celina stood beside him on the step as they watched the coach, the two corded trunks securely strapped on behind, travel down the drive and turn into the main drive toward the road beyond the gates.

Somewhat to her surprise he turned with her and came into the house.

"How nice of you to stay for a few moments, Edmund," she said. "I confess the house seems quite empty already. How I shall support her absence for a month I can't quite think." She laughed shakily. "Shall I ring for something? Some Madeira, perhaps? There's a bottle of Father's in the dining room."

He shook his head impatiently. "I want to talk to you."

I really cannot support another discussion of Nelly's grievances, she thought, and wished she could simply say as much. But she knew she couldn't refuse at least to listen to Edmund. She sat down again and fixed her eyes, in which there was now no amusement, on him.

He was curiously tentative, as though he did not know how to begin. At length he ventured, "Are you happy, Celina?"

The question was so at variance with what she expected that she laughed. "Don't jib, Edmund. I laughed only because I did not expect such a question from you."

"From whom, then, if not me?" he demanded.

"Well, now that I think of it, not from anyone."

"I'm serious, Celina."

"I can see that. My apologies, Edmund. Truly I am not laughing at you." She took a moment to consider and finally said, "Yes, I think so. I am as happy, I suppose, as I have ever been." Or am likely to be, she added silently.

"Will you be content to live here in the Dower House all your life?"

"What are you getting at, Edmund? Surely you don't wish me to remove from this house?"

"Of course not. You know it would be yours as long as you want it even if your tenancy wasn't a provision of Father's will."

He took a couple of turns around the room. If her visitors didn't sometime sit down, she thought wildly, all this pacing would wear a track in the carpeting, just like an oval race track.

"What will you do if Mary finds a husband? She's likely to, you know. Will you find another companion?"

Mary can find a husband, thought Celina, but my dear brother does not think I will. He's right, of course. I'm independent, with more than ample means, and perfectly contented with my life as it is.

But just the same, his words stung a bit.

"I hadn't thought that far, Edmund. Suddenly you make me wonder. Are you in Mary's confidence? Is she—going to wed?"

"No, no. It's just that—well, I don't suppose you know, but—well," he concluded lamely, "it's about Lyddy."

"Lyddy? What about her?"

"Well, Eleanor, you know her, she's so damned anxious to get the girl married off. I myself don't see any harm in Lyddy staying at home if she wants to. Maybe she's not inclined to marry."

She felt a rush of sympathy for him. His eldest daughter was, as Nelly had shrewdly observed, his favorite. And Celina understood why. Lydia was quite the most spectacular beauty in the county, if not in the entire country. Her hair lay in golden curls, cascading in lovely profusion to her shoulders. Her eyes were violet, large and appealing, her skin soft as swansdown, and she was possessed of a beguiling sweetness of disposition. One might have thought that the *ton* would have stormed the steps of the house Lady Forsyth had taken in Green Street for the Season. To look at her was eminently pleasing. But the most charitable of observers could say no more than that the beautiful Miss Forsyth was not above the average in wits.

"And here is this business of Nelly. She wants to get married to that captain of hers."

"Do you object to the match?"

"Not at all. But Eleanor insists that Lyddy get married before Nelly. I tell you, Celina, it's not going to be easy."

"Well, Edmund, I really don't know what I can do."

She had the liveliest suspicion that just as she had spoken these same words within the past hour she would likely be called upon to speak them again more than once in the future.

"Nothing, I suppose," he said gloomily. "Only if that brat Nelly comes to complain about her mother, I wish you'd talk some sense into her."

Celina saw no reason to inform him that his second daughter had already come with that purpose in mind, nor did she tell him that it would not be an easy task to impose common sense on such a white-hot feeling of indignation as Nelly was nursing.

After a while Edmund was ready to leave. At the door he turned. "I forgot to tell you. Eleanor's aunt Tibby is descending on us at week's end. For a long visit."

"How nice! I like Lady Gaunt."

"She interferes."

Lord Forsyth's terse statement was true. Aunt Tibby, widow of Eleanor's uncle, was a woman of lively wit and excessive leisure. Naturally she turned her hand to giving advice where it was needed, whether or not it was desired. A happy thought struck Celina.

"Of course she interferes, Edmund. It is up to you to see that she does so on the right side of your problem."

His pale eyes lit up as he reflected on her suggestion. "Of course! That's it!"

He was almost jovial as he went down the steps.

Chapter II

Celina was alone at last. The sounds of the house seemed small and far away. Mrs. Elkins was in the kitchen; Carrie, the parlormaid, doubtless setting things to rights upstairs; and Ford, probably at loose ends now that her rival, Mary's Polly, was gone, most likely was dealing efficiently with Celina's wardrobe against the coming cooler weather.

But most distressing of all was the positive quality of the silence left behind by dear Mary.

Edmund had left Celina with thoughts that did not lend themselves to the support of serene contentment. Six years of retired living in the country had left its mark on her, she supposed. It was true that she had cultivated an enviable equipoise of disposition and until now had considered herself if not happy at least content.

First, of course, she strove mightily not to display however subtly the scars of two fruitless Seasons on the Marriage Market. It was obvious at the time that while she had a small success or two, she was not taking the bachelor world by storm. Rather than suffer a third Season, when her status as ape-leader might well be established for all the world to see, she chose to take up her residence in the Dower House, the life lease of which her father had left her.

At first she had felt lonely and cloistered in the charming little house, far away from the bright and lively family activities at the Manor. Then, as the years wore on and Lydia and Nelly, growing up, came more and more insistently to the Dower House to beg advice, comfort, and partisanship, she began to wish occasionally and guiltily that the Dower House were not quite so accessible.

She had endeavored without complete success to stay uninvolved and neutral in the family squabbles. But her sister-in-law, Eleanor, nonetheless regarded any advice as *de trop*. Mary's arrival had been a godsend. Recently Mary had given firm voice to her conviction that Celina's family, all pulling at her for their own ends, took advantage of her good nature.

Thus it was more important than ever for Celina to preserve the calm demeanor behind which she hid.

She had reflected on Edmund's unsettling words long enough, although it was clear that his concern was not for Celina, companionless, but for Lydia, harried by her mother. But at least he was now doubtless deep in a scheme to bend Aunt Tibby's penchant for interference to his own good use.

Tired of her own thoughts, Celina picked up the latest issue of the *London Magazine*. There was a new editor, she remembered, one William Hazlitt, who had promised spectacular changes in the periodical. Ordinarily she would have reveled in the silence, in settling down uninterrupted for a long two hours of reading. But today she was too restless. She looked around her at her parlor, furnished in quiet tones of beige and ecru. The room, for the first time, did not soothe her.

She was discontented, that was all. She had grown to depend too much on Mary for amusement. Well, it was a good thing that she would be gone for a month. Time to adjust her habits.

She had been reading one of the new Waverley novels that had appeared this year. She had thrilled over *Ivanhoe*, but the newest one, *The Monastery*, did not seem as exciting.

By sheer exercise of will she sat down with the book. A sad falling-off on the part of the author, she decided. Surely the author of *Waverley* should have sufficient art not to have to resort to a supernatural agency!

Nevertheless she persevered. She had had enough of unsettling interruptions this morning. She considered instructing Carrie to turn away any callers, but decided that there was little chance of more visitors at least until afternoon. She was wrong.

When, conscious of someone in the room, she looked up, she was surprised to see her niece Lydia standing just inside the door with a woebegone expression on her incredibly beautiful face. Tears did not mar that unearthly beauty. Instead, the brimming eyes seemed merely a more intense, rain-washed violet.

"Lydia!" exclaimed Celina. "What's amiss?"

"They're all so cruel to me!"

"Cruel?" Celina echoed. What now?

It was futile, Celina knew from past experience, to try to get to the core of Lydia's perturbation until the girl's distress had abated sufficiently for her to hear her aunt's voice. Instructed by questions recently brought up by Nelly and by Lord Forsyth, Celina eyed her niece with somewhat less than her usual approval. Why had not the girl been besieged with offers during the last few months, instead of dancing the nights away in London?

Her spectacular beauty was set off at this moment by a round dress of blue jaconet muslin, fashioned neatly over her delicate bosom. The full skirt was trimmed at the hem with a ruffle of darker blue muslin that moved gracefully at every step. Her headdress, now sadly alop, was made in a style called the Parisian Mob, ornamented with a garland of flowers, and tied fetchingly under the chin with pink ribbon.

She made an excessively appealing picture, one would think. In truth, Celina was reminded of a confection concocted by a French pastry cook. Why on earth wasn't

Lydia at least a countess by now? The puzzle defied solution.

Lydia, although invited to sit, stood in the middle of Celina's parlor, a figure of vulnerable helplessness, great tears brimming from her violet eyes.

"How can they all be so heartless?" she lamented.

Celina said, "Not heartless, surely. I cannot think that your parents are quite gothic, you know. You can have no doubts that they wish you nothing but happiness." Since Lydia continued her shuddering sobs, Celina, drawing on past experience, suggested, "Are you sure you have not misunderstood something they said?"

Lydia said in a muffled voice, "How can I have been mistaken?"

Her tears subsided, without a corresponding return of coherence. The only way to live through these storms of Lydia's, Celina knew, was to wait and think firmly of something else.

Her thoughts, guided by the current crisis, slipped to her avoidance of Lydia's ball. She had of course been invited to London to attend Lydia's introduction to Society. She had refused. It had seemed to her that her own single status might well bring to Lydia's ball the question of a flaw somewhere in the Forsyth family. Why hadn't Celina herself married? It was a question bound to arise, she believed. At any rate, now she had a feeling akin to Lydia's, especially since Edmund had only this morning revealed his own questions about Celina's state. Besides Edmund's disapproval, no longer disguised, there was her own restlessness that consumed her today, an unease she could not put a name to.

Lydia, as though she had read Celina's mind, protested further. "It was not my fault! Truly, I am not an antidote!"

Since her niece's outburst ran so closely to Celina's own thoughts, she was startled into indiscretion. "But why didn't you take?"

The explanation, at least as far as Lydia was concerned,

came in fragments. Put together, it was understandable to Celina.

"I didn't know what to say to any of them," she wailed. "I liked to dance, you know, and as long as that was all we did, it was all right. But when they talked to me, you know, I couldn't think of anything to say, and Mama was furious. But I could not help it, you know."

She had stopped crying at last and was persuaded to sit in a blue-striped satin chair. "I did have beaux, although not quite an offer. And Mama kept on at me about all the expense Papa had gone to and told me I was ungrateful, and you know that's not true, Aunt Celina, I am not, and Mama said it was all for nothing and it was all my fault—"

"Now, now," soothed Celina, hastily forestalling another storm of tears, "I am sure it was not."

But she was well aware of the expense involved in introducing a daughter to Society—hiring a house on a fashionable street for six months, maintaining two carriages, riding horses for the daily promenade in the Park and a wardrobe full of new gowns and gloves and slippers, and the cost of entertaining—and remembered that Eleanor Forsyth had five daughters to launch into the Marriage Market. It did not bear thinking of.

Again Lydia echoed Celina's thoughts. "Mama would have me wear that pomona-green spencer on the day Lord Beaumont took us to see those poor animals at the Tower. I am persuaded that hideous color put him off."

Faintly Celina echoed, "Pomona-green?" That particular shade was an ugly color, reminding her of a dish of figs left too long in a warm pantry. With Lydia's fair coloring, the hue, no matter that it was the crack of fashion, would be a disaster.

"I know it was all the thing." Surprisingly, Lydia had now found her lost composure. "I do think, no matter what Mama says, that the green put him off. He—he did seem to like me."

Celina, fascinated by Lydia's revelations about her Season,

which she had not before heard, urged the girl on. "What did Mama—I mean, your mother—what did she say?"

"She said that it was the animals that repelled him. I do hope not." She added ingenuously, "Perhaps it was all for the best. I am glad he did not offer, for truly, Aunt, I might have wished for a marriage with him. But a dislike of animals shows a sad lack of sensibility."

Spellbound, Celina quavered, "The animals? At the Tower? Pray what had they to signify to anything?"

"Well, the poor things looked so sad, you know, all caged up like that. Just—just like me, you know, made to do what they did not in the least wish to do. And—" Her voice faded away.

"Come, Lydia, I shall not allow you to stop there. What happened?"

"I could not help it. I cried. And Mama was so ashamed of me. And Beaumont grew so red, for I caused such a scene, Mama says. And now they're all determined to punish me for making such a coil of it all. And I never can think of anything to say to anyone I am not well acquainted with, you know, and I hated London and I was so frightened. Aunt," she confided, "I have never been so frightened in all my life."

"Surely not for the better part of six months?"

Lydia nodded. "Every day. I was so happy to come back home." She remembered the complaint that had brought her to the Dower House. "But now it's as bad as ever."

Celina understood Lydia well. She had never considered the girl as possessed of a powerful intellect, but it had not occurred to her that with such beauty and a substantial dowry she would not be besieged by suitors. Now she could better understand Lydia's distress. She had little comfort to give to her niece.

But comfort, while it might be welcome in time, just now was not Lydia's prime concern. She had finally been able to speak about her pent-up unhappiness in London, and once the dam had burst there was no stopping her.

"Besides, you know, I cannot abide the thought of being married. You know what I mean, Aunt, for I am persuaded you feel the same. Mama talks so much about duty, and what I must be prepared to endure, and I do not understand it in the least, but whenever Mama tells me about duty, then something very unpleasant is bound to come of it."

Celina could only agree. It seemed to her that Eleanor had begun wrong with Lydia and was compounding her mistakes daily. But there was nothing Celina could properly say either to her troubled niece or to her sister-in-law.

"Besides," Lydia went on, "I have given this much thought and I have determined that I shall not in the least like a husband. Imagine putting up with his cigars! I wish to grow old like you, Aunt."

"Like me?" Celina echoed faintly.

"I would have my needlework, you know, and my dear kittens. Perhaps I could even come to live with you. Think of it! You and I could go out to visit our friends. Perhaps we could get a cart with a dear little donkey to draw it."

Lydia had become quite eloquent. She had always trusted her aunt and was most truly herself when alone with her. Celina had been secretly pleased with Lydia's preference for her, but that same affection now hung on her neck like a yoke.

Lydia prattled on, while Celina's thoughts turned inward. Was this a true picture of herself? A spinster, eschewing the company of men and content to play with a kitten and pay calls in, of all things, a donkey cart? Celina grasped at the fact that in her stable stood a gig in the latest style and a smart carriage, and Welsh grays to draw them, as well as a pair of chestnut riding horses. A donkey cart! Preposterous!

But her own ruffled feelings aside, Celina was touched by this glimpse, probably vouchsafed to none other, into the depths of Lydia's soul. Granted, the depths were no more than shallows, clear and open, subject to rippling at the slightest breeze. But ponds have their uses as well as do oceans, and who is to say which is best?

At length, somewhat calmed and believing without cause that she had gained her aunt's unqualified support against her mama, Lydia went home, leaving Celina to brood over her niece's artless revelation of how her life appeared to others. Not that Celina ordinarily would care about appearances, but she had not realized that she had fallen into such a sterile routine. Now she reeled under the shock.

If Mary had been home, she would have teased her out of her mood. But there again, how long would Mary stay with her? An unfamiliar feeling of impending change came to her. She had mentioned that sense of change to Mary fleetingly, as though it was merely the shadow of a passing cloud. Now that uneasy feeling returned like an incoming tide.

She was inordinately glad when the Honorable Lawrence Coleraine was announced.

"How pleased I am to see you, Mr. Coleraine," she said, offering him her hand. "You find me very low in my mind today."

"Then I am indeed happy to be of service," said the curate. Lawrence Coleraine was the youngest son of the Earl of Rommillies. Since there were four brothers standing between him and the title, and two of those had found careers in the army, there was little choice for young Lawrence but to enter the ranks of the clergy.

Indeed, he fitted the conception of minor clergy quite well. He was tall but willowy, giving a deceptive appearance of frailness. Actually, he kept himself in fine physical condition and in his preclerical days had given a good account of himself at Jackson's gymnasium.

His advancement in the Church, considering his breeding and his comfortable income, must have been much more rapid had it not been for his great shyness. He would rather have been put to the torture of the Iron Boot than stand before his handful of parishioners on Sunday and exhort them to a better life. He forced himself to do the job he was required to do, but every Sunday he was more than ever conscious of his failings. Only in this house, tenanted by kindly ladies of his own background, could he feel easy.

"You see, Mr. Coleraine, my dear Mary has gone for a month, and already I miss her sadly. Would you be kind enough to join me in a glass of my father's sherry? I am sure it will lift our spirits."

With glasses of wine in their hands, they were more comfortable. Celina was grateful for his company, for she had had a sufficiency of her family for the morning. Certainly the curate had brought her no problems. He would know well enough she could not solve them for him.

She was wrong. Mr. Coleraine indeed had something on his mind. Setting his empty glass down firmly on the table at his right hand, he leaned forward, his hands on his knees, and addressed her earnestly, like a man who had come to a desperate decision.

"Miss Forsyth," he began, "I am sadly in need of advice—of your opinion, in fact, formed as I know it will be by common sense and a strong intellect."

Taken aback, Celina suppressed an urgent wish to refuse to listen to him. "I fear—" she began, with the intention of turning his confidence aside as gently as she knew how.

He continued as though she had not spoken. "I believe I am not the man for this parish. I have the strongest feelings of failure. I am not accepted. I should never have come here. But then, if I had refused to heed the call of my bishop, I should never have made the acquaintance of—of both you ladies. That in itself is worth all the efforts that I have made here in vain."

Celina said truthfully, "My dear Mr. Coleraine, you are wrong. I know that your parishioners have a strong respect for you."

She remembered one of the older men in the village telling her, "He's naught on the preachin', mind, but he's strong on the visitin'. Aye, all we be glad when he comes in the door, when they's trouble come. We like him fine."

Her protest left him unmoved. "I feel I should do better in a parish in the heart of London. At least there is much work to do there."

When he fell silent, she asked, "Do you really want to work in that kind of parish?"

"I have thought a long time on this, Miss Forsyth. I do not wish to go. Is it not a sign, then, that what one wishes to do the least, that is the best to do? Is not the very fact that I feel unworthy, that I do not know in the least how to talk to people like that—is not this in itself a call to serve?"

How pompous he is, she thought. And yet how very real his doubts and his ambitions are to him.

"I should think the contrary," she said sensibly. "But you are appreciated here, you know, and it seems too bad to deprive our villagers of a man they like and trust in order to serve strangers."

He looked up with something like hope in his eyes. "You may be right. I could not of course take a wife to London, to expose her to the hazards of violence and disease. I confess I have been much troubled on that account."

With conviction Celina told him, "The right kind of wife would do. I protest the thought that women must be placed on a shelf and taken down at certain specified times—to entertain, or to run a household." Certain other occasions occurred to her. She was gratified to see that he was too engrossed in his own thoughts to notice her flushed cheeks. "Surely a woman has a right to serve where she is called."

"But a woman is not likely to be called, is she?" he said earnestly. "I believe it was Samuel Butler who said something *à propos* here. 'The souls of women are so small, that some believe they've none at all.' A great wit." He smiled kindly in apology for plain speaking. "But I suspect that the right kind of woman would be more at home in this parish. You have set my mind greatly at ease. I must thank you for this little conversation, Miss Forsyth. Since you will be lonely while Miss Remington is gone, I shall make a point of dropping in, so to speak, from time to time."

He left her alone. What a strange conversation! He had never opened his thoughts to her before. This was surely a morning for baring the soul, she thought, and she would not protest if another such morning didn't come for twenty years.

She puzzled over the visit for some time. Finally the key she sought came to her. She had just received an offer of marriage! Not quite an offer, she amended, but at least she believed she had seen a preliminary scouting expedition. "The right kind of wife"; she regretted her own words. But obviously Mr. Coleraine was thinking seriously of marriage! And he knew that she would be alone because of Mary's journey, and—oh dear, how all things joined together to support her suspicion.

If this was the alteration that she had felt coming, the change that caused her such unease, she considered it less than favorable!

Chapter III

A few days later Lady Gaunt arrived at Forsyth Hall for a visit. She was Eleanor's aunt by marriage, her deceased husband having been Eleanor's uncle. Possessed of a substantial fortune of her own, she had made it a great one by her marriage settlement.

She liked her children in inverse ratio to the time she spent with them and therefore was constantly on the move. She owned a house in London and one in Bath as well as a country house, none of which saw her for more than a month at a time.

Her orbit of visits brought her to Forsyth Hall for a month once a year. She was not overly fond of Eleanor, but she found life there comfortable, since the Forsyths were careful not to cross her. Besides, she had a great liking for Celina, who treated her like an equal and even at times like a good friend.

On the evening of her arrival, the Forsyths dined *en famille*, with Celina the only guest. The dinner was unpretentious—only two removes. It was too much to hope that the dinner conversation might be equally unremarkable. Even before the sweet, Aunt Tibby was aware of certain tensions crisscrossing the table like taut wires. Inevitably, and to Celina not in the least surprisingly, the quarrel currently occupying their minds erupted.

Lady Gaunt unwittingly provided the spark that set fire to the tinder, lying ready to kindle. In an attempt to introduce a diversion, she leaned forward to address Celina across the table.

"My dear Celina, how very well you look! I do like that shade of misty green. Quite like the first buds of spring, you know. I am gratified that you did not, like all the sheep in London, follow the fashion and take up that ugly pomona-green. Quite insupportable, especially for ladies of fair complexion."

A strangled cry escaped Lydia, on Lady Gaunt's left, and all eyes turned in her direction. Muffling the sobs rising in her throat with her napkin, Lydia fled the room, leaving her family in various degrees of astonishment. Celina kept her own counsel. Pomona-green was the reason, so Lydia had thought, that Lord Beaumont's ardor had cooled, and while Celina deemed it unlikely that Lydia's heart was deeply involved, yet clearly there had been much family discussion in recent days on the subject of Lydia's failure to bring him up to the mark.

Lady Gaunt, somewhat shaken by the unexpected consequence of her harmless remark, eyed those around the table with speculation. Eleanor's pale cheeks wore an unaccustomed rosy glow, likely because of Lydia's lack of decorum. Nelly's eyes shone brightly, and Aunt Tibby immediately turned thoughtful. When that young lady wore that particular expression, it was well for all those nearby to make sure of accessible cover close at hand.

"I declare," said Edmund at last, mindful of the guest at his table, "I do not know what comes over young ladies. Eleanor, my dear, pray explain Lyddy's vapors to us."

Lady Forsyth stiffened. "I wonder at your tone, Edmund. I have done my best with her and I do not quite like to be criticized, especially at my own table. I cannot understand why a compliment tendered dear Celina should send Lydia into hysterics." She gathered her family together in one embracing glance before she turned to Celina. "Can you explain, dear sister?"

Celina, knowing exactly what had gone through Lydia's mind, said mendaciously, "I cannot conceive of any reason. Perhaps she is feeling not quite the thing."

Nelly intervened. "She's been like this since Mama said she must marry."

"Marry!" said Lady Gaunt, startled. "I have heard nothing of this Who do you have in mind, Forsyth?"

Edmund turned thoughtful, choosing unexceptionable words to clothe his real resentment of his wife's dictum. But Nelly forestalled him. "Mama says that Lydia must marry before I can be betrothed to dear Henry. I say it's monstrously unfair, and Aunt Celina agrees. Don't you, Aunt?"

Eleanor's sharp, resentful glance fell on Celina. Celina opened her mouth to deny Nelly's statement, but at that moment Lydia returned to the table. At once there was an uproar. Lady Forsyth began scolding and insisted that Lydia apologize for her abrupt departure.

Edmund's voice rose above the others'. "Lyddy, my dear, are you well? Shall we send for Mr. Emerson?"

Nelly interpolated, "See, Mama? I told you Lydia doesn't want to be married, but I do!"

"Well, young lady?" said Lady Forsyth ominously. "I am waiting for your explanation. I never thought the day would come when a daughter of mine would show such a want of civility. I lay the blame entirely on that governess—what was her name? A good thing I dismissed her. Lydia?"

Lydia persisted in looking down at her plate. In a muffled voice she said, "Ask Aunt Celina. She knows."

Celina wished strongly that Lydia had held her tongue. Her brother and sister-in-law turned eloquently accusing eyes on her. Eleanor tightened her thin lips. "Apparently," she said, "Celina knows more about what is going on in my family than I do."

It was useless to protest, Celina knew. Either she must accuse her nieces of falsehood before their parents or she must accept the onus of appearing to side with the girls against their mother. Either way she was caught in a distinctly uncomfortable position. There was nothing to do but keep silent. She was uneasily aware of Lady Gaunt's speculative eye on her, but any way she turned, the effect would be disloyalty to one or another.

Nelly's clear young voice broke the silence. "Aunt Tibby, you must see that Mama is not trying to marry us all off. But she won't even let me be betrothed until Lydia is married. It is so unfair!"

Lydia, seeing that she was being put definitely in the wrong, protested. "Unfair! You have no idea—" Her words failed her. With a desperate gesture she turned to Celina. "Oh, Aunt, you tell them, pray, how unfair it is of Nelly to torment me so!"

Celina, thus appealed to, was in a cleft stick. "I do not wish to interfere—" It was a badly chosen word. Interference was not only what she never had any intention of doing but also a word that inevitably heated Eleanor's always simmering resentment into a rolling boil.

"Interfere?" said Lady Forsyth ominously.

Nelly, clearly seeing that her cause was apt to be swallowed up in what she considered irrelevancies, interrupted. "Aunt Celina knows the right of it. It is grossly unjust to Henry to expect him to wait forever, just so Lydia can find a husband. She's had her chance—"

Eleanor said repressively, "She has had one Season. Your Aunt Celina had two, you know, before she retired to the country, and I shall insist that Lydia have another."

Rashly Nelly pointed out, "One or two, what difference does it make? Either you take or you don't."

Celina, in spite of her iron self-control, felt a shamed flush creeping up her cheeks. Two Seasons, and she did not take. It was useless to point out that she had indeed had three offers but had chosen to accept none of them. She was twenty-six, after all, and the gulf between that advanced age and Nelly's seventeen was too wide to be bridged.

Lydia, turning drowned violet eyes on her, sniffed delicately and said, clearly feeling betrayed, "But you agreed with *me*—"

Celina had had enough. "Lydia, I did not agree. Nor did I take Nelly's part." Her voice trembled from distress and growing anger and could hardly be heard except by Aunt Tibby. That lady, wearing an expression similar to that of a spectator at a very bad play, was watching the scene.

Edmund, always slow to act, said heavily, "I am quite sure my sister is not so lost to propriety as to take a partisan stand on what is after all a purely domestic matter. Eleanor, I shall expect a decent silence during the rest of our meal from your daughters—"

"So. When they misbehave, they are *my* daughters. Let me tell you, Edmund, if you were not so indulgent to your sister—"

Too late Eleanor realized that she was approaching deep water. The question that had often occupied husband and wife in late-night discussions had no business being aired in front of the subject of it. Lamely she said, "I did not mean precisely what I seemed to have said, Celina. I assure you we are both excessively fond of you."

It was unfortunate, thought Celina, that the apology sounded so much less sincere than the remark it was intended to erase.

The end of the meal came at last, and the family adjourned to the sitting room for coffee. As soon as was decent Celina excused herself and departed for the Dower House, refraining with some difficulty from running down the driveway as though fleeing the devil.

Eleanor, conscious of having made a gaffe of some dimensions, lapsed into a subdued mood. Lady Gaunt, who had said nothing since her inoffensive remark about Celina's looks, was now in possesion of the core of the crucial question. There was always a crisis in Eleanor's household, she remembered, but this particular problem had not before arisen.

Eleanor Forsyth, with five daughters to marry off, had quite clearly succumbed to panic, in Lady Gaunt's opinion. Lydia should have been betrothed by now, leaving Nelly the next eligible miss. After that, in steps only a year or so apart, came Sophie, Catherine, and Amelia. The two boys that Eleanor had at last produced were still in the nursery or in leading strings. Lady Gaunt felt not the slightest pang of sympathy for Eleanor. If she had managed Lydia's debut better, the girl would now be preparing for her wedding.

Such a spectacular beauty should have gathered suitors as a honeypot gathers bees. What if the bridegroom had found out after the vows had been exchanged that Lydia's understanding was minimal and confined for the most part to her apparel and her exquisite needlework? Many another man had received such a surprise and survived it.

The crucial question, to Lady Gaunt's mind, was not the internecine squabbles over the orderly procession of brides in the Forsyth family. Instead, her thoughts clustered around Celina. The girl deserved much better than this family of hers, not one of whom had the loyalty of a snake, Lady Gaunt told herself. Even Edmund lacked a proper feeling for his young sister. While Lady Gaunt did not expect him to abandon his wife for Celina, any man worthy of consideration should not have crumpled entirely under Eleanor's malicious glance.

Complacent Edmund refused to see the deep wounds that Celina had suffered. If anyone in the family needed rescuing, it was not Nelly or even Lydia.

Lady Gaunt retired early, pleading fatigue from her journey. Once in her room, however, she appeared to be marvelously refreshed. She extracted her correspondence folio from her luggage and sat down at the desk. Tapping her pen against her teeth for some moments to collect her thoughts, at length she began to write, a small smile touching her lips.

Chapter IV

In due time Lady Gaunt's letter arrived at its destination, an address on Portman Square in London. The house had been recently opened for the return of its owner, Jervis Henry George Blaine, son of the Duke of Lynton and newly come to the title Marquess of Wroxton.

When the letter arrived, Jervis was at the breakfast table, idly turning over the morning's delivery of mail. An observer would have seen a weary, handsome face with lines of disillusionment around the resolute mouth. The hooded eyes held a lively intelligence that their owner took pains to conceal from most of his acquaintance. Only on rare occasions did he allow a darting, oddly keen glance to betray the quick wit that provided him with much private amusement.

At the moment his good friend—in fact Jervis considered him his only trustworthy friend—Adrian Sadler was pouring himself a cup of the thick Turkish coffee that his host favored.

"I see the *ton* has discovered that you have returned," said Adrian, surveying the pile of cream-colored envelopes that spoke eloquently of balls and routs and outings to come. "I wager that in a week you'll scarcely find a moment to sleep!"

"I'll take your wager, Adrian," said Jervis. "My patience will scarcely endure more than a tenth of all these." He waved a negligent hand in the direction of the invitations.

Silence fell between them, broken only by the sound of tearing paper as Jervis opened his mail. At length he stopped short and pursed his lips in a soundless whistle. "Now here's one I can't quite ignore," he announced. "Remember my aunt Tibby, Adrian? Lady Gaunt?"

Upon being assured by a vigorous nod, since at the moment Adrian's mouth was full of the most delicious Devonshire ham, Jervis continued, "She wants me to come down to the country house she's visiting. In Wiltshire, I gather."

"Wiltshire?" mumbled Adrian. "Whatever for?"

"I'm not quite sure." Making up his mind, he rang for his butler. When that worthy, Gibbs, appeared, his master asked, "Do we know anyone in Wiltshire?"

"Not to say know, my lord. But there are a few small manors belonging to us near the village of Ludgershall, my lord."

"Strange," mused Jervis. "Lady Gaunt seems to be domiciled at least for the moment near that same place. That will do, Gibbs, thank you."

The butler vanished as silently as he had come. Jervis wondered whether he would again be able to accustom himself to the very high quality of English service. He had spent some years traveling on the Continent and beyond, having as a son of a marquess and grandson of a duke few responsibilities and a great deal of money. He had spent a good amount of time in Constantinople and had even taken the hazardous route, which few English traveled, to Baghdad, where he had become well acquainted with Claudius Rich, the Resident.

It was with real reluctance that he had left the noisy, uproarious bazaars of the Middle East to return to his homeland. He would much rather have faced bedouin bandits than the sea of anxious, acquisitive female faces at Almack's.

"My aunt's letter is most timely, Adrian," Jervis said. "She wishes me to come and visit her at Forsyth Hall, near Ludgershall. Says it's my duty to present myself to her."

"I suppose it is," said Adrian judiciously.

"Who are these Forsyths, do you know?"

"The name is familiar," said Adrian, frowning in his effort to remember, "but I was not in town for the Season, you know. My grandfather stuck his spoon in the wall in February, and I had a good deal to do."

Jervis sent him a glance full of sympathy. "I can well imagine. But Yorkshire in winter?"

"Spring, you know. And summer. No place like it. I should not have come to London at all, save that you invited me to. It's been a long time, Jervis, since we've met."

"Too long. So you can tell me nothing about the Forsyths. Well, I shall simply have to brave the unknown."

"As though you were a green one! But what of all those?" He gestured toward the pile of invitations.

"Easily taken care of."

When Gibbs appeared again in answer to his master's ring, Jervis gave him instructions. "Tell Pollard to pack for two weeks in the country, and tell Brewer to arrange for relays. I suppose it's more than a day's travel." He gave further instructions and finished, "And these things, Gibbs."

"The invitations, my lord?"

"See that someone answers them all. My regrets, of course, but civilly stated." He turned thoughtful. "Two weeks might be more than enough, and I should not like to be ignored entirely if I come back to civilization a bit early."

Adrian stole a glance at his great friend. He was a little younger than Jervis and had experienced the benefit of his protection at Oxford. The friendship that had sprung up between the two oddly assorted men had not flagged, even though Jervis's absence from the country had intervened.

The Jervis who had come back, Adrian sensed without knowing how he knew, was not the same man who had left. Now he seemed weary, empty of feeling. If Jervis had perhaps suffered from unrequited love, the details would never be known. Adrian worried about him. Now, in a gentle attempt to lift his spirits, he suggested, "Civilization? I do believe all those ruins at Baghdad are more real to you than people."

Jervis looked inward for a moment. "Perhaps you are right. But I do not know how to alter." Then, grasping at a diversion, he said, "I expected to find you wed or at least betrothed. Is there no one? Or am I soon to wish you happy?"

Modestly Adrian explained, "I have not a lot to offer."

"You surprise me. Your fortune cannot be gone. I have found, myself, that fortune alone provides all the eligibility a man needs."

Adrian was completely without envy. "You can surely take your pick of any lady in London. Besides, not many would overlook your title, you know."

Jervis turned thoughtful. Almost to himself he murmured, "There must be more to marriage than a simple financial contract. If I had wanted to buy a bride, I could have remained in Turkey."

Adrian laughed. "I suppose they come by the dozen there!" Neither Jervis nor his devoted friend noticed that Jervis did not deny that he could make his choice among all the eligible females in Society. His exalted title and his great wealth were an Open Sesame to the heart of every ambitious mother in town. The marquess was well aware of the magnetic power of his name. Unfortunately he had not yet learned that complacency has its own perils.

At length Jervis laughed. "Time enough for entering the marriage stakes. I'll come to that in due course." And on my own terms, he added silently. At least I shall make the best bargain possible. "And if I find this family—Forsyth, is it?—deadly dull, as I am sure I will, I can always plead business at my new manors."

"Jervis the Fox!" said Adrian admiringly. "Always sure

of a bolt hole. Do you ever think that some day you may be caught out?"

"Never!" But in spite of his vigorous denial, he was aware of a passing touch of an emotion he had not had before, a sort of wistfulness, a wish that the world had been made differently.

Her nephew's letter was gratifying to Lady Gaunt. He promised to come to see her, and the first step in her campaign to liberate Celina from the entangling demands of her family was accomplished. The small matter of informing her hostess that she had without so much as asking permission invited Lord Wroxton for an indefinite stay gave her no pause whatever.

She told Eleanor at breakfast. "I hope you do not mind," she finished civilly. "I promise you he will be no trouble. He will bring his own cattle, I suspect, and a groom, besides his own man."

Her niece gazed vacantly at her. Automatically she responded, "Oh, no, there's plenty of room. No trouble at all." Then, pulling her wits together, she set her coffee cup down quickly, for her hand had begun to shake. "Marquess, did you say? Lord Wroxton, I have heard that name recently, have I not?"

Lady Gaunt, hugging her scheme to her ample bosom, informed her, "Jervis was in foreign climes for several years, until not six months ago his elder brother succumbed and he succeeded to the title. I dare say he will be happy enough to spend a month or so in an English family again."

A month or so? thought Eleanor. Surely that means—

Lady Gaunt examined the letter again. "The mails are abominably slow!" she exclaimed. "He says he will be here by the seventh—that's tomorrow! How uncomfortable to give us such a short time!"

She had intended to do some vigorous spadework with Celina before Jervis's arrival. But now there was not enough time to bring Jervis's many attainments and virtues to the girl's attention. Perhaps it was better, she sighed, this way. Sometimes too much forewarning spoiled the plot. Engaged on her own thoughts, she paid too little heed to Eleanor.

"Dear Aunt," she was saying when Lady Gaunt attended to her again, "how excessively thoughtful! I should never have doubted that our little problems would engage your interest. I must tell Edmund at once!" She left the breakfast room, leaving her aunt to mull over her parting remark.

"What does she mean, thoughtful?" wondered Lady Gaunt. "I myself should like more than a day's notice to welcome a gentlemen of the first consequence." She was not unduly perturbed, however, since she knew that Eleanor, mindful of possible alterations in the Gaunt will, would have pretended to be delighted even if she had been presented with a brace of African elephants to be housed in the salon.

Lady Gaunt was far too shrewd to pursue her scheme, at least in the presence of the Forsyths. Eleanor was already immersed in plans for entertaining the marquess. "We'll have just a small family dinner tomorrow night. He will be weary from traveling, I make no doubt."

Since Jervis was well inured to riding twelve hours a day in a bedouin saddle with only a handful of dates for sustenance, it was not likely that two days in a well-sprung phaeton would exhaust him unduly. But Lady Gaunt said only, "Perhaps Celina would like to come, since her companion is not at home."

"I vow I had forgotten. Besides," Eleanor said ingenuously, "I shall need her help in arranging the ball."

"Ball?" echoed Lady Gaunt.

"Oh, yes. We cannot have a gentleman of Lord Wroxton's eminence finding us dull, you know. He must see that we know quite how to do things, even though we do keep country hours for the most part. You must tell me, Aunt Tibby, just who of our neighbors are likely to please him."

Eleanor was going to spoil everything, thought Lady Gaunt, making so much of him that he would turn away in disgust. Well, she had a few strings left to her own bow; she would deal with complications as they arose. She set herself to deal with the first.

"I haven't seen him in some years, you know. As I recall him, he was excessively cultured, enormously well read. I wonder whether it might be well to wait until he arrives to see what his wishes are."

Eleanor was disappointed, but conceded gracefully, "Perhaps you're right. Well, at least we can offer him a dinner that will not be inferior to any he may enjoy in London."

Eleanor said no more until she and Edmund were safely private in their bedroom that night. She had spent the day harrying Cook and making sure the large bedroom the honored guest would occupy was freshly aired, the linens warmed, the fire laid in the grate. She could do no more until the morrow.

Now she sat at her dressing table brushing her hair. Edmund pottered in his dressing room beyond. She called to him, "I vow I did not expect Aunt Tibby to come so swiftly to our rescue, did you?"

Edmund appeared in the doorway. "Rescue? You mean saddling us with a nephew of hers that nobody ever heard of? I do not like to see you put to such trouble, and without so much as a by your leave."

She turned in her chair to look at him with astonishment. "Edmund! Is it possible you don't see what a great stroke of luck it is to have Aunt Tibby in the house?"

"I find it hard to consider it good fortune to have that meddling old woman here at any time."

"But this time, Edmund, you must admit she is meddling to good purpose. She heard about our little problem with Lydia only a sennight ago, and already she is providing us with the answer. My dear Edmund, you cannot be thinking!"

Edmund sat on the edge of a chair, recognizing his wife's tone of voice. He was about to be instructed, and once begun, the lesson would grind on to its appointed end. In the ordinary way he found it necessary to listen with no more than half his attention, but Eleanor's next words jarred him into alertness.

"Fancy your eldest daughter a marchioness, if you please!"

"Good God, woman! Have you lost your wits?"

"Not at all." Eleanor's superior smile was not lost on him. "I will admit I shall be much happier when Wroxton makes his offer, but surely he cannot resist her. Lyddy's looks were noted as unusual even by His Majesty, you know."

"She is a beauty, isn't she?" he agreed with satisfaction.

"I cannot be mistaken, Edmund. Aunt Tibby has sent for him to come to Wiltshire for a visit. Now that he has the title, he must be looking around for a wife. Even in the little season he could find plenty of eligible belles. How clever it is of Aunt Tibby to fetch him right away from London! And I wager you, Edmund, that one look at Lydia will make him forget all those Turkish women."

"Turkish women? I should hope, Eleanor, that you know nothing at all about Turkish women," said Edmund oppressively.

"Well, of course I don't. But Aunt Tibby says . . ."

What Lady Gaunt said took half an hour in the narration. At length, defying all the laws of probability, Edmund succumbed. "You must have the right of it," he sighed. "But it must be handled very carefully. Besides, I must be very sure Lyddy will like the match."

"That has nothing to do with it," said Eleanor sharply. "It is time for her parents to make the decision. She had every opportunity to follow her own inclinations, and you see what that led to: nothing! Don't fret so, Edmund. I shall see that Lyddy understands what—that is, what is best for her."

"You've to be careful, Eleanor. Don't throw the child too much in his way. Best tell her—"

"Tell her what?" interrupted his wife in an ominous tone of voice. "Are you instructing me on how to manage my daughters?"

Stung, Edmund forgot himself. "You haven't done so well thus far, have you? One daughter in London for the Season, and nothing comes of it. The next daughter throwing herself at the head of an army captain with only his pay to support him—"

"Plus," said Eleanor acidly, "a good allowance from his father the general."

"And God knows what the rest of the girls have in their minds," fumed Edmund, ignoring his wife's interruption. "I myself, in your place, would not take amiss a little advice."

"Wouldn't you? I doubt that. Let us see what you make of this advice, Lord Forsyth. Leave the girls to me and busy yourself with your farmers. They are more suitable company for you!"

Since Edmund enjoyed visiting his various farms and scarcely let a day go by without looking into one detail or another, his wife's taunt struck a vulnerable spot in him. So Aunt Tibby's great thoughtfulness, as Eleanor's unlimited capacity for self-deception led her to believe, resulted in Lord and Lady Forsyth, while occupying the same bed, lying ostentatiously back to back in mute and mutual resentment.

Chapter V

Celina did not learn of the impending arrival of Jervis Blaine, Marquess of Wroxton, until the next morning. The news came in the form of a summons to dinner that afternoon to welcome the honored guest.

"I have half a mind not to go!" she muttered, tossing the invitation onto her desk. But she was in the mopes, no question about it, since Mary's departure, and she believed she should certainly accept any possibility of recovery.

She picked up the short note and read it again curiously. The unusual warmth of its phrasing was suggestive. If Eleanor offered an olive twig, then Celina was generous enough to accept it. Eleanor wanted something, she was convinced. Celina began to smile. It was curiosity that would bring her to the Manor, not gratitude for being included in a family entertainment.

Indeed, her inquiring spirit suggested that she should go up to the Hall this morning to hear more about the expected visitor. But news from the Hall came to her first in the person of Lydia.

The girl was at her most fetching, thought Celina as she brought her into the small salon and rang for tea. Lydia was once again regarding her world through moisture-filled eyes. Celina refrained from any but the most ordinary conversation, uneasily aware that the slightest tactless word would bring tears brimming from the beautiful violet eyes. No use to tell the girl not to be a watering pot, thought Celina, and not for the first time. Such an admonition simply increased the flow.

But Lydia held her tears in check until Carrie had come with the tea and gone. The door was scarcely shut before Lydia wailed, "I simply won't do it, Aunt Celina, and you've got to help me. There's nothing left but to run away!"

"Nonsense!" said Celina more sharply than she intended. "Run away to where?"

"Won't you go with me? We could go to Bath. You've often mentioned removing for the winter to take the waters. Mama would not send after me if she knew I was with you, would she?"

Lydia's glance searched the corners of the room as though expecting to find a Bow Street Runner behind every chair.

"We shall never know, for the occasion will not arise."

Her niece spoke through her sobs. "Then will you hide me here in the Dower House? I promise you I'll be no trouble!"

No trouble!

Strong measures were clearly indicated. "Lydia, such fustian I never heard. One would think that a cruel parent was forcing you to marry a wicked baron."

In a strangled voice Lydia corrected her. "He's a marquess."

"*What?*"

Through endless coaxing, Celina extracted the elements of the plot as Lydia understood it. Indeed, her tale had certain facts to support it: the family's wish that she be married soon, Aunt Tibby's sending for an eligible male.

"But he's so old, Aunt Celina! Aunt Tibby says he's over thirty!"

Celina bit her tongue. Thirty was not unduly far from twenty-six after all. "Are you sure he wants to marry you,

Lydia? Not that you're not a lovely girl, but he's never seen you."

"They all say I must. I cannot say no to Mama. Aunt Celina, I'm so afraid—"

"Nonsense!" said Celina bracingly. "Now, dry your tears and drink your tea, although I expect it is cold by now. And don't worry. If the man is all that dreadful, your papa won't force you to marry him. Who knows? You might even fall in love with him."

Her attempt at raillery fell on ears closed against all but her own misery. The girl sank to the floor before Celina and, clasping her hands pleadingly on Celina's knees, said imploringly, "Please help me, dear Aunt."

Guiltily Celina stifled an unaccustomed wish stirring in her, a wish that somehow Edmund's family would settle their own affairs without involving her. Lydia pulled her strongly one way, and Eleanor and Edmund quite likely would exert equal pressure the opposite way. But finally, stroking Lydia's pale, silky hair as the girl sobbed wetly into her skirt, she admitted defeat.

"I'll go up myself and talk to your papa." No matter, she thought, that I have been told that I interfere. This is all in a good cause.

Restored to her usual sweet disposition, Lydia returned to the Hall. Celina gave way to reflection. Had she ever seen this Wroxton? she wondered. Of course, when she was in London, six years ago, he was simply Jervis Blaine. She summoned up the faces she remembered and found none that answered to that name. Well, she would see him soon enough.

But before Lydia's nemesis arrived, she must go to Edmund, and even if she could not sway him from his intent to marry Lydia to the stranger, she could at least beg him to deal gently with the girl. Sighing, she rose to find her cloak. "I'm just going up to the Manor, Carrie," she said to the maid, and stepped out onto the graveled drive.

* * *

She found her brother in his library, sunk in gloom. He did not even glance up when she came in.

"Edmund, I do not quite like to disturb you—"

He lifted his head, startled. "Oh, it's you. I thought it was Eleanor come back to ring another peal over me."

Celina stifled a pitying smile. Poor Edmund! He would never be master in his own house. She realized that she had very little hope of success for her mission. But she had promised Lydia, so she pressed on.

"Lydia tells me a tale that I find very difficult to credit, Edmund," she began with guile. "So I have come to hear the straight of it from you."

Edmund gave every appearance of a hare cornered in an inadequate covering of brush. "What kind of tale?"

"She insists that you are forcing her into marriage."

Feebly he protested. "You believe that I would do such a thing?"

"Lydia thinks so. And I must tell you that I had a great deal of difficulty in keeping her from hysterics. I fear I did not convince her that you would at least take her wishes to heart."

"Good God, does she think I'd drag her to the altar myself? What kind of sentimental twaddle has she been reading, eh? I'm not that gothic!"

Celina beamed on him with approval. "My exact words, Edmund. She will be much heartened when you tell her as much."

Edmund got up to stride back and forth behind his desk. She watched him carefully. He turned at last. "Eleanor's got the bit in her teeth. I tell you without exaggeration she's already planning the wedding."

Celina's heart sank. Lydia, for once, had the truth of it. "Wedding? The man's not even here yet! What do you know about him? I don't recall ever meeting him myself."

Edmund grumbled, "I'm not surprised. As far as I can tell, nobody recalls him. Of course, he's been out of the country for some years in outlandish places, from what Lady Gaunt tells me. Of course, she also tells me he's rich as a nabob and elegant of figure, as though that signifies anything."

"Then," pursued Celina, her heart sinking, "Aunt Tibby is encouraging the match?" If Lady Gaunt was supporting Eleanor, poor Lydia had little chance of wriggling clear.

Edmund reflected. "To be honest, she has not mentioned the match. Eleanor says there's no doubt of it. Lady Gaunt knows we're in a coil because Nelly's turned rebel, and Eleanor insists that her aunt is providing the solution."

"Well, Edmund, I shall not try to dissuade Eleanor from her course."

"Better try to stop an avalanche," muttered Edmund, once again sunk in gloom.

"But I shall expect you," said his sister repressively, "to remember that Lydia is not to be forced."

"I shall not sell the girl, if that's what you mean."

"Of course," said Celina slowly, "if he's as elegant as you say, perhaps he has sufficient address to overcome Lydia's objections."

"God knows I hope so, because if he doesn't," said Edmund inelegantly, but with feeling, "Nelly's apt to blast the roof off."

Celina turned to leave. She stopped at the door and smiled mischievously. "Eleanor is partial to old tags. Has she thought of the one about unhatched chickens?"

He smiled ruefully. "She'll have the second generation of chickens in the pot in a sennight." He straightened, as though shaking off unwanted thoughts. "Never mind, Celina. He's likely a monster. After all, he's not yet married."

He stopped short, watching the flush mantle his sister's cheeks. "My dear, I meant nothing by that. Just a thoughtless remark. I know you had offers—" He realized that with every word he was digging himself in deeper, and his voice died away.

Gently Celina said, "No matter, Edmund. I should be used to such remarks by now." She believed that Edmund said what he thought, but also she recognized that many of his thoughts were shaped by his wife's strongly expressed views. Rightly, she suspected that her sister-in-law had been dwelling heavily on Celina's spinsterhood, regarding that state as a horror from which Lydia was to be delivered in spite of herself.

She had fulfilled her promise to Lydia. She had spoken to Edmund, urging him to make haste slowly with his daughter, making use of another of Eleanor's favored adages. Now there was nothing more she could do.

She went slowly down the steps and walked across the gravel sweep before the entrance to the Manor. Not for the first time she decided that it was far better to live alone, or at least with Mary, than to have a marriage like Edmund's.

Still wrapped in her unpleasant reflections, Celina began to hurry down the drive toward the Dower House. Her flight bore some parallel, she thought, to a wounded animal hastening to the safety of a dark and comforting burrow.

She was not prone to feeling sorry for herself, but the unexpected stab of Edmund's words still stung. Trying to argue herself into a better frame of mind—he really did not mean that anyone unwed must be a monster, did he?—she did not hear the sound of carriage wheels on the graveled drive.

The curve just ahead hid the approaching phaeton until it was at hand. She glanced up at the last moment to see dead ahead a pair of horses looming like a mirage. With a muffled shriek she leaped to the side of the driveway. Unfortunately the sudden desperation of her movement did not allow for any choice, and the thick shrubbery resisted her intrusion. The heavy branches supported her at first, before, cracking ominously, they broke and dropped her unceremoniously to the ground.

She was dimly aware that the equipage had stopped a little way beyond and the driver had dismounted. She had no wish to be seen in such a humiliating posture, her bonnet knocked awry, her skirt rucked up above her knees. She scrambled to her feet.

Before her stood not the groom she half expected but the very mirror of a gentleman. He was elegantly dressed, his coat obviously fashioned by Weston, his Hessian half-boots mirror-bright with polish.

His features, however, disappointed. They were handsome enough, she conceded, but there was an expression of weariness about the well-shaped firm lips. She had no time to consider him, either the strong shoulders and the powerfully muscled thighs or the intelligent eyes that regarded her with a keen intentness at odds with his languid pose.

She fumbled with her bonnet strings, still tied around her throat. "I am sorry," said the stranger. "You will allow me to inform your mistress of this unfortunate accident."

His condescending tone restored her wits. "I must indeed look all of a jumble," she said. "But I assure you there is no need to inform anyone of your incompetent handling of a pair of goers!"

Her feelings still raw from Edmund's unfortunate remarks about unmarried monsters, and dreadfully aware that she looked as though she had been dragged backward through a briar thicket, she found herself speaking to him with a tartness calculated to erase that cool, expressionless look from his face.

"I daresay it would not occur to you to watch where you are going," she added with spirit. "A bending drive often provides surprises not easily dealt with!"

"As you see," said the stranger easily. He regarded her with speculation. "I have it!" he exclaimed, as though the idea had just struck him. "You are mortified because I thought you a serving wench at the start. My apologies."

"That has nothing to do with it!" she stormed, aware as she spoke that she was protesting too much.

"I wonder," he said, amusement now in his eyes, "whether you will take it amiss, ma'am, if I were to inquire whether you have suffered any injury. Due, of course, to my abominable handling of my cattle."

"It is only civil of you to inquire, of course," she

responded. "Pray do not concern yourself. I am quite all right." She had suddenly realized that this man—with, as Edmund had said, an elegance of figure that would make him noticeable in any company—must be the expected visitor, Lord Wroxton himself.

Full of curiosity about Aunt Tibby's nephew—Lydia's intended husband, if Eleanor was right—Celina looked levelly and critically at him. She would not have been gratified had she been able to read the thoughts behind his cool eyes.

Lord Wroxton it was, of course. He had come in two stages from London, sparing his cattle. He had enjoyed seeing again the marvelous English September, with its lovely muted colors of gold and bronze and soft green under the bluest of northern skies. How far removed from the desolate, colorless landscape of Mesopotamia, relieved only by mounds of debris and mud brick!

He had turned into the Forsyth drive in a state bordering astonishment at the luxuriant foliage of the thick shrubbery growing right to the graveled track. He had not the slightest thought that anyone was within miles of him, to say nothing of someone idly strolling down the center of the drive, as lost in thought as he was.

It was fortunate, he knew, that no damage had been done—at least, no more than a tear in the skirt, a bending of the bonnet, and a ruffling of the feathers of the lady standing before him.

A lady of quality, beyond question. Only a female of excellent breeding could muster such a level look from her eyes, those great, beautiful, luminous eyes of a dark gray not often met with. He was conscious that his *amour propre*, if not quite shattered, at least had suffered a crack.

Jervis had gained great experience in reading expressions, for occasionally his life had depended on accurate assessment of the immediate future. If he was not entirely mistaken, the lady before him appeared to look quite through him, and moreover she seemed not to like what she saw.

His immediate impulse was to inform her quite baldly

that she had no business marching like a madwoman down the middle of a drive, no matter that it was not a public road, and that he cared not a fig for her opinion, whatever it was.

But since the lady had turned without a word and was now well on her way, while he stared in moonling fashion after her, he drew a breath of relief. At least he was not likely to see her again, he told himself, and immediately was sorry he would not.

Bemused by his own startling reactions to what was after all a most commonplace incident, he drove on to the manor house.

Chapter VI

Two days after the accident Celina sat in her small salon entertaining a morning caller.

She had not gone up to the Manor for dinner the day of the honored guest's arrival, pleading indisposition. She did not lie, for the fall through the bushes had jarred her unpleasantly, and even yet she was conscious of soreness in various muscles.

Besides, now that she had met the famous marquess, she did not wish to renew their short acquaintance. She considered him dull, arrogant, self-centered, ruthless—not ruthless, perhaps, she amended, but doubtless he was possessed of vices she did not even know the names of.

After two days of fruitless mulling over every word, every intonation of the short dialogue with him, with the ostensible purpose of finding some weakness that could be exploited to save Lydia from marriage with such a selfish man, she was glad of the diversion of a visitor, even Lawrence Coleraine.

Fortunately the curate's conversation required no attention from her. He seemed content simply to prose on, much as if he were rehearsing his sermon for the next Sunday. From time to time she paid him heed in the interests of a coherent comment when that might be required.

Today's text, she thought, privately amused, seemed to be taken from Saint Paul and dealt crisply with the role of women if not as a whole, then at least in the future life of the curate.

"A helpmeet," he informed her, "to serve her lord in any way she can . . ."

Admirable, thought Celina, until with a start she realized that Mr. Coleraine's "lord" was spelled with a small letter.

". . . to minister to his needs, to comfort him, to . . ."

Celina's mind, sternly disciplined, moved to contemplate far horizons, lest she deal too tartly with those at hand. At length, seeing he had a long way to go before his peroration, she inserted a diversion.

"I am thinking of removing permanently to Bath," she said, grasping at the first thought that came into her head.

Her caller ignored her. "To set the wavering on the right path—what a triumph for a man engaged in the work of the Church!"

"Or," she said distinctly but without effect, "a woman."

She must be going mad, she thought, to listen to this fustian. She had joked with Mary about marrying the curate, but after a morning like this a leap from the church steeple would be more to her liking than a ceremony at the altar within.

At her wit's end, she caught sight of her butler in the doorway. "Yes, Elkins?" she inquired, much relieved.

"Lord and Lady Forsyth," he said, "Lady Gaunt. The Marquess of Wroxton."

The room was suddenly filled with people. Of them all, her eyes caught only Jervis's. There was no surprise in his expression. He had long since, she gathered, discovered her identity. She scarcely knew how she had made her new visitors welcome. Somehow Mr. Coleraine was presented to Lady Gaunt and her nephew, and all found chairs.

After a few false starts the conversation began to flow well. Eleanor Forsyth was full of plans for the entertainment of her house guests, and Lady Gaunt seconded her admirably.

Edmund found much of interest in contemplating morosely the pattern of the rug, and Celina was blushingly aware of the marquess's steady gaze on her. Perhaps he was merely concerned to see that she had survived his reckless driving.

At length the curate judged he had been ignored long enough. Surely, he thought, as the younger son of a peer of the realm as well as a man of the cloth, he need not be shy in the company of a marquess.

He plunged into speech. "Wroxton, I understand that you have spent some time with Sir Robert Ker Porter. I have read some portions of his book, which I believe is soon to be published. How amazing it is that we daily discover the Bible's truths are true indeed. The desolation of Babylon." He sent a fiery glance around the circle of listeners. "Those who deny the Lord, you know, their fields and their monuments, all gone. At any rate, this is what Ker Porter found. Perhaps you would be kind enough to enlighten me further." He eyed Wroxton steadily. "I should like," he added complacently, "to prepare a series of sermons on the subject, perhaps pointing out that even doubters must now admit that the Bible is infallible."

Edmund forgot himself sufficiently to snort. Eleanor's minatory eye fell on him, and he remained silent.

It was at this point that Celina, avoiding a direct glance at her brother or the curate, caught Jervis's eye. He was looking at her, and in his hooded eyes she read an invitation to share his amusement at the spectacle of such a ridiculously pompous clergyman making a fool of himself in a lady's drawing room. It was a curiously intimate glance from a man who had no claim to more than the barest acquaintance with her, and she steeled herself against responding to it.

But she could not still the sudden flutter somewhere

within her. She hoped desperately that her expression revealed no more than a civil acceptance of her guests and their well-known crotchets.

Instead, from an impulsive need to give Jervis a well-deserved set-down, she spoke kindly to Mr. Coleraine and gave the conversation a vigorous turn in another direction.

Edmund had been trying to catch Eleanor's eye for some time. Failing the subtle approach, he said bluntly, "Eleanor, I think you wish to extend this gentleman an invitation."

Thus urged, Eleanor invited the curate to the dinner, a sennight hence, in honor of Lady Gaunt. "And, of course," she added, "for Lord Wroxton as well."

"Why, ma'am," beamed Mr. Coleraine, sending a glance of gratification at Wroxton, "I shall be most happy. I shall prepare a short agenda of questions that occur to me about your travels, and perhaps we may find a few moments apart from the company."

Celina dared not look at Lord Wroxton. She was certain that his startled expression must send her into gales of laughter.

After Mr. Coleraine left, pleading the incessant demands of his flock, Eleanor visibly relaxed. "Now at last," she sighed with an arch glance at Jervis, "we are *en famille.* Celina, I do not understand how you can suffer the company of that man. So prosy! I vow every encounter with him is precisely like suffering a sermon!"

Celina murmured, "He's really very kind."

"I had to invite him, you know," continued Eleanor. "I believe in living at peace with one's neighbors. And of course, Lord Wroxton, you must know that Mr. Coleraine's father is the Earl of Rommillies. Quite eligible, in fact." She lifted her eyebrows in an arch glance at Celina.

"Eleanor . . ." said Edmund futilely.

"How careful we must all be of one another's sensibilities! Celina, I shall make sure you are paired with him at my dinner, even though it may upset the seating. I daresay you will not wish to be preached at after dinner. I have it!

I shall tell Mr. Coleraine that I wish you to take the general off my hands."

"Eleanor—" Edmund repeated in a firmer voice, without result.

Lady Gaunt, in the interests of diverting her niece, interrupted. "The general? Who might he be?"

"General Sir Robert Gordon. Henry's father, you know." She turned confidingly to Jervis. "Henry is quite taken with my second daughter, Nelly. Although with Sir Robert as an example of what Henry may be in later years, I shudder at the prospect!" She laughed. "My sister-in-law does exceedingly well with him. She has a flair with elderly gentlemen."

Jervis had not taken his eyes from Celina almost from the moment of arrival. How well she had handled those two complete boors, both her brother and the preposterous curate! Now, however, he noticed a flush of vexation creeping into Celina's cheeks.

Lady Gaunt came to the rescue. She rose, clearly putting an end to the visit. "My dear," she said kindly to Celina, "do come to the Manor to see me. I should like your opinion on the new embroidery I am starting."

Celina smiled gratefully. "One day soon, I promise."

"Don't let your visit go, Celina," said Eleanor, "until the end of the week. I shall wish you to deal with Cook at that time about the dinner. With so many guests expected, she is bound to turn stubborn."

Edmund, sensing disaster if their visit was prolonged further, took his wife by the elbow. "Come on, I have promised to visit one of the farms."

Eleanor suffered herself to be removed from the salon. In the foyer she paused. "And we must find out Lord Wroxton's favorite dish, mustn't we?" The implication was clear. *Now that he is to be one of us.*

Jervis repressed a shudder. The Forsyth woman was quite beyond belief. He wondered at her breeding and remembered that she was no kin of his, since his aunt had married her uncle. Thank God, he thought fervently. He saw no valid reason why he should stay longer at the Hall than civility to his aunt required. He opened his mouth to inform the group firmly that he would be gone from their midst long before the dinner planned for a week hence.

"Celina, pray do not forget, too, that the invitations must be written. You have such a clear hand!" Eleanor added.

To Jervis's great surprise, he heard himself saying, "After some of the meals I have had in recent years, my palate has deteriorated sadly. I should not like you to take special pains on my behalf."

Why hadn't he told them he would be gone on the morrow, and that not a moment too soon? He suspected that the reason lay in that flush of irritation that had mantled the cheeks of Miss Forsyth upon Eleanor's words. Miss Forsyth should, if she had any regard for herself, simply have told her sister-in-law that if after twenty years Eleanor could not manage a simple country dinner, it was no longer her province to do so.

The tangled web of relationships he saw between Celina and the others of her family seemed, at least on the surface, about to enmesh her in the way that a grapevine stifles its host tree. He made up his mind that he would stay for the dinner—after all, he had the excuse of visiting his manors in the vicinity—and he would be much surprised if he could not at least thwart Lady Forsyth's plan to hang the general around Celina's neck like an ox-yoke.

Watching her visitors disappear down the short drive that connected with the drive to the Manor itself, Celina allowed herself to sag against the door. Assured that none of them had forgotten anything and would return for it, she turned back into the hall. Elkins hovered.

"Tea, miss?"

She nodded gratefully. "Hot and strong, Elkins. And at once, please."

"I think the Bohea would be best, miss."

Sipping the hot, fragrant tea, she laid her head back and

closed her eyes. She wished that Mary were here. Mary knew how to talk to Mr. Coleraine, how to divert him from his absorbing preoccupation with himself and what he was pleased to term his high calling.

Although her irritation stemmed from the curate's want of conduct, the face that smiled at her from inside her closed eyelids was not his thin, ascetic one. Instead, the strong, intelligent features of the man marked by Eleanor as Lydia's future husband came to her and would not go away.

How would Lord Wroxton and Lydia suit? Not at all, she believed. Lydia had as sweet a disposition as a child and was in all things the soul of amiability. But not even her partisan aunt could claim that she had wit enough even to manage a household. And surely Wroxton, widely traveled and widely read, must expect more of a wife than a lovely, smiling face.

The thought of Lydia's smiling was optimistic in the highest degree. It seemed to Celina that of the past six times she had seen Lydia, five of them had consisted mostly of uninhibited shedding of floods of tears.

Suppose Wroxton were indeed infatuated with the girl's beauty. What then, when he discovered that she was no bluestocking?

She tried to picture Lydia as a marchioness, far from the familiar faces of home, and Wroxton himself off to Baghdad or London or indeed, speculating from the little she knew of him, anywhere away from his child-bride. He would neglect her, break her spirit, or even worse.

"I cannot let this happen to her!" said Celina aloud.

Edmund was partial to Lydia. He would never give her away to such an unsuitable husband. But also he was no match for Eleanor, even in such a small matter as trying to stem the spate of her conversation this very morning.

There was no question about it, she told the amused eyes of Jervis's image floating before her mind's eye. I shall quite simply have to stop the marriage myself.

The first step would be to speak cogently to Edmund.

But she had already done so without effect. She could tell him that Wroxton was cruel. But he had been kind today to Mr. Coleraine, even though she suspected that his civility had been due more to his own consequence than true kindness.

There was only one solution. In order to speak convincingly to Edmund she would have to become better acquainted with Lord Wroxton and ferret out all his faults.

Chapter VII

Three days passed, much like other days in the past and, although Celina would not contemplate it, very much like days to be expected in the unchanging future.

Once again, and Celina could not count the number of previous occasions, Nelly sat on the edge of her favorite chair, complaining hotly about her elder sister.

"She pretends to be frightened to death of him! She says," mimicked Nelly, "that he looks at her in *such* a *way*! What does she expect? I myself never heard of a suitor who refused to look at his intended. And when I point this out to her, she simply acts terrified. I make no secret of it, Aunt Celina, when I tell you I am quite out of patience with her."

"I must say that you have little understanding of her. You've been baiting her again."

Nelly started guiltily. She glanced at Celina with some doubt. Her aunt was more accustomed to sympathize than to correct, and she did not quite like the turn the conversation was taking.

"No, I haven't! At least, not really. But if I don't, then who will? Someone should take her in hand."

"You feel your mother is not capable of managing her children?"

Nelly looked up through narrowed eyelids. "I don't understand you this morning, Aunt Celina. Do you have the headache?"

"No, I merely suggest, Nelly, that your mother is the best judge of what is good for Lydia." She realized that her thoughts for three days had run in exactly the opposite direction, but she did not even blush for shame.

"Everybody knows what's best for Lydia," complained Nelly in a moment. "Wroxton is a great catch. Money. An elegant presence. A title. But nobody knows what's best for me."

"And what is that?" inquired Celina, knowing the answer full well.

"Henry, that's what. But if Wroxton comes up to the mark, then Henry and I will be married at once."

Amused, Celina suggested, "What if your mother insists on a London Season for you? After all, your acquaintance with eligible suitors is so small as to be nonexistent."

"I know Henry," she said stubbornly.

Celina remembered a word of Nelly's that had slipped past without comment. She inquired now, " 'If Wroxton comes up to the mark,' you said. Surely nobody expects him to make up his mind in a week."

"My mother does," Nelly revealed. "She's hoping to have Papa make the announcement at her big dinner. In truth, that's why she's planning the affair."

"But it was to honor Lady Gaunt!"

Nelly was sufficiently well brought up not to contradict her mother, not precisely. She said only, "A very *proper* reason, don't you think?"

Celina fell into an appalled silence. She had no idea that the affair had progressed so swiftly. Had Wroxton in only three days found in Lydia his heart's desire? Every fiber of Celina's being insisted that Nelly must be wrong. But it occurred to her that if all were settled, then Nelly's complaints had no foundation.

"So," she probed, "Wroxton has offered?"

"I don't think so," said Nelly frankly. "But if he does,

and Lydia turns him down, as she probably will unless Mama insists, he'll never offer again."

"Not much of a catch," protested Celina, "if one refusal turns him off."

Nelly ignored her comment. "I'll do anything to marry Henry. I can bring Mama around if she does talk about London. And if I have to, I'll elope."

"I should hope you have more sense than to run off to Scotland. A marriage over the anvil will not do Henry's army career a great deal of good."

"There are ways," said Nelly darkly. "But if Lyddy would only get over the mopes, I won't have to worry, will I?"

"I think," said Celina as a final pronouncement, "you are stirring up a tempest in a very small teapot."

After Nelly had left, Celina's thoughts remained in some turmoil. From past experience she could accurately assess Nelly's concern. Nelly's primary interest to the exclusion of all others remained Nelly herself. She believed Henry to be necessary to her and therefore she would have Henry. It struck Celina for the first time that she had never been made privy to Henry's own thoughts. She was quite sure, however, that either Henry Gordon was not as much in love with Nelly as that young lady thought or that he was a master of the stiff, unrevealing countenance.

But whether Wroxton had offered or not, his lingering at the Manor was not easily explained. He had been out of the country for some years, it was true, and perhaps he found the companionship of his aunt especially beguiling after his absence. She wished she could simply dismiss the entire family to their fate. But they were, after all, her only near relatives, and unfeeling as they often were, she believed Edmund and the children at least were fond of her.

It was time to walk up to the Manor and ask Eleanor what her wishes were for the dinner menu. It was too late to tell her that she did not wish to act as liaison between the mistress of the house and her cook.

She put on her new walking costume. For the first time she realized what an ugly color it was. How could she have been so misguided as to think that a pelisse of gray kerseymere lined with white sarsnet was becoming to her fair complexion and light hair? She remembered then that she had thought the color matched her dark-gray eyes. It did, of course. But gray was a fading color, reminiscent of half-mourning. Grieving for her spinsterhood, she thought acidly.

She hurried out of the house before she could yield to the impulse to change her costume. It did not matter what she looked like—a quite proper attitude, she remembered, for the wife of a curate. She had by design not seen Mr. Coleraine alone since that tentative conversation. She did not wish in the least to marry him. But she was more aware than before of that certain uneasiness that had come upon her recently.

A glance at the overcast sky told her that rain before she returned home was a real possibility. She hurried up the drive to the Manor. The carefully manicured lawn was just ahead of her when she caught sight of movement to her left. Two people were strolling along one of the paths cut through the woods to display more effectively Eleanor's imported rhododendrons.

She recognized them and stopped short—Lord Wroxton and Lydia! Lydia was looking her loveliest in sapphire blue and hanging on Wroxton's arm! Celina, at the last moment, refrained from gaping in astonishment.

"Oh, dear Aunt," said Lydia in a breathless little voice. "Did you come—have you seen—of course they are not in bloom now! H-how foolish of me!" She blushed charmingly.

Informed that Lydia shrank from Wroxton, even feared his presence, Celina was given a rude shock by the present amiability of the pair before her. Her unguarded glance flew to Wroxton. His eyes expressed, as though he were sure of her understanding and sympathy, a quizzing humor that locked her into an intimacy with him she did not expect.

She felt as though she had received a powerful jolt in some undefined manner. Shaken, she fought to conceal her surprise.

"Aunt Celina," breathed Lydia, the picture of shy happiness, "Lord Wroxton is so kind. He has been telling me about his travels."

Amused appeal deepened in Wroxton's eyes. Celina ignored him. "How nice. I am so glad you are enjoying your stroll." She felt a complete fool, mouthing such commonplace words. Quite like Eleanor, talking idly without significance, she thought in self-disgust. Burning to establish her dignity again, for her own gratification, she turned to the traveled Lord Wroxton and quoted, " 'I will a round unvarnish'd tale deliver'?"

" 'Her father oft invited me,' " he answered. The aptness of his quick answer shook her.

"I do not understand," Lydia complained, her lovely face wearing a puzzled expression.

Immediately Wroxton bent to her and smiled. "Your aunt chooses to quote *Othello*, even though it is nothing to the point."

"Oh," said Lydia, relieved. "Only Shakespeare."

Feeling she had the worst of the exchange, Celina hurried up to the Hall. She did not see the long, speculative glance that he sent after her.

At the Hall she came upon her brother wearing an odd expression she suspected to be one of triumph. "Come into the library, Celina," he said in a low voice, as though he did not wish to be overheard. He closed the door behind them.

"Well, Edmund, are you plotting against the government? Why the air of conspiracy? Which, I must tell you, is not sufficiently well concealed to fool a child in leading strings."

"Did you see them?"

"See? The only persons I saw were Lydia and the marquess. Are they plotters, too?"

"Don't be foolish. You know I mean them. I sent them out together."

Her father oft invited me, indeed!

"Far better to be alone, you know, than to have Eleanor hovering over them, making all kinds of hints. I vow it's enough to turn a man off matrimony for life! How did they seem to you?"

So Edmund was promoting the match that only a couple of days ago he had been dead set against. And Lydia herself seemed more than ready to accept Wroxton's offer, if he made one. There seemed no doubt that he would. Celina refused to admit that the sight of the two strolling along in complete amity had upset her.

She had promised Lydia that she would try to convince Edmund that the girl was completely opposed to any marriage. She had believed herself to be Lydia's last resort, even though she refused to entertain the notion of riding in a donkey cart. She was somewhat nettled to have seen her niece quite openly hanging on a gentleman's arm and sending him a shy glance of admiration and trust.

It would all end well. Lydia would be a marchioness before the year was out, and Nelly could marry her soldier. No more would they come to beg her help, pulling her in opposite directions, demanding her partisanship against their parents. This was what she wanted, wasn't it?

"How did they seem?" repeated Edmund.

"In total charity with each other," she snapped. She could not refrain from adding, with an unexpected waspish twist, "Lydia seemed much like a child toddling after her dear papa."

She left Edmund, his mouth agape, and sought out her sister-in-law. She found Eleanor in the back parlor that she used for the ordinary business of her day, small pieces of paper strewn over the table. She saw that Eleanor was already becoming undone.

"Invitations," she explained in response to Celina's question. "I cannot conceive how we can entertain these hordes to dinner. But Edmund insists that we live in all charity with our neighbors, you know."

"Yes," murmured Celina. "I recall you said as much after you invited Mr. Coleraine."

"General Sir Robert and Lady Gordon, because Nelly would ring a peal over me if I didn't include them," enumerated Eleanor, "and the Ashburtons and the Middletons and the Lyttons and the surgeon, Mr. Emerson, and his wife—you know she is connected closely with the Sawbridge family—"

Stemming the tide, Celina said firmly, "I know that at first all seems a muddle, but you always come straight in the end." She thought a moment. Her reassurances sounded somewhat inadequate in her ears. With shameless flattery, she added, "Your dinner parties are quite the envy of all your guests."

Gratified, Eleanor visibly relaxed. "I believe you are right, because I recall only a month ago that Lady Middleton asked me the recipe for those French chicken cutlets that Mrs. Pardoe makes so well. Do you think you could persuade her to make them again?"

Celina sat. "Tell me what you wish to serve, Eleanor, and I will tell Cook."

Eleanor searched her papers and found one on which she had scribbled a few notes. "I thought we might start with carrot soup à la Crecy and soup à la reine. I know it is customary at this time of year to have a dish of stewed eels. What do you think? And perhaps for an entrée vol-au-vent of chicken."

She moved on past the entrée into the second course—rump of beef à la jardinière, for one dish—and the third course, including grouse, pheasants, compote of peaches, scalloped oysters.

At last Celina surfaced from discussing the technical details of a dinner for twenty-four. She gathered her notes together. "I'll tell Cook your wishes, Eleanor."

"She is much more amiable if she thinks the menu is of your contrivance, you know."

Celina's emotions were mixed. The unsettling feeling of

impending change had come to her again. If Lydia and Nelly were to marry and move away, as they gave every sign of doing, she would feel their loss keenly. On the other hand, it was becoming clearer to her that it was past time that she look beyond the confines of Forsyth Hall and make some kind of satisfactory life for herself.

Without intending it she asked, "How long is Wroxton staying?"

Eleanor smiled in a self-congratulatory fashion. "He says only until after the dinner. But I have no objection to telling you, Celina, since you are after all almost family, that Edmund may have a very interesting announcement to make to our friends then."

Almost family? When a day did not go by but what one or another of them stormed down to the Dower House, giving vent to the most unbridled emotions, complaining bitterly against parent or offspring. Almost family? She did not trust herself to answer. Eleanor was waiting for the inevitable question, but Celina did not oblige her.

Her own observation, an hour since, told her that Lydia, far from rebelling against the proposed match, now, like Desdemona, listened enthralled to the tales of her Moor, and was falling in love with "what she fear'd to look on."

"One favor, Celina," said Eleanor. "Pray find out from Wroxton what his favorite dish is. Whatever it is, no doubt Cook can manage."

Celina said tartly, "That is far too intimate a question to ask him. At least he would consider it so."

Her sister-in-law demurred. "I think not." She glanced at Celina with scarcely concealed scorn. "I daresay I know better what gentlemen are accustomed to." Having brought Celina to a renewed sense of her jejune spinsterhood, she moved on. "I shall of course pair you with Coleraine. I cannot think it will cause talk."

Celina held her tongue. Edmund was right. His lady had the bit in her teeth, and there was no reasoning with her. She was convinced that Wroxton had come to Forsyth Hall to offer for Lydia and she would not allow herself to be diverted from that belief.

In truth, Celina thought, if Lydia was agreeable, then there was nothing for it but to accept Eleanor's arrangements. But the relief she should feel, now that the family quarrel was well on its way to resolution, did not come. The marriage was wrong, but she did not know why.

In the meantime, there was still the dinner—the announcement dinner, as Eleanor had hinted—to arrange. She went to find Mrs. Pardoe in the kitchen. Cook greeted her entrance with satisfaction. Once again Mrs. Pardoe had brought Lady Forsyth to a recognition of the importance of the cook to the smooth running of the establishment. She made much of walking the ragged edge of defiance of Lady Forsyth's orders, finding ways of thwarting requests for special dishes: the berries were too green to pick or the eels had gone off or the stockman had not provided the butcher with a suitable sheep.

But for Celina, whom she had known and loved since her childhood, she would do anything.

"Ah," she said, after Celina had gone over the plans with her, "quite a fancy party. But after all, to tell about the marriage, I suppose it's called for."

"Marriage?" echoed Celina. Had the world gone mad? The man had been here less than a week, and he was all but wed. It was true that Celina had not seen much of the family, except of course for those disaffected members who came to the Dower House, and it was clear that affairs had marched more swiftly than she had suspected. But just the same, it had not seemed to her there in the park that Wroxton was mad with love for his Desdemona.

It is not your affair, she told herself sternly. So engrossed in her own thoughts was she that she nearly missed Cook's last remark. "Although I shouldn't think he'd be raiding the schoolroom, not with all them travels I hear about, and women galore, I doubt not."

"Women?" Celina repeated faintly.

"Stands to reason, don't it? You go to Turkey, you got to live like the Turks. And everybody knows what they are. Now," she continued, dismissing all manner of heathen foreigners with a shrug, "about them little cakes you mentioned. I've got the saffron on hand already . . ."

Chapter VIII

The night of the dinner party arrived, even though Celina on occasion believed it never would.

Besides expecting Celina to deal with Cook about the menu, Eleanor gradually extended the areas of, as she said, her sister-in-law's particular abilities, so that the table settings, the placing of the guests, the arrangements for refreshments later in the evening, and, as the date drew closer, advising the Forsyth ladies on the proper costume to wear—all was in Celina's hands.

By the time the night of the dinner party came, she was exhausted. She longed simply to lie down on her bed and sleep at least for two days. But she was expected to pair with Coleraine, to keep General Sir Robert Gordon amused, and—Eleanor had said only this morning—to keep old Lady Ashburton from asking too many pointed questions of their honored guest, Lord Wroxton.

"I thought the dinner was in honor of Lady Gaunt," Celina pointed out.

"Circumstances have altered," said Eleanor loftily.

Celina had pulled from her wardrobe the newest evening dress she had, quite in the highest fashion of two years before. She could not remember even the occasion for which it had been made. Whatever country gala it had graced, she had not donned it since.

Now, an hour before the guests were to arrive, she examined herself from head to toe in her mirror. The net frock was worn over a blue satin slip. The body of the gown was cut very low at the neck, with an extremely short waist, and was marked by a row of blond lace just under the bosom. The sleeves were becomingly short and decorated with ribbon knots, and the full skirt was trimmed with a rich flounce of blond lace embroidered with satin cockleshells.

She laughed ruefully at herself for taking such pains with her appearance. No one would look at her, especially since all eyes would be fastened on the prospective bride. Lydia's proposed happiness did nothing at all to raise Celina's spirits.

It was only because she was excessively weary. Or perhaps because she missed Mary. Surely there could be no other reason for her mopes.

She was early at the Manor. She checked the table once more, with Pardoe at her elbow, and pronounced the arrangements good. "At least," said Celina, "if aught is amiss, it's beyond time to set it right."

The rooms were unfamiliar in their party guise. Huge palms had been brought in from the conservatory, which was attached to the side of the house and formed an extension from the larger parlor, and stood around the walls. She expected guests to wander from the parlors into the conservatory. Perhaps she should see that the gardeners had rearranged the remaining greenery into a presentable facade and covered up the gaps left by the abstracted trees.

Pardoe caught her at the door. "Begging pardon, miss, but this just came from Lady Ashburton."

She read the missive swiftly. "Oh, Pardoe!" she cried. "Another change. The Ashburtons have house guests and they're bringing them! We'll have to rearrange the table again!"

"Very good, miss," he said without expression. Later, to Mrs. Pardoe, he exclaimed with some heat, "Blessed if I wouldn't take a tuck out of that messenger, not getting it here till now!"

She turned to look longingly into the conservatory. The greenery lining both sides of the center walk beckoned, promising, to her fevered imagination, the solace of inarticulate things. Nobody in the conservatory would demand of her that she change the table again at the last moment, adding three places after she had already arranged to remove two because of the defection only this morning of the Lyttons.

"Give me a moment, Pardoe, and I'll come."

"Very good, miss."

The scent of fresh-turned watered earth and the subtle aroma generated by living plants met her at the door. At once she felt calmer, if not restored to high spirits. She moved slowly along the walk, letting her thoughts drift as they would, as long as they avoided the dinner party.

Suddenly she was aware that she was not alone. She looked up, startled, into the face of Lord Wroxton.

"Oh!"

"My apologies, Miss Forsyth. I did not mean to startle you." Looking more closely at her, his expression altered. "Is something amiss?" he asked anxiously.

She closed her eyes for a moment. To her surprise she found herself confiding in him. "Only that wretched Ashburton woman. She's calmly announced that she has three house guests who will accompany her tonight. She ought to be put in the stocks in the village square!"

With an amused twitch of his lips, Jervis agreed. "Or perhaps, more appropriately, be presented, herself, with a dozen uninvited guests on the verge of starvation."

"Delightful! Especially if the incident were to take place in a violent snowstorm, so that they would be unable to leave for a sennight!" She chuckled. "How ridiculous this is!"

"I don't believe I have heard you laugh before," he said in a commonplace tone. "But I surmise you have been far too busy to find amusement."

"My sister-in-law, you must know, is subject to nervousness."

He inclined his head gravely. "I am sure her frailty quite incapacitates her."

She glared suspiciously at him to detect any sign of inappropriate laughter at his hostess. He gazed back, his demeanor quite unexceptionable. She relented all at once. "She does depend too greatly upon me, I know. But it seems to be a habit, and the fault is not entirely hers." She thought a moment, smiling to herself.

"I should very much like to hear," he said after a moment, "the thought that amuses you."

Why not? she thought. After all, he is about to become one of the family. "It's Cook. Mrs. Pardoe, you know. She carries on such a continuing quarrel with Eleanor. If it were not so uncomfortable, it would be quite diverting."

"Then you are required to deal with Cook, I gather," Jervis probed delicately. "And, I notice, all else dealing with this entertainment."

It was not so much the words he spoke as the tone of voice in which he spoke them. There was a note of concern in it, a genuine interest in her affairs, even indignation on her behalf, that nearly undid her. No one had ever before noticed what she did for Eleanor's parties, to say nothing of considering the unfairness of Lady Forsyth's demands on her. She felt moisture prickling behind her eyelids.

She pulled herself together with an effort. "Old family servants," she explained. "I know their ways."

"But," he objected gently, "you have your own establishment."

She looked up. He was watching her, his eyes intent upon her with an expression that unexpectedly caused a tumult in her breast like nothing she had experienced before. If it were not anatomically impossible, she would have thought her heart had turned over.

She could not take her eyes from his. He took a small step toward her and reached out one hand in a most daring, unconventional, and welcome gesture. She trembled suddenly, feeling herself on the brink of the unknown, aware of the most ridiculous longing to hurl herself into his arms and cry on his shoulder.

Not cry, she amended, a more delicious possibility occurring to her.

It was a very special moment, she thought afterward, and who knew what might have come of it? Certainly, had Pardoe not appeared at the conservatory door, clearing his throat with significance, the events of the next few weeks might well have taken an entirely different turn.

As it was, she whirled, feeling her cheeks growing scarlet, and said, successfully concealing her irritation with him, "What is it, Pardoe?"

"It's Captain Gordon, miss. Lady Gordon sent word that her son will come with them to dinner."

Suddenly shy, she exchanged a glance with the man who was expected to marry her niece. The precious moment was shattered, but perhaps she could salvage a few iridescent fragments to keep in her memory.

"I'm just coming, Pardoe."

After she had dealt with the table, she hurried up the broad, curving staircase. She did not dare chance meeting Lord Wroxton until they were both surrounded by hordes of people. Not that Wroxton would have any reluctance, she told herself, for he was a man of great and varied experience and formidable poise. But she herself had no assurance that she could maintain the aplomb expected of a twenty-six-year-old spinster of excellent breeding.

She found upstairs the confusion and incipient panic that could be expected thirty minutes before guests were due to arrive.

Lydia called out, asking Celina's opinion of her gown. It

was a round dress of white crape spotted with white satin over a white sarsnet slip. At the hem the full skirt bore a double row of flowers and leaves in pale yellow silk. "Much better," murmured Celina, "than pomona-green, I assure you."

Prettily Lydia asked her aunt to fasten her pearl necklace. Thanking her, she whispered, "A favor, Aunt Celina? I do wish you will protect me this evening."

"Protect you?" echoed Celina. "In your own house?" Seeing the girl's obvious distress, she added, "Against what, dear?"

"It's Wroxton, you know. He must in civility greet everybody and talk to them, and it would look excessively odd if he were to stay with me the whole evening."

Then it was settled, thought Celina, and that little episode in the conservatory meant nothing to him. He had the instincts, it was obvious, of the Grand Turk. Well, she thought indignantly, he had chosen Lydia, and Lydia he should have. But he would not also have Celina.

She was shocked at the direction her unguided thoughts were taking. A simple look of concern, an intimate glance of understanding, and she melted like the greenest girl!

Lydia was still talking when Celina paid heed to her again. "Wroxton is so kind, you know, and I do not mind talking to him at all. But I dread the general. He booms so at one and he quite frightens me." Changing the subject, she added, "Mr. Coleraine, too. He does not boom precisely, but he looks at one as though he believes the worst. Mama says you are likely to marry him, and I shall be most unhappy if you do not like him excessively."

"Never fear, Lydia," said Celina, scarce knowing what she said. "I shall marry no one I do not like."

She moved down the hall. Nelly's door was open, and Gurney, the maid who served both girls, was busy hooking up Nelly's gown. The apricot crape set off the girl's dark hair to perfection.

"Aunt, I'm so glad you're here. Tell me, is that Pamela

Ashburton really coming? Gurney said she heard so. That homely girl! I saw her once, standing at a gate, and I declare I thought at first she was a pony."

"Nelly! That's disgraceful!" Celina suppressed the strong remarks that leaped to her tongue. It was Eleanor's right to discipline the wayward Nelly. But, Celina had to admit, it was beyond possibility that Nelly would ever feel the rough side of her mother's tongue.

Still, expressing her displeasure in the only way open to her, Celina left Nelly without a word. She must make Eleanor acquainted with the latest news from the dining room, and there was little time left.

Her news was entirely unwelcome. "Mark my words, Celina, that Ashburton woman sent word to her granddaughter and her parents after she received my invitation. She won't admit it, you may be sure, but she heard that Wroxton was here and she didn't waste an hour. That Pamela is such a dowd! I cannot think that Wroxton could ever be taken in by Lady Ashburton's machinations!"

The same lady, remembered Celina, that he wished to provide with half a dozen ravenous guests. She dared not think about Wroxton. He was Lydia's.

"Of course he is quite committed to Lydia," Eleanor hurried on, "and there's nothing to worry about. But I'm counting on you, Celina, to see that Wroxton is no more than civil to any of those Ashburtons." Suddenly she turned, as an appalling thought came to her. "Good God, Celina, you didn't seat them next to him, did you?"

She was becoming a bit weary of them all, including Wroxton. "I shouldn't think," she said, tartness edging her voice, "that Wroxton would need much protection."

Eleanor's eyes narrowed. "I wonder at you, Celina. I shouldn't think being a guest at a small dinner party would set you so on edge!"

Celina stared at her in unbelief. A guest? Small dinner party? She shook her head. There was no talking to the woman. They simply traveled on different roads.

She stopped at the door on her way out. "By the way, Nelly's captain will be here too. Lady Gordon sent word not an hour ago."

Eleanor became aware that she owed Celina some acknowledgment of her efforts. "Dear sister, you must not think that I am ungrateful for your help. Edmund sets such a high value on entertaining, you know, to keep up the Forsyth name. He does not care that I become quite ill with the strain. All day I have suffered the most dreadful headache. I am sure I am quite out of looks tonight. And I have no help from the servants—"

She stopped short guiltily. She knew full well who had done all the arranging of the dinner. And not only this dinner, but nearly every entertainment of any size that had been given since her arrival at Forsyth Hall as a bride. But she had pointed out to Celina that her efforts were primarily to be considered as a Forsyth responsibility for dear Edmund and the Forsyth name. Surely this was reasonable.

She would have been surprised had she been able to read Celina's mind at that moment. Far from caring inordinately about the Forsyth name, Celina had become aware that the hairline crack in her peaceable life was widening. Now that she could pay heed to the fracture, she could recognize a burgeoning resentment of Eleanor's burdens placed heavily on her own shoulders. For perhaps the first time she thought seriously of removing from the Dower House permanently. She could take a house in Bath, she could do all manner of things. But not tonight.

Eleanor was watching her in the mirror. "Celina, you did pair yourself with Coleraine?" At Celina's nod, she went on, "I should like a favor, dear Celina. Oh, no, not for me, but really a duty to the family."

Celina lifted her eyebrows.

"Keep an eye on Nelly and Henry, dear, if you will. Nelly is so impulsive, and I wish no scandal, especially in Wroxton's presence. I shall not let anything or anyone stand between my Lydia and such a magnificent catch as Wroxton."

* * *

The guests arrived, and the dinner party was *en train*. Celina's wits went scampering. The rooms were hot, and the high-pitched hum of a dozen conversations at once rang in her ears. Pardoe and his staff silently dealt with the serving of the many courses, and Celina could relax, letting her mind empty itself.

She still had tasks to perform. Lydia asked for protection, Nelly wished Pamela Ashburton removed from Henry's vicinity as well as Sir Robert and Lady Gordon diverted.

Eleanor insisted that Wroxton be delivered from any kind of *ennui*, especially that generated by the predatory Lady Ashburton. And underneath all, Celina must steel herself against the announcement that Eleanor had told her to expect. She watched her brother to detect the first movements toward rising to proclaim the great good fortune of his daughter Lydia.

But the moment did not come.

At length, when the guests surged toward the parlors, Lady Gaunt caught her wrist and drew her aside. "My dear Celina," said Aunt Tibby, "I've been wondering where you could have got to. But then I was told that you were slaving in the dungeons to concoct this perfectly dreadful meal."

"Dreadful? You do not flatter me, you know."

"Nor do I criticize. I know Eleanor's touch when I see it. All you are required to do is move the work forward, is that it?"

"Something like that," she admitted. "But Aunt Tibby, when is the announcement to come?"

Lady Gaunt's mouth tightened grimly. "Not tonight, anyway."

"Then he has not offered?"

The older woman looked closely at her. "He's a fool if he does," she said in a downright fashion. "The girl's got the brains of a peahen."

"But—" Celina was on the verge of a question indecorous in the extreme. How could one ask an elderly lady acquaintance, no matter how fond one was of her, the details of her matchmaking endeavors?

One couldn't.

"What a motley group Eleanor has assembled!" sniffed Lady Gaunt. "If these are all close neighbors, then I thank God I live in Surrey. At least, I suppose my own friends might well look quite as odd as these if I did not know them so well," she added generously. "Tell me, Celina, should you rescue Jervis from that willow-wand Coleraine?"

Celina looked across the room to where Jervis, his back toward her, was caught in conversation by the curate. She felt her heartbeat falter. Was Lord Wroxton arranging with the clergyman for the wedding service Eleanor expected to announce? Her cheeks flamed.

The older lady kept her gaze fixed on her nephew and Mr. Coleraine. The latter was talking at length, and Jervis gave every indication of intent listening. "I have been told, dear Celina," murmured Aunt Tibby, "that Rommillies' young sprout intends to marry you. It is not clear to me whether he has spoken to Edmund or not."

Celina's irritation was visible. Lady Gaunt smiled to herself. "I wager he is speaking about saving souls, or some such subject that should never be brought into a drawing room. Could you do me the greatest favor, my child? Go and rescue Jervis from that idiotic man for me."

Reluctantly Celina made her way slowly across the room. Jervis would certainly not relish her interference. She would like to tell him that it was at his aunt's bidding that she came, but she knew she would not. Let him think what he would; it made no difference to her!

As she drew closer, she caught bits of conversation. The curate was listening to Jervis as though the Pythoness at Delphi were reporting for the oracle.

"Yes," Jervis was saying, "my cousin is quite settled at Ely Cathedral for the present. I have not of course had occasion to visit him since my return to England."

"I am sure I would have much in common with His Grace the Bishop," said Mr. Coleraine with purpose, "even though my *churchly* rank is lowly. But that fact, fortunately, could be changed by a word in the proper ear, so to speak."

Good Lord, thought Wroxton, appalled, the man's touting for my influence! He required a set-down of the first order! Wroxton opened his lips to deliver the much-needed rebuke, but the words never came.

Judging from Jervis's expression, thought Celina, as she arrived at his elbow, it was time for rescue.

"You must forgive me, Mr. Coleraine," she said sweetly, and added without truth, "I think the general will be glad of a word with you."

The curate looked around him, startled, as though suddenly brought back from a far place. "Oh, yes, yes, of course. My lord, I shall hope to continue this enlightening conversation at another time. The general, you said? I wonder—yes, yes, I shall go to him at once."

He was gone then, weaving his way through the crowded room to the far wall, where General Sir Robert Gordon had found a comfortable chair and did not intend to move from it.

Suddenly shy, Celina realized she was trapped. She could not remove Jervis's companion without offering him someone in exchange. She mumbled something. When he did not answer at once, she looked up at him curiously.

He was watching her with a quizzical expression. "I am not quite sure," he said in a low voice intended for her ears alone, "whether you were talking fustian, but it has occurred to me that the general does not wish to speak to anyone. In fact, I should judge he is at this moment expressing to Lady Gordon an intolerant wish to be home."

She glanced across the room, taking care not to be noticed. "Oh, dear," she said, "he does look excessively cross. And I sent Mr. Coleraine to him. He'll be furious!"

Jervis nodded. "The general or the curate? No matter. But I am quite sure you had some purpose."

Belatedly it occurred to her that he believed she wished to talk to him herself. "Surely—but I didn't—I thought you were bored—"

"And of course you were quite right. How could you know that I was longing to talk to you rather than that pallid excuse for—" Remembering the family gossip, he cut his words short.

"But I didn't think so."

She looked up at him and lost her words of explanation. His expression did not change, but the warmth that kindled in his eyes jarred her.

Jervis, seeing in her what he believed to be alarm, made haste to repress his amusement. He was moving too fast. Indeed, he had become conscious in the last week of a strong wish to inform her sister-in-law that Celina was not to be used as a drudge for this wretched family. He knew from judicious inquiry that she was far from financially dependent on her brother. But the habit of her lifetime was undoubtedly powerful, and resistance must inevitably lead to loneliness.

He had engaged in furious thought since he had spoken to her in the conservatory. Even exhausted as she was, she had spirit and more charm in her little finger than existed in all of Forsyth Hall. If he could make her see what was happening to her—that she must not allow herself to be catapulted into marriage with the greatest bore in England . . .

He was wryly amused at himself. Never had he seen himself as Sir Galahad, but now that he thought about it, such a role might suit him well.

They were both turned slightly away from the company and had fallen silent, she from shyness and an overwhelming sense of his presence, and he because he dared not frighten her away. Thus they were both in a position, as others were not, to have a clear view of the door to the conservatory.

Nelly, flushing angrily, emerged first. Just behind her,

also with reddened cheeks reflecting some kind of emotion, came Henry. The two of them together in the conservatory! Quite beyond the bounds of decent behavior.

"What can Henry be thinking of!" exclaimed Celina, quite forgetting she was not alone.

"I should think there was not much doubt of that," said her companion dryly. "But perhaps you did not notice. The young man looked quickly over his shoulder. No, pray do not move. I think our drama is not yet over."

After a few moments the next act proceeded. Tentatively, looking carefully around and believing she was not observed, Pamela Ashburton came in from the conservatory. She was not flushed, as Nelly had been, but there lurked in her secret smile a hint of triumph.

"What shall we conclude, Miss Forsyth?" murmured Jervis in Celina's ear. "That the daughter of the house has discovered her soldier making forays into enemy territory? I have seen just such a look as Miss Ashburton wears at the moment," he mused, "on the face of a bedouin hunter just after he caught sight of a fresh game track."

"How horrible!" said Celina in a muffled voice. "Truly, Lord Wroxton, this is not an amusing diversion!"

"You surprise me," said Jervis, "particularly since I perceive, with great approval, that you are choking with laughter."

She turned, to him, eyes dancing. "You quite undermine my decorum," she accused, "and I dare not think what Eleanor will have to say to me. I was particularly charged with observing Nelly this evening."

"Indeed?" Jervis raised an eyebrow. "I can affirm that she was indeed observed." Suddenly he perceived real distress beneath her rueful laughter. With concern he asked, "Will any harm come of this, do you think?"

"I devoutly hope not. But I see Pardoe coming for me. Pray excuse me."

Every instinct informed him that his dearest wish was to stand in the center of the room, coldly ring a peal over

Nelly's mother—who was she to delegate chaperoning her own daughter?—and carry Celina off to the Dower House where he could, over a restoring glass of sherry, tell her . . .

Tell her what? He was not quite clear in his mind yet. It was just as well, then, that he stood where he was, watching Pardoe speak quietly to her, and following her with his eyes as she hurried out of the room.

Chapter IX

If Celina had hoped that the days following Lady Forsyth's dinner party would signal a return to the routine tenor of country life, she was wrong. Indeed, she had scarcely opened her eyes on the following morning when the aftermath of the party burst upon her.

Her maid entered Celina's bedroom with an early cup of tea and set it down on the stand next to the bed. "Go away, Ford," groaned Celina. "I have just now got to sleep."

With some indignation in her manner, Ford explained, "Believe me, Miss Celina, I should not have in the ordinary way come to wake you. You need your rest after such a large entertainment. But better I come up and wake you with your tea than with what's waiting for you downstairs."

Celina had closed her eyes, the better to warn Ford away, but after the maid's unclear explanation she opened them again. "What do you mean, Ford? I must be woolly in the head this morning. Did you say something is waiting downstairs?"

Ford did not answer directly. She opened the curtains. "The day is fair enough. At least to start out."

Celina pulled herself up against the pillows and reached

for the teacup. "My robe, Ford, as long as I must wake up. What is downstairs that needs to be dealt with?"

At the door Ford struck a dramatic pose. "It's Miss Nelly, miss, and in a rare taking. She wanted to come right up and wake you," she added in a horrified voice, "but I told her right out, over my dead body you'll wake Miss Celina."

Her expected morning of repose vanishing, Celina nodded, resigned. "Quite right, Ford. Although I should hope it would not come to that. What can possibly be agitating Nelly?"

She did not realize she had spoken the last words aloud until Ford answered. "I'm sure I cannot say, miss, but to tell the truth of it, I've not seen her so wild."

The teacup empty, Celina threw back the coverlet and swung her legs out of bed. "Help me dress then, please. And ring for Carrie. Ask her to tell Miss Nelly I shall join her in a few moments."

All the while Ford was dressing her in a round dress of jaconet, made with a full skirt that moved pleasingly around the ankles, trimmed at the hem with a double row of buttons, above which was a trimming of the same rose material as the dress itself but arranged in diamond-shaped puffs, Celina recalled in detail the evening before. Searching for the cause of the reputed storm in the salon below, she found none.

Ford finished brushing her curls into fashionable ringlets, one falling before each ear. "I cannot imagine what maggot has got into her head," said Celina frankly. "But doubtless I shall soon learn."

She found Nelly in the salon, pacing back and forth. Catching sight of her niece's expression, Celina's heart sank. Ford's description of Nelly's mood had not given the full picture.

"Aunt Celina! How could you sleep so late? It's nearly ten o'clock!"

"I had expected," said Celina in a calm voice, "to sleep until noon."

"But I *need* you!"

Celina did not try to hide her resigned sigh. "Very well, you need me. But if you expect me to champion your cause, whatever it may be, with your mother, let me tell you that knights in shining armor are quite out of fashion."

"But you must tell me what to do!"

"Very well. The first thing is to sit down. In that bergère chair, I think. I shall not need then to turn my head to follow your conversation."

Instantly all sympathy, Nelly flew to her. "Poor aunt! I knew Pardoe made that punch far too strong. Does your head ache?"

"No," said Celina, "but I am sure, when you tell me what brought you here at an outrageously early hour, that it will."

Nelly recognized a note in Celina's voice that she had heard before, not often, as it happened, but frequently enough for her to understand that her aunt was in an unusually sharp mood.

"Perhaps I should not have come so early," conceded Nelly, "but the truth is I haven't slept a wink! All night!"

"How unfortunate," said Celina. "But of course I quite see your point. Sleep is quite unnecessary."

"Well, it is, when your whole life is lying in pieces."

"Very well. I see I shall have to hear it. Nelly, pray make it short. But first another cup of tea will do us both good."

By the time Elkins had brought the tea tray and left, manfully concealing his intense curiosity, Celina had recovered her usual good spirits. Something had clearly stirred Nelly to a high pitch of agitation. "What can have happened, Nelly?"

"It's Henry!"

Celina was startled. "He's not had an accident!"

"No. At least, not yet. But if he thinks he can flirt with that dreary-faced Pamela Ashburton in the conservatory, he may have one."

Nelly looked quite fierce. Celina almost laughed, but

something about the intensity of the girl's indignation set off alarm bells. Nelly, overwrought, bore a close resemblance to a festival girandole, ready to explode in all directions at once. As the nearest bystander, Celina had a duty to redirect the blast and confine it to harmless display.

"I remember," she said, "that you came out of the conservatory with Henry. Surely Henry has sufficient decorum not to be caught in *flagrante delicto*?" Deliberately she suppressed the memory of Pamela herself emerging in a surreptitious manner through that same door, a sly smile on her thin lips. Whatever had gone on in the conservatory last night, Celina was sure she did not wish to be informed.

"He says not," said Nelly darkly.

"Perhaps you should reconsider marrying Henry," ventured Celina, "if you cannot trust what he says."

"Oh, I believe what he says happened, which was nothing at all. But I do not trust Pamela an inch. Henry is quite innocent, and he cannot see through that simpering slyness. He thinks that he was simply seeing that the girl was not lonely! Can you believe that?"

"It may be true, you know."

"He thinks it is true. What Pamela thinks is that she's got her big foot in the door and she'll winkle him out before I know it. This tea's cold."

"I'll ring for a fresh pot."

Nelly's arguments had produced a thirst, and she gulped down the first fresh cup without stopping. In the meantime, Celina cast about in her mind for soothing solutions to a problem that seemed at least on the surface to be excessively trivial. Her advice was not called for.

"Lord Wroxton is the answer," said Nelly in a matter-of-fact way. "He's got to offer for Lydia."

Celina felt sick. She did not know why she had this morning taken such a loathing to the thought of Lydia in the arms of Lord Wroxton. It was a most suitable arrangement. Everybody said so. Aunt Tibby had sent for him for this specific reason, Eleanor was ecstatic over the match, and Lydia, to her surprise, had confided shyly that she was most comfortable with the marquess.

Why then did Celina boggle at the idea? She had exchanged only a few words, some of them thorny, with him. She reflected on those few moments in the conservatory before the guests arrived the night before. It was his real concern for her weariness that had laid balm to the sore places in her mind. He would have, she told herself firmly, done the same for any serving girl. His behavior to everyone was in the highest degree courteous. She had no doubt that his own servants adored him, for he had a flair for making each one feel that his interest was personal.

The feeling was not confined to serving girls. She felt an unwelcome warmth in her cheeks.

"There's no sign that he's coming up to the mark, though," lamented Nelly. "I told Henry last night that Mama expected to announce the betrothal." She fell silent for so long that Celina prodded her.

"What did Henry say?"

"He said that frog wouldn't jump." At Celina's inquiring glance, she explained, "He means that Wroxton will not offer."

"I know what that dreadful phrase means," Celina pointed out, "but I am curious to know what makes him think so."

"I asked him, and he turned all huffy and said if I had the wits of a flea I could see that Wroxton was not interested in Lydia but only putting on the civil act because he's a guest in the house. Besides, he says, Lyddy's no more than grateful for his paying some attention to her when her family—and he meant me, you know, I could have thrown a soup tureen at him—did nothing but harry her."

Many a marriage was built on a weaker foundation than gratitude, thought Celina. If this was a sample of Henry's shrewdness, she wouldn't be surprised to see him leading his own brigade in five years.

Just before Nelly rose to leave, she made a remark that

would come back to Celina later. "There are ways," said Nelly, "to make an unwilling frog jump."

"For example?"

"I haven't thought them up yet," said Nelly candidly, "but you may believe that I shall."

The Dower House was comfortably silent after Nelly left. From the kitchen came subdued noises of housekeeping, and upstairs Carrie was setting Celina's bedroom to rights—all sounds of a well-run household.

Celina's head, as she had prophesied, had begun to ache. Nelly's visits were becoming less welcome than a trip to the tooth-drawer. But there was no sending her away, for she had the persistence of a mosquito. The only remedy was to hope that the girl's problems would be quickly solved.

Nelly was not Celina's only visitor that day. Late in the afternoon Lady Forsyth and Lady Gaunt arrived. Celina expected to see her sister-in-law steeped in gloom, since Wroxton had apparently not offered. She was surprised to see Eleanor in the highest of spirits.

"I declare I cannot believe the delicacy of Wroxton's sentiments," she announced. "He is the very essence of propriety."

"Commendable," said Celina faintly. She glanced at Lady Gaunt for a clue to Eleanor's elation, but that lady refused to meet her eyes. The overwhelming probability that occurred to Celina was that Wroxton had at last offered.

"He is leaving Forsyth Hall this very day. I insisted of course that he stay as long as he wished, to get to know Lydia better, you know, but he said that he felt it the thing to remove himself from the Manor."

"If he is going back to London," ventured Celina, "then I cannot understand why you are pleased. Unless—"

"That is it, Celina. He is not returning to London. Quite the contrary. He is settling in at Beechknoll, his own manor. So he has not truly left us."

Seeing that an answer was expected, Celina murmured,

"But I do not quite see this as an example of the highest sensitivity."

"He did not wish to offer for Lydia under her father's roof!" (Where else? thought Celina.) "It would put her in a most uncomfortable position, don't you know."

Lady Gaunt, glancing at Celina and seeing what she had hoped to see, took a hand. "Eleanor, once again you have leaped your fences before you got to them. Jervis has not offered for Lydia, that is true. And he is moving to Beechknoll. That at least is true. But all the rest is fustian."

"Then why is he staying in the neighborhood," demanded Eleanor with an air of driving a final nail in a protracted argument, "if not for Lydia?"

"Quite likely he wishes simply to look over his new holdings. After all, he succeeded to the estates only a few months ago."

(And former years on foreign strands, thought Celina, make of a traveler a magnificent raconteur, certain to hold spellbound even the shyest of maidens. Like Othello, ensnaring Desdemona with similar wiles. He has not bothered to spin me an adventurer's tales! But then, why should he?)

"I shall be most relieved when he offers," continued Eleanor, "not because I fear he won't, for he seems much taken with her, but then Nelly will stop going into alt at the slightest excuse. She is such a schemer, you know, that I quite quail when I think of what she might do."

"Meddler is the word," said Lady Gaunt, grandly ignoring that it was her scheming letter that had brought Jervis.

Eleanor might indeed have done worse than quail if she had known the thoughts that lay in her second daughter's head. Nelly, not basically inclined toward religion, nonetheless had a firm belief in one tenet: The Lord helps those who help themselves.

She found the peace of the gazebo beyond the rose garden, out of sight of the house except for a view of three of the chimneys, conducive to solemn reflection. She sat for a long time, her cloak wrapped around her against the chill in the shade of late September, turning up plan after plan and then discarding them one after the other.

There was nothing so sure to result in a declaration of love as a rescue from danger. If Wroxton found Lydia in peril, it would move him, Nelly believed, to avow his love on the spot. To be binding, of course, Wroxton's confession must be made in the presence of witnesses, her father for preference.

But since Lydia led such a sheltered life, it would be most unlikely that chance would provide both the peril and the opportunity for rescue. This unlikelihood daunted Nelly not at all.

Chance must be helped, and an opportunity contrived. A runaway team would be easy to manage—a burr under a collar, for example. But the other elements required on the scene, Wroxton and Papa, would be more difficult.

A blazing house? Not to be considered, for the Manor was Nelly's home too, and she was not prepared to make undue sacrifices. Footpads, of course, were an ever-present danger on the public roads. Stagecoaches were always being stopped at pistol-point, and the passengers robbed of their jewels. Try as she would, Nelly could not envision Lydia on a public stage or even traveling in her father's private coach. There was also the small matter of providing false footpads. Jem, the groom? The stablehands?

She was about to give up when the most sublime plan entered her head. An assignation! What of all things could be more romantic? The very thing, and much easier to manage.

She examined the plan from all angles. As she considered it, it appeared more and more suitable. Only the smallest doubt entered her mind. The plot did require a little deceit on her part—to say true, quite a lot of deceit. But this was for Henry, and there was nothing she wouldn't do for him.

Nothing in the world!

Chapter X

Several days later Nelly's crisis seemed to have eased. Her family, while saying nothing, yet were sensible that somewhat of a calm prevailed over the family gatherings.

If Celina had attended any of these, she might have become suspicious. Life at Forsyth Hall had never before been unruffled, and an intelligent observer might have wondered at the appearance of peace.

But Celina remained at the Dower house. She decided that only upon definite invitation would she walk the half-mile of drive to the Manor, and such an invitation did not come. She told herself that her reason was simple and valid. She had already done recent and heroic service in planning the dinner. If she appeared at the Manor, in however casual a manner, she would likely not come away without some further task to do.

Sufficient reason, she told herself, without adding her reluctance to hear the daily speculations on the expected offer of Lord Wroxton for Lydia's hand. Wroxton had moved to his manor of Beechknoll. Lady Gaunt had offered, in a way calculated not to be taken seriously, to remove herself and her maid there to keep him company. Assessing her offer in its true light, he had refused, saying his house was not comfortable enough.

There was little time to be lonely at the Dower House. The curate called every day. She could not in conscience refuse to receive him, but by the fourth day she was giving serious thought to avenues of escape. Just now, Mr. Coleraine had delivered himself of a most curious remark. "I have often been tempted to render myself up as an offering to the Church, that is to say, to follow the exhortations of Isaiah. 'The Lord has anointed me to bring good tidings to the afflicted.' "

"Admirable," murmured Celina absently.

"It is most interesting to see that good Saint Luke phrases it in a most poignant way. He quotes Jesus as saying, 'Preach good news to the *poor*.' "

"But," she pointed out, "there are not many poor in this community."

Mr. Coleraine smiled in a superior fashion. "Ah, the old argument. It is, my dear Miss Forsyth, the poor in spirit whom I must reach. There are many such unfortunates even here, my dear Miss Forsyth. Although it is an uphill climb. At times I rather imagine that I can understand Pilgrim in his many travails. I suppose that you, dear lady, cannot have read such uplifting tracts as I refer to?"

And why should he suppose that? she wondered. She recognized in herself the signs of waning patience. She ignored his question. She took forcible hold of the conversation.

"I shall leave for Bath," she said recklessly, "in two days."

Her ploy achieved success. Sitting up stiffly, Mr. Coleraine wore an expression of pained shock. "Leave? But you cannot! I have something—I must tell you—I should like all settled first—"

She interrupted ruthlessly, if untruthfully. "I shall be gone for some weeks." At least by that time, she thought, Wroxton would either have become part of the family, as Eleanor believed, or he would have left the neighborhood, possibly to return to the Near East.

Mr. Coleraine took a moment to absorb the shock of

interruption. "But it is not the season for Bath," he objected. "Nor is it the thing to go alone."

"I did not precisely say I was going alone."

"Indeed," interrupted a voice from the doorway, "I should be very much obliged, Miss Forsyth, were you to postpone your departure for a few days."

Elkins hovered helplessly behind the broad-shouldered figure of Lord Wroxton. He had opened his mouth to announce the visitor when he was gently set aside and Lord Wroxton announced himself in what Elkins could only consider a hasty and improper manner. But, Mrs. Elkins pointed out later, who is going to tell a marquess to mind his manners?

Jervis's manners appeared flawless. He bowed to his hostess and said civil things to the curate. It would be difficult to explain exactly what he said, thought Celina, but suddenly the curate was no longer there, and Jervis was looking down at her with a smile that brought a flush to her cheeks.

She struggled to regain her composure. "Pray tell me," she said, "how did you manage that? I confess I have been wishing him gone for this long time."

"I am not quite so kindhearted as you, Miss Forsyth," he said. At her invitation, he sat down but declined tea. "I was startled to overhear your plans. Can your departure for Bath be postponed?"

Since the Bath journey was at this point only a suggestion pulled from the air, Celina said, "I suppose it could be, if there were a reason."

Jervis leaned back in the chair opposite Celina recently vacated by Mr. Coleraine. Leisurely he pulled a note from an inner pocket. "I have received a rather odd missive," he told her, "and I find myself badly in need of advice."

"I cannot think I am able to advise you on any subject."

"On the contrary. It is precisely your counsel I need." He held the note out to her. "Perhaps you can make more out of it than I can."

She refused to take it from him. "Something so personal

as your correspondence—I think not, Lord Wroxton. Surely we are not so well known to each other—"

He smiled with warm intimacy. "I shall hope to improve our acquaintance directly." For the moment he seemed to have forgotten the letter in his hand. "I am not an unobservant man and I have noticed during my short stay at your brother's that your family reposes much confidence in you. And therefore, since this is a matter that concerns one of them, I thought it best to confer with you as to the proper thing to do."

He had sounded the right note. "One of my relation?" she inquired, her interest fairly caught.

"May I read this to you? It is ill writ, and since I have taken the time to puzzle out its meaning, we shall save time. And time, I think, is an element here."

He looked at the note and shook his head. "I must tell you that there are some words I cannot make out. But the kernel of it is this: 'Meet me in the spinney at three.' You see my need of your advice. I am not sure, you know, what spinney is meant, or how to find my way there."

"You cannot mean the spinney on my brother's land!"

Jervis lifted an eyebrow. "On the contrary, I should think that is exactly the spinney. You see I was right in coming to you."

"Is there more?"

"Not a great deal more. I can make out the words 'utmost importance,' but of course any assignation in a spinney takes on an aura of urgency, don't you agree?"

She was mystified. "But you indicated one of my relations sent this—this entirely improper note. How do you know that?"

"That, of course, is the crux of the matter. The signature is less than revealing." In answer to her questioning expression, he added, " 'One who greatly admires you.' "

She could not repress an ironic comment. "I should think that description might well take in half of England!"

"Not quite half," he objected gravely. "But if you were

to enlarge the area to include Mesopotamia and Constantinople, I should not venture to contradict you."

She gurgled with laughter. Suddenly the serious puzzle of this note, addressed in the most shocking way to Lord Wroxton, ceased to trouble her. She was struck sharply by a sense of strength in him, a powerful intellect at work. There was, she believed, nothing in the world that would overset him.

The atmosphere turned lighter. "I gather that you yourself did not write this," he asked.

"Of course not!"

"Ah, well," sighed Jervis, "I must extinguish my hopes. But who, then?"

He watched her expression carefully. He had at last gained her interest and he was content to bide his time. In a moment he said, "I see you suspect someone."

"Well, I must say it sounds like Nelly. She does have a romantic tendency." On a sharper note she added, "If indeed the wretch wrote that—that compromising note, I shall be very angry with her. How do you know it came from the Manor?"

"It was brought, according to Pollard, who received it, by a Forsyth footman." He hesitated. "What shall I do, then?"

She said at once, "Ignore it."

Pensively he said, "Do you know, I don't quite feel I can. I confess to a good deal of curiosity on this head. If you are correct, and I must bow to your intimate knowledge of your niece, then there must be a purpose to this proposed meeting. One never has sufficient admirers, you know, and I should not like to ignore any." He frowned at the letter. "Even one with such an atrocious hand as this."

"You're bamming me!"

Imperturbably he said, "Of course."

"The whole thing is preposterous!" she said after a moment.

"But the note is real." He tapped his knee with the folded paper and then, appearing to come to a conclusion, he said, "I wonder whether you can give me directions to this spinney."

"It's a small stand of willows along the stream—oh, this is ridiculous. I think it is best if I accompany you. Should you mind?"

He smiled broadly. "It is what I wished above all things. In case my unknown admirer gives way to injudicious impulse!"

She laughed outright. He nodded approvingly, his eyes warm. She tore her gaze away, suddenly uncertain.

He only said gently, "Best put on a heavy cloak. The wind is rising, and it is possible that we may have to wait."

"I should hope not," she retorted with humor. "She is probably pacing the ground at this moment."

They went out to his waiting phaeton. "I hope you are not concerned at riding with me without a groom or your abigail?"

"I am six and twenty," she said with dignity, "much too old to need a chaperone."

He climbed in beside her and took up the reins. He turned to her, his eyes kindling. "I shall hope to discuss such a nonsensical remark at a more suitable time. Now, Miss Forsyth, where is this famous spinney?"

By crowflight the spinney was not far. By road and lane they drove for half an hour before they came near enough to see it.

"We must tie up here," directed Celina, "and walk the rest of the way."

While he was tying his horse, she looked carefully at the willows clustered at the curve of a small stream. Nothing moved. If Nelly waited, she had hidden herself well. Jervis came to stand beside Celina.

"Do you know where we are?" she asked in a low tone.

"Not precisely."

She pointed. "That stream forms the boundary between our Home Farm and our Upland Farm. And beyond those trees along the horizon lies Blaine land. Right here you are our nearest neighbor."

He nodded in comprehension. "And now to the spinney. I believe we must be early to the rendezvous."

Celina had enjoyed the short ride. Jervis had made her laugh more than once, and it had come as a surprise to realize that she had not felt so lighthearted for a long, long time. No one clamored for her support against one parent or another or a sister. No one envisioned large dinner parties and said, almost as an afterthought, that Celina would plan the affair with Cook and Pardoe. No one—a darker thought here—hinted that an unmarried person must perforce be a monster. It was quite a delicious feeling.

They walked to the spinney.

"No one here." Celina added, "Perhaps your admirer's nerve failed her at the last moment."

He reached to tuck the collar of her loose cloak close around her throat. She knew she should frown upon such an intimate touch, but a part of her protested that his gesture seemed exactly right.

"Your cloak is very becoming," he frowned, "but I fear you will not be warm enough."

"I'm quite comfortable." Indeed she was. He stood quite close, blocking the wind from her. The September sun had broken through the overcast sky and fell warmly on her shoulders. All around them was the peace of the autumn fields, and the only sounds were the small bustle of the stream through the reeds at water's edge, and the faraway cawing of rooks.

Minutes went by. Jervis gave no sign of impatience, and she was content simply to lean against a tree-trunk and wait. The clean scent of his shaving soap mingled with the smell of fallen leaves and the indefinable scent of the dying season.

The spinney was in a hollow shaped like a cupped hand. The land rose, so that no one could overlook them until he arrived at the lip of the hollow, only yards away. Whoever intended to keep the rendezvous would not shy off because of her presence until it was too late to avoid recognition.

After a time she began to realize that she had without much question followed a man she hardly knew to a deserted stand of scrubby trees with not a soul in sight. She turned, suspicion in her voice, and said, "Are you sure that you did not write that note yourself?"

"It would have been more legible if I had," he said, unruffled. "Perhaps we have mistaken the day."

"Utmost importance, indeed," she scoffed. "I collect this is a jape—"

His hand clutched her arm, demanding silence. She listened. From a short distance away, still out of sight, came a sweet, anxious voice calling, "Kitty, kitty . . . where have you got to? Come, Muffin. Here, kitty . . ."

Celina looked at him with eyes wide. "It's Lydia!" she whispered.

Comprehension moved in his eyes. Lydia, not Nelly!

Chapter XI

Celina tore her gaze away from him. How shamed she was by her family! Such a havey-cavey trick as summoning Wroxton to a secret rendezvous would be abominable in Nelly, but if not expected, it would at least occasion little surprise. But Lydia!

She was hardly aware when Jervis moved her to scant cover behind the tree and himself stood in front of her. She dared not look.

Lydia came closer. "Kitty—?"

She stopped short with a little gasp when she realized she was not alone. "Lord Wroxton!" The name was only a breath on the air.

"Miss Lydia," he greeted her formally. Stating the obvious, he added, "Are you looking for your kitten?"

"Oh, yes, have you seen her? A darling white kitten with a bow around her neck, and she's gone from her basket!"

"I shall be much surprised, Miss Lydia, if she has managed to travel this far from the house."

"I did not think so either," confided Lydia in a rush, "but Nanny said she had."

He was sure that Lydia was as much an intended gull as he, being summoned to a place of assignation for a reason that was not entirely clear yet. However, he suspected it would very soon be made lucid to them all.

Gently Jervis probed. "Did Nanny see the kitten?"

Celina's patience fled. Stepping into the clear, she cried out, "Lydia! How shocked I am to see you here. Looking for a kitten! Was ever anything so ridiculous?"

Lydia was startled beyond speech. Her lips moved—Aunt Celina?—but no sound came from them. Her flawless complexion reddened and then paled. Her hand at her throat, she could only gaze unwinking at her scolding aunt, while large tears brimmed over and slid unnoticed down her cheeks.

Celina steeled herself against the tears. She did not recognize the unreasonableness of her anger until Jervis touched her arm. "A scheme it is, of course," he said quietly. "But, Miss Forsyth, do you really think that Miss Lydia plotted this affair herself? I see you have not considered the possibility that she is also an innocent victim. No, my dear, this speaks of a finer hand—forgive me, Miss Lydia—than she is capable of."

Celina cooled from a rolling boil to a simmer. "But she came to this place. Surely you don't think by accident."

"If I am not mistaken," he said, listening, "we are about to be visited by those more acquainted with this situation than we are." He thrust Celina quickly into her former place of retirement. "Do you, Miss Lydia, leave everything to me!"

An irate face appeared over the brink of the rise. Celina peered unseen from behind Jervis's shoulder. Edmund! What had brought him here? The reason was simple enough. Made privy to the supposed assignation, he had lost no time in investigating it. Such vulgar behavior, such deceit, such—she could not think of words severe enough to do justice to the enormity of the plot.

Edmund, it developed in a moment, was not alone. Behind him came Nelly, her eyes afire with excitement.

"Lyddy!" roared Edmund. "Get away from that man!

What are you thinking of, sir? I shall drag your name through all the mud in London before I'm through with you. Let me alone, Nelly, don't pull at my sleeve. Thank God I've got one daughter who's got some sense of proper behavior. Lyddy, girl, what did he say to you? Did he hurt you? My God, Wroxton! I thought you a man of honor."

Jervis bowed slightly. His back, intended as a screen to conceal Celina, touched her. She was astonished to feel a trembling through his body. He could not be afraid of Edmund! It was such a coil, she could not think straight.

"And you, Lyddy, I shall have a word with your mother about you. Of all the hen-witted females, to rear you with such a scandalous notion of how one goes on—I can't believe it of her. Haven't you any sense? Where's your abigail? Although," he continued gloomily, "what good is an abigail? Does what she's told!"

He glared at his eldest daughter, who promptly covered her face with her hands.

Jervis's shaking subsided, and suddenly Celina realized that he was, with some difficulty, stifling untoward laughter. Wretch! She raised her fist and struck him sharply between the shoulder blades. The situation was not in the least entertaining!

Edmund's bullish anger was an emotion she had not before seen in her brother. He must be greatly moved. "I suppose," he said nastily to Jervis, "that you were persuading her to set off for Gretna Green. What on earth for? Why didn't you speak to me if you had a *tendre* for her? God knows I put enough opportunities in your way."

"My dear Forsyth," began Jervis. The innocuous words fed the flame.

"Meeting here alone! I cannot believe it. By God, I cannot believe it! All right, Wroxton, marquess or not, you've ruined my Lyddy. The House of Lords shall hear of this."

All was not going according to Nelly's scheme. If her

father came on too strongly, then Jervis would defect and Lydia would be farther away from marriage than ever.

"Papa—"

"Stop hanging on my sleeve, Nelly."

"But Papa—"

"I know, I know. Only one way out of this. You think I was born yesterday? Now, Wroxton, you've got a choice. You'll stand trial in Westminster for this insult or you'll marry my girl."

He was breathing heavily. Jervis hoped he would not suffer an apoplexy on the spot. The man seemed to have run out of words at last. While his fires were not out, at least they seemed banked for the moment.

"Have you quite finished?" asked Jervis in an unemotional voice. When Edmund did not answer, he went on, "Much as I regret to inform you, I do not wish, at this moment, that is, to marry anyone. You know, Miss Lydia and I should not suit. I am deeply sensible of the honor you pay me when you think I would be a suitable match for her. But, really, I shall choose my bride in my own time."

Celina was shaken by mixed emotions. He was not planning to marry Lydia. But from her vantage point she could see Lydia clearly, and the expression on her incomparable features was disturbing. Lydia's violet eyes were fixed on Jervis and held a look of utter adoration.

"I really cannot think why you believed that I should offer."

Edmund explained, "Lady Gaunt said so."

"Ah, I see I shall have to have a few words with my aunt. To resume, Forsyth, I have not tarnished your daughter's reputation—"

Edmund burst out, "A mile from the house? In a deserted clump of trees? Untarnished? Only because I arrived in time. By the grace of Providence I learned of this—"

"I recommend strongly, Forsyth," said Jervis, growing irritated, "that you listen to me. I did not come to meet

Miss Lydia. In truth, I did not know she expected to be here."

Edmund was listening now, as Jervis explained the note he had received. "I do not know who wrote it," he finished, "nor do I wish, at least at this moment, to know. But I can tell you that Miss Lydia came only in search of her lost kitten. She was quite surprised to find us here. I should imagine she can tell you just when she discovered her kitten had strayed in this direction."

Edmund caught the word Jervis intended he should. "*Us?*"

Jervis stepped aside to reveal his companion. "You see I did not come alone. Certainly such a threadbare ruse as an anonymous note demands caution on the part of the recipient. You agree? So Miss Forsyth was kind enough to come with me."

Celina's presence provided a shock that turned Edmund speechless. When he found his voice, he gabbled. At length he became somewhat coherent.

"Celina? Good God! Women! I'd think you had enough to do without jaunting all over the countryside. What will your fiancé think? I'll not be surprised if he cries off!"

"Fiancé?" echoed Celina faintly.

Jervis did not trust his voice. He had heard nothing about a fiancé. He could not think that Celina would have succumbed to the questionable blandishments of that blockhead who seemed far too often to plant himself in her salon.

"Fiancé, Edmund?" repeated Celina in a firmer voice. "I do not know what you mean."

"Damme, that church fellow asked me only an hour ago for permission to make you an offer. In fact, he was with me just before I heard about this—mess! He'll cry off, Celina. Mark my words."

"Edmund, you have quite exceeded yourself—"

She stopped short, feeling a regrettable impulse to throw herself on Jervis's chest and sob. She stifled the unbecoming urge, for the poor man had suffered enough today at the hands of the Forsyths. But the unshed tears in her throat prevented her from further speech.

Her brother, however, wished for further enlightenment. "I am not sure, Wroxton, that I understand about the note. I cannot believe that anyone of my family could be so depraved as to make an assignation with you. Certainly you are welcome at the Manor." He considered a moment and added, "At least, you have been till now. No reason on God's earth why you couldn't talk to Lyddy anytime." He raised suspicious eyes to Wroxton. "If you're bamming me . . ."

Celina recovered her voice. "Edmund," she said, ignoring Jervis's quick, restraining touch on her arm, "you have lost what little wits you have. Lord Wroxton has been the dupe of one of your girls."

"Not *dupe*, precisely," murmured Jervis.

"I consider it quite beneath contempt for you to come here and ring a peal over him, when he has done all that is proper to preserve Lyddy's reputation. He brought me, did he not? And pray for what reason other than to lend a little countenance to what I can only call a idiotic plot to enmesh him?"

Jervis, a small smile on his lips, stood back and folded his arms. There was no need for his interference, for Celina was competent to defend his interests. He allowed his gaze to focus entirely on her, admiring the precise manner in which she demolished her brother's puffed-up indignation. He was right; she had a lively spirit. Too bad it took a contretemps like this to bring it out.

Secretly he cherished a hope that one day she would deal in such a forthright fashion with that leech Lady Forsyth. If she did not, it was likely that he himself must do so.

Suddenly he was shaken by an unalterable conviction that came to him like sunlight bursting through heavy cloud. He had come to see himself in the light of a rescuer of a fair maiden, with the admirable purpose of shielding Celina from the exigent demands of her sister-in-law. Much like, he thought, stretching out a sturdy limb to one sinking in quicksand. A simple rescue, no more.

But what he now knew beyond any doubt was that he himself was enmeshed and there was no way out, even had he wished to escape. Celina was the woman he had longed for and had given up hope of finding.

Jolted by his discovery, he came to himself to see that she had successfully put Edmund to rout. Edmund appeared abject, as well he might. Jervis glanced at the others.

From where he stood he had an unimpeded view of Nelly. Inexperienced in hiding her emotions, she made her disappointment obvious. That wretched girl had written the note and arranged to bring Lydia and then her father to this rendezvous. So much was clear to him. But he was not certain of the reason.

To compromise her sister? To what end?

He must consider the question later. Just now his dear Celina had fallen silent. He stepped to stand beside her, so close that he could feel her body trembling. He dared not touch her, not yet.

With only a half-hearted gesture of farewell, Edmund gathered his daughters on either side, with a tight grip on the forearm, and marched them toward home. Jervis noted the rigid disappointment apparent even in Nelly's straight back, but Celina saw only the woebegone, miserable face of Lydia as she looked back over her shoulder at Jervis, her eyes full of appeal.

They were alone again in the spinney. Suddenly Celina felt cold creeping into her bones. She began to shiver. Jervis turned her toward him. She refused to meet his eyes. He put one finger under her chin and gently lifted her face to his.

"What is it, my dear?"

"I'm so ashamed," she murmured, "such a dreadful scene. I wonder any of us can ever face you again."

"Your family's faults are not yours. Nor, I thank God,

are my aunt's proclivities for mischief-making anything to do with me."

Her distress moved him as nothing in his life had done. He put his arms around her and drew her close, feeling her trembling against him. Hiding her face in his shoulder, she felt the warmth of his body comfort her, the security of his arms tight around her holding her safe. At last she stopped shivering.

She was conscious of the moment when his mood changed. She could hear very clearly the purling of the stream nearby. The wind had come up and sang a little tune in the willows. She could almost hear her own heart pounding faster. She lifted her eyes to meet his, and the light in his eyes was bright enough to banish all the shadows of her mind.

His lips came down on hers, and insensibly her arms stole around his neck. A measureless time later she pulled away. Suddenly her situation struck her: in the arms of a man whom she had known for less than a fortnight, the man her niece adored, and worst of all, enjoying it.

"We sh-shouldn't—" she stammered, "I—I c-can't—"

With a small sigh he set her away from him. "A bit incoherent, my love, but I expect I shall get used to translating."

In a very small voice she protested, "I am not your l-love."

"We'll see," he said comfortingly, and they turned to walk back to his phaeton.

The journey home was accomplished in silence. Sober reflection told him that he had moved much too fast—except that she had responded to him! But now he remembered a bit of news that Edmund had flung into the pot as he ranted.

"What will your fiancé think?" he had shouted. "He'll cry off, mark my words."

"That church fellow" could only be Lawrence Coleraine. Jervis could not believe that his Celina had developed a *tendre* for the tedious cleric. Well born enough, he was a consummate bore.

Inwardly Jervis laughed at himself. He already thought of her as his Celina. Was he to lose her to someone else just as he had found her?

He glanced at her. Her features were set, he judged, in melancholy. Dark circles appeared under those spectacular gray eyes, denoting weariness. She had been chilled through this afternoon, and though he had done his best to warm her—and he had, no doubt of that!—he must make sure she took no harm from it.

They pulled up in front of the Dower House. He helped her down, not letting his hands linger at her waist.

"I am grateful to you," he said softly, "for coming with me on this distasteful mission. I trust you will not be ill from the effects of the weather. May I call tomorrow to inquire?"

She should not see him again; there were so many reasons against continued acquaintance. She could not speak over the lump in her throat that refused to go away. Finally she nodded. He put her into the care of Elkins and hurried down the steps before his impulse could betray him. At any rate, he thought as he drove away, he would come tomorrow and declare himself.

By this time tomorrow, he thought with rising cheerfulness, he would be a betrothed man!

Chapter XII

Celina had taken no harm from the outing, at least as to her health. She was not ordinarily prone to infections, and an early bedtime and a good sleep put her quite to rights again.

If only, she thought over her morning chocolate, she had not had such frightful dreams! Strange, shapeless beings had pursued her the night long, with faces that changed even while she watched them. Edmund and the vicar and Lydia, and changing again to Edmund, but her rescuer always wore the face of Lord Wroxton. Unfortunately, just as he threw out his shield to protect her, he faded away, and the pursuit began again.

She could not, now that she was awake, gloss over any of the events of yesterday afternoon. Meticulously she searched her memory for every word, every nuance of tone. She knew the skeleton of the affair. Nelly, beyond a doubt, had sent the note luring Wroxton into what she hoped would be a compromising position with Lydia, with the guaranteed outcome that Wroxton must marry the girl, clearing the way, Nelly obviously planned, for her own marriage to Henry.

But Wroxton was too wary to be thus snared. Her own presence was the element that foiled the plot, and Lydia was saved from a marriage that she had at the beginning loathed. But Celina could not forget that look of entreaty from Lydia as Edmund drew her away toward the Hall. That look of appeal, one that Celina knew well because it was usually directed at her, was this time sent directly to Wroxton. Lydia had clearly changed her mind as to the horror of marriage to him. Shocking to Celina, that longing look gave evidence that she had more than an ordinary affection for him.

In fact, it was a look of unconcealed, unbridled adoration! Othello had told his tales to good effect.

But how, then, to explain those fond terms with which he addressed her all afternoon? "What is it, my dear?" Even "my love"! She should have put him in his place at the start, but she had thought it better to ignore the endearments.

Still, she shied like a nervous colt at the remembrance of that embrace, that soul-disturbing kiss, and worst of all, at her sheer delight in it. Her cheeks burned. He had asked if he might call this morning. She could not face him again, that was the long and short of it.

Summoning Elkins, she instructed him, "I shall not wish to see any callers today." A sudden thought struck her. She added, "Particularly any of the family." Let the butler make what he would of that, she thought testily. She did not wish to see either Nelly or Lydia in the foreseeable future. Or, if it came to that, Edmund.

She had not been specific enough. Late in the morning Elkins sought her out in the small morning room. "Miss, Lord Wroxton has called."

"I told you, Elkins—"

"Indeed, yes, miss," said Elkins virtuously. "Miss Nelly called and Mr. Coleraine. I refused both of them."

"Then why Lord Wroxton?" Her voice shook on the name.

"Because, miss, he will not go away."

She suspected that Wroxton had made a friend of her butler by judicious application of generous vails, thus guaranteeing his admittance to her parlor. The servant sustained her glare with impassivity.

"Very well, Elkins. Since you cannot remove him from my parlor, I shall do it myself."

Her purpose was not easily accomplished. Jervis rose the moment she came into the salon.

"Your butler did try to dissuade me," he told her, "but I wished to see for myself that your health is not impaired by our jaunt yesterday. The air proved chillier than I anticipated."

His hooded eyes held little warmth today. Perhaps he deliberately held his emotions in check, and perhaps, she thought, he regretted his demonstrativeness at their last encounter.

He must have come to apologize for his forwardness. He would take care, he would assure her, not to offend in the future. Of all things she did not wish to be reminded of her scandalous lapse from decorum, especially by the cause of it! She was aware of an uneasy stirring in the region of her heart.

He crossed to the door she had left open behind her. To her inquiring gaze, he answered, "I have something very particular to say to you and not to your estimable butler."

"Something particular?" She managed a frosty note.

A fleeting doubt slipped across his features. Rarely was he uncertain of his next words. "I would like to ask—" he began, then started anew, blurting out the words from his heart. "Will you do me the honor of becoming my wife?"

She felt the room tilting around her. She groped for a chair and sat staring at the carpet. "Wife," he had said. Of all things it was what she ached for. If only she hadn't seen that look of Lydia's!

"But you said," she protested at last, "only yesterday that you do not wish to marry anyone!"

"At that moment, I believe I said."

He had also said he didn't want to marry Lydia. Suppose he didn't. But why would he want to marry Celina? Madness was the only explanation. Celina's two unfruitful

Seasons in London had left their mark. She could not believe that he was in love with her, and indeed he had not mentioned love.

It was all wrong! He should be speaking so to Lydia! Celina had not been caught so off balance since the Prince Regent, now King George IV, had run his fat hand down her back.

Celina chose her words carefully. "We are both too old for romantical flights of fancy, and I suspect you are impatient of roundaboutations."

He watched her intently. "I protest your first statement, my dear. Although neither of us is green, I grant you."

She held up her hand. "Pray do not stop me. I cannot—I should dislike—" This would not do. She had enough poise to get her through only the baldest statement. It would be fatal for her composure, to say nothing of her strong feelings, to lapse into argument.

"But, although—although I am sensible of the high honor involved, I must tell you that we should not suit. Pray, do not press me. I am not the wife for you."

He stared at her. Clearly this was not the answer he had anticipated. His mouth twisted wryly. At length he spoke in a voice reminiscent of dried leaves crushed underfoot. "Thank you for putting it so plainly. You mean that I am not the husband you wish. Very well, I shall not distress you by remaining when you clearly wish me at the antipodes." He turned at the door and said, with a curious appeal in his demeanor, "Is it—is it possible that your feelings may change?"

The feelings she had were strong. She suspected they would stay with her, haunting all her days, forever. But she could not live with the thought that she had devastated Lydia's life, either. Besides, she felt at this moment incredibly aged. Too old for romantical nonsense, too young to retire from the world.

She dared not answer. She regarded the toe of her slipper with the greatest of interest. Her mind shouted Go away! There was no sound, but in a few moments she realized she was alone. Not surprisingly, she realized she had a screaming headache. And there was soreness elsewhere, as well.

She had now, she was convinced, fathomed the reason behind this abrupt offer. Her cheeks flamed as she recalled that moment—that long moment—when she was held tightly in his embrace, his lips demanding on hers, and her own willing response.

He *had* to offer, being a man of honor and she no lightskirt, and even though the intimidation was solely due to his high sense of duty, it was of the same order as Edmund's insistence at the top of his lungs that Wroxton marry his daughter or stand trial in the House of Lords.

She, Celina Forsyth, a resigned spinster of the utmost propriety, had lost her balance. She was not so lost as to accept the offer he felt forced to make.

She had never been so wretched in her life.

Jervis rode down the gravel drive to the junction with the main drive to the Hall. How ironic it was, he thought ruefully, to think that only yesterday he had looked upon his future with the most sanguine expectations. The wife he wanted, the happiness he hoped for—now wiped away by a few words from her lips.

Familiar objects seemed curiously strange to him. He knew that he would from now on be able to date his experiences from this watershed: before Celina and after Celina.

Had he gone wrong? Or was it simply that she found him unacceptable? The possibility that she would refuse him had simply not occurred to him. Adrian had told him, a fact he already knew, that with his wealth and his title he could marry anyone he chose. He had answered Adrian modestly, but his present reaction now informed him that he had seen himself in a false light.

How serene she had appeared at first, a quiet center where a man could find peace after his travels. Witness her astounding patience with that curdling family! But there were fires banked under her calm exterior. Even Celina had a limit, and the shabby ruse of that appalling niece of hers had exposed that strong spirit.

In his memory her lips moved warmly and, if he were not much mistaken, willingly again under his. By the time he had cantered up the long drive to Beechknoll, he had made up his mind. She was worth whatever effort it would take to win her. Spirit she had, but he reserved for himself the right to bring those fires to glowing and tender life.

Too old for romantical sentiments? She should be privy to his thoughts just now!

Chapter XIII

The only question in the mind of Lord Wroxton was how to accomplish his designs. The long night had told him only that he wished to reverse Celina's decision, longed to feel again and forever that pliant body in his arms, those sweet lips moving on his.

The storm in his blood had kept him awake until nearly dawn. Only with the cold autumn sunlight falling pale on his breakfast table did he remember the qualities that had attracted him at the first.

The ready amusement that lurked in her eyes, her incomparable grace in dealing with her brother's brood, the peace that lay at the core of her. After the tumult of his recent years, the hazardous journeys, the wretched circumstances of travel, the loneliness, he needed her as a tempest-tossed sailor needs a calm harbor.

How could he get her to change her mind? It was a puzzle deserving of his best efforts.

His ruminations were cut short. Pollard had just poured his second cup of coffee when a visitor was announced.

Celina, come to tell him she had changed her mind? Impossible. Such an unconventional visit would never occur to her.

Lady Gaunt entered the morning room. "Aunt Tibby!"

he exclaimed in surprise as he rose from his chair to greet her. "Just in time for breakfast. Pollard, another plate."

"No, Pollard. But perhaps a little coffee. Hot, if you please, for it was deucedly chilly driving over here."

"I wonder you did not send for me if you wished to see me," said Jervis. "Surely the cold must not be good for you."

"Rime on the grass already, and it's only the last week in September," commented Lady Gaunt. Pollard set coffee before her, the steam rising from the surface, and tactfully vanished. "But I did not come here to talk about the weather, Jervis."

He smiled. "Whatever the reason, I am glad you are here. I suppose you are escaping from that hornet's nest."

She made a *moue.* "Hornet's nest describes it. I gather that you are the cause of the latest swarming."

"Swarming? Oh, bees." Had they already heard about his offer to Celina? He doubted very much that she would hurry up to the Hall and make them privy to what was a very private conversation. He spoke cautiously. "I have not visited the Manor for several days."

"I know that. But something has happened. Did you offer?" She regarded him without favor. "I see by your expression that you did. No wonder Lydia came back from her walk in a daze. I have never seen her in such a state. Jervis, I am gravely disappointed in you."

"Lydia?" he echoed faintly, surprised out of his wits.

"Lydia," she repeated firmly. "I must say that Edmund mopes around frowning, and Nelly looks like a damp squib that has failed to explode."

"Most trying," murmured her nephew. He gathered himself together. His aunt's news was unsettling, at the least. "Let me understand this. Forsyth says I offered for Lydia?"

She set down her empty cup. "I should have talked to you plainly at the start. But I did think you had some sense. Your father was an idiot, but I liked your mother. Now you've ruined everything."

"Now, Aunt Tibby—"

"Don't Aunt Tibby me, Jervis. Tell me straight out. Are you going to marry that spectacular face with an empty head behind it?"

"Lydia," he repeated, to set the record straight. "You mean Lydia."

"Of course, haven't I just told you? Are you?"

"Not in my wildest nightmares would I consider it."

She leaned back, satisfied. "Well, that's settled. Ring for Pollard, will you?"

"But you're not leaving so soon."

"I simply want another cup of coffee. Do ring, Jervis."

Her hands holding the refilled cup for warmth, she said, "Then what do you think has got hold of them all?"

Warily he inquired, "You know of no reason?"

"You've not been listening. If it isn't an offer for Lydia, then I have no clue. But," she continued musingly, "there was some taradiddle two days ago. A great deal of fuss about a kitten, of all things, and Lydia went out, and after a bit Edmund stormed out with Nelly at his coattails." She narrowed her eyes. "Jervis, you do know something about all this."

He nodded. "I did not for a moment think of offering. For Lydia."

She peered suspiciously at him. "I shall not move from this room, Jervis," she said impressively, "until I hear it. The whole of it."

There was nothing for it but to oblige his aunt. Besides, he was aware suddenly of an urgent need to confide his heart's desire to her. His own resourceful mind had failed him thus far. Perhaps Lady Gaunt, a woman of some worldly experience, could tell him what he needed to know.

"It started," he began, "with a note brought here by a footman from the Hall."

He related with accuracy the events of the afternoon two days previously, omitting only a few details that were not pertinent. There was no need for Aunt Tibby to know of that moment when he held Celina close and warm and responsive. "So you see it was hardly the time to declare myself, even had I wanted to. Forsyth roared like the bull of Bashan. Not at all the place for romantical sentiments."

Lady Gaunt regarded him with wonder in her eyes. "And that's all of it?"

"Enough, isn't it? I confess I did think he would have an apoplexy on the spot and I did not wish Celina to see such an incident, but the danger soon passed."

"As soon as he was made aware of his sister's presence," concluded Lady Gaunt. She lapsed into thought, drumming her fingers absently on the table. "Well, I see nothing for Lydia to preen herself about, if that's all that happened."

He shook his head. "I cannot decipher it myself."

Lady Gaunt caught a glimmer of the truth. "If Lydia thought you were rescuing her . . ."

He looked up quickly. "But that's nonsense!"

"I quite agree. Especially when I—" She cut her words short guiltily.

Enlightened, he pounced. "Aha, now perhaps you will explain a thing or two to me, Aunt. Especially when you—sent for me to come? Is that what you were going to say? I see it is. And why, dear Aunt, did you send for me to come? Not only to visit you, I daresay."

"I had my reasons."

"Come now. You have said too much not to finish. I was to come to Forsyth Hall, but not to offer for Lydia. Am I correct? Then why?"

She sighed. "I may as well tell you. It didn't work out, anyway. I thought if you came and met Celina, who is a darling, you might develop a *tendre* for her. She needs to get out of the toils of that clunch Eleanor, and . . ." At the expression on his face she faltered. "What's the matter? What is so amusing?"

He controlled his laughter. "Your scheme did not fail, Aunt Tibby. No, indeed. The truth is that yesterday afternoon I declared myself."

"You offered? To Celina?"

He nodded, sober once again. The subject was far from amusing. "And she refused me."

For once Lady Gaunt could not find words. "Refused?" she repeated at last. "Celina refused?"

"We should not suit, she said."

"Nonsense! You would suit admirably."

"You reassure me," he said dryly. "But your opinion, forgive me, is not the relevant one."

"I know that!" She brushed his remark aside. "What did you say to her?"

He wished to rebuff her. What he had said to Celina was none of his aunt's affair, but to his surprise he heard himself answering her seriously. "Do you know, I don't remember. I know I asked her to be my wife."

"Naturally. What else?"

He shook his head, puzzled. "I cannot recall."

"That's a good sign," Lady Gaunt said briskly. "Now, Jervis, put your mind to it. Did you tell her you loved her?"

"I don't think so."

"More to the point, do you? Or are you simply after a gracious lady for your family seat?"

"Of course I love her!" The protest burst out. "She is everything I have wanted these years. Impeccable breeding, a sweet disposition, a—a kind of quietness about her."

Lady Gaunt, inelegantly, snorted. "You could say the same thing about a mare." She shook her head. "Don't look so surprised. I see I shall have to take a hand in this. Good God, I would think that a man of over thirty would have sufficient address not to bumble a simple offer of marriage." She paused to reflect. "Although I suppose that very ineptitude speaks of an elevated emotional state."

Jervis had sustained more than one shock in the last twenty-four hours. His aunt's strictures were only the most recent. But he had wit enough to realize that a lifeline was at hand. He would be ten times a fool if he did not grasp and hold on as if his life depended on it. As it did.

"I offered her marriage." He swallowed. The lump in his throat may have been the remnants of his pride. "What did I do wrong?"

"For one, you cannot think that Celina has not had offers before. She refused them. Can you guess why? Don't trouble, for I am determined to tell you. She has not married because she does not need to marry. She has an ample fortune, all the comforts she wishes. But what she does not have—I wish you to listen to me, Jervis—she does not have a man who loves her." She regarded her nephew without emotion. He was listening intently, hanging on her words as though she were an oracle. She was satisfied with what she saw in his eyes. Celina, she thought with satisfaction, had indeed caught this man in her toils, even though she did not know it.

In a gentler voice Lady Gaunt continued. "I suspect, Jervis, that all you have thought of to this point is what Celina will bring to you—breeding and the rest of it. What you must convince her of is that you have something to give her. Giving, not taking, Jervis. You are not simply arranging for a superior kind of housekeeper."

She rose, gathering her gloves and cloak. He sprang to help her arrange herself and walked with her to her carriage. After he handed her in, she leaned forward and said, "I thought you would be the right man for Celina. But now I'm not so sure."

"Why not?" he demanded.

"You offered her everything but the right thing."

Humbly he asked, "Is it too late?"

She regarded him thoughtfully for a long time. At last she said, "Never too late until she weds someone else."

Revelation came to him. "That bombastic idiot Coleraine! She cannot be serious about him!"

"Edmund thinks so, as does Eleanor." She touched his sleeve in a gentle gesture. "I can help you, Jervis, in some ways, and I will, I promise you. Jervis?"

"Yes, ma'am?"

"If you love her, you must prove it to her!"

* * *

Jervis stood on the drive, watching until the carriage vanished from his sight. Chilled by the weather and chastened by his aunt's frankness, he turned and entered his house, a subdued man.

He had not been chided thus since a plain-speaking tutor had pointed out that, even though he had intelligence enough for half a dozen boys, he would be nothing but an empty-headed fribble unless he chose to work at his studies.

Again today he had been weighed and found wanting. This time the prize was an elusive lady with speaking gray eyes—and he was determined to win her.

The house was stifling. He put on a warm countryman's jacket, and set out for a walk to clear his mind. He crossed fields brown with stubble, pastures where curious sheep raised long, inquiring faces to him. He reached the line where his lands marched with Edmund Forsyth's—that bag of wind!—and paused, looking across the gently rolling land to the chimneys of Forsyth Hall.

Coleraine had already requested permission from Edmund to make his offer to Celina. The curate was a man with money and the youngest son of an earl. Could he appeal to her? Was he the kind of man Celina needed?

A deep gloom settled over Jervis. His defenses fell, and he began to think reasonably about the needle-sharp accusations his aunt had made. Had he indeed been as arrogant as she had said? Had he gone to Celina, expecting her to swoon with delight at his feet? Now that Lady Gaunt had ruthlessly dealt with the unedifying underbrush of his thoughts, the answer came clarion-clear. Yes, he had. Adrian had told him he could have any woman he wanted. He had not expected Celina, living in a backwater and serving as a drudge to her family, to be the exception.

At last he turned toward home. As he went, he knew he had found what he had searched for. He could make her happy. If happiness came to him because of her, he would be enormously grateful.

No more than a fortnight ago his great goal was to

deliver the maiden from the dragons of her family. Now his quest was simple: to give her all the love he had, to make her as happy as lay within his power.

It would take all his efforts to convince her of his devotion. Mere words would not suffice. His powerful mind stirred. Suddenly as impatient as a green lover, he lengthened his stride as he neared the house.

He had things to do.

Chapter XIV

Celina felt as though she were clinging to a great pendulum swinging to the limits of its arc. From elation stemming from Jervis's offer of marriage she swung to the opposite extreme, the conviction that he had offered only because his honor drove him.

That kiss in the spinney—she examined it from all sides. They had been alone, since the Forsyth party had returned home, squabbling all the way. The kiss itself was far from chaste—and here her thoughts fell into a pleasantly rosy muddle. She had believed she was too old for romance, that love was a sentiment fit only for adolescent dreams. Jervis had proved to her that she was as susceptible to tender passion as any green girl nurtured on Minerva novels.

A flush of shame mantled her cheeks as she remembered her response to him, her wholehearted response. No matter how one looked at it, she had flung all her standards of decorum to the winds.

And Jervis, being a man of honor, conceived it his duty to offer marriage to her. No gentleman could take such liberties, could permit such a compromising and embarrassing occurrence to develop, without making the amende honorable.

It would be of no use to protest that she had not been harmed, for Jervis would never admit that his offer was prompted only by his strong sense of duty; to confess that would negate his apology. Suppose he were in love with Lydia, but wed Celina . . .

One part of her, a large part, longed to say yes, to contemplate a blissful stretch of years in his arms. Or side by side with him, privy to his thoughts, his wry humor. She had turned him down, now and forever. Her emotions were too muddled, but she was sure of one thing—she could not accept a proposal forced by duty.

Well, she thought the next morning after a sleepless night, he offered and I refused. That certainly puts an end to the whole episode. The darkling suspicion remained, however, that she would not quite so easily dismiss certain warming memories from her mind. The warmth of affection or the heat of shame? How could she have been so abandoned?

Several days went by in gray sequence. The rising wind that had buffeted them when they went to the spinney had brought with it the first of the mournful autumn storms. Great walls of silver rain, swept by the gusting wind, pounded against the house, and to step outside the house was to become wet through in a moment.

At length, her thoughts proving execrable company, she decided to walk up to the Manor. She had avoided them all since that dreadful meeting, but she could not stay away forever. Lydia must by now have regained her equipoise, and Edmund, always more bluster than substance, would likely have moved on to worry some other trifle.

Housebound by the weather, the Forsyths were gathered in the small sitting room toward the back of the ground floor. Celina, directed thither by Pardoe, stopped on the threshold to contemplate her nearest relatives.

The weakness of the morning light filtering into the room required the lighting of numerous candles. Her presence unnoticed, she saw the inhabitants of the room for a revealing moment as though they were strangers. Eleanor, her fair complexion marred by lines of selfish petulance. Lydia's spectacular beauty, lifeless as though painted on canvas. Nelly, her very body tense with unspent energy, rather like a small, mildly dangerous explosive. Aunt Tibby and Edmund—suddenly she felt she did now know them at all!

She had traveled a great distance since Jervis had requested her company at the notorious assignation in the spinney.

Edmund was the first to catch sight of her. He greeted her abruptly. "Well, what have you got to tell us?"

Sifting through several appropriate but uncivil answers, she chose to say, "Regarding what, Edmund? If you mean the weather, I have not the words to describe it."

"You know what I mean. Have you—has he come up to the mark?"

All eyes were turned toward her. How had they known?

She was convinced that Jervis would not have galloped up to the house to proclaim far and wide that he had offered marriage to a spinster who was somewhat long in the tooth and might be presumed desperate to be married and had been refused! But what then? Were her emotions clearly limned on her forehead?

"W-who?" she temporized.

"Coleraine, of course," said Edmund impatiently. "I told you he asked permission to speak to you."

Coleraine? With an effort she wrenched her thoughts out of their Wroxton groove. Jervis had usurped her mind, but now, prodded by Edmund's brusque demand, she recalled certain unwelcome news he had flung at her that day in the spinney.

Fiancé, he had said. Your fiancé is bound to cry off if he hears about that scandalous meeting.

"Oh," said Celina with creditable calm. "Mr. Coleraine! No, of course he has not offered."

Gloomily Edmund looked at the floor. "I knew he'd cry

off. Who told him about that havey-cavey scheme of your daughters, Eleanor? Don't tell me the girls thought such abandoned behavior was something to boast about, for I shan't believe you. Not after the peal I rang over them both."

"My daughters?" cried Eleanor, rising quickly to the bait. "Only when you are displeased with them are they mine. I confess I do not understand the right of that whole matter and in truth I do not wish to hear more about it. To think that Lydia would run off to meet Lord Wroxton is beyond belief. Even my Amelia would know that such a great lord as Wroxton would not be entangled by a transparent schoolgirl's trick such as that. I am quite persuaded that he would never allow himself to be compromised!"

Ah, thought Celina darkly, but he did! No matter that he chose to embrace a woman of mature years rather than the naive Lydia, he had felt compromised, or he would never have harkened to the voice of duty.

How extravagantly my thoughts phrase themselves, she thought.

Eleanor was still prosing on. "But certainly no scandal can arise. I do think, Celina, it was very sensible of you to accompany Lord Wroxton to that rendezvous. It shows a nice feeling for Lydia's reputation, quite as careful as I myself would be."

What about me? Celina thought. "I gather that the point of the exercise was to compromise Wroxton. Have you," Celina said, turning to Edmund, "found out who sent that abominable note?"

"No," he fulminated. "Although I have my suspicions." He glared at his second daughter. "There's only one in this family who has a want of decent feeling. If he wishes to offer for Lydia, then all he has to do is speak to me."

Lydia, who had been silent to this point, said, "He is all that is kind and good."

Aunt Tibby exclaimed, marveling at Lydia's change of heart, "Wroxton?"

"I am most comfortable with him." Lydia stood up and faced them all, looking, Celina thought, like an absurdly indignant kitten, her violet eyes brimming with tears. "I like him quite as much as Beaumont." Hastily she left the room.

Celina's heart dropped into her slippers. If she had doubts before as to the rightness of refusing Jervis's offer, she had none now. Lydia was a dear, sweet girl, the niece whom she had loved since the first sight of her in her cradle. And Celina, of all ironies, was the one person Lydia came to with her troubles. It seemed only yesterday that Lydia had begged Celina to protect her against her father's brutal wish to marry her to Wroxton.

Well, Wroxton had wrought a miracle. The girl was in love with him! In her mind Celina heard Lydia saying that she liked him as well as she had liked Beaumont—the man she wanted to marry in London, who had been put off by a green dress. Celina had not recognized until now that a small hope of a future in which Jervis might again offer, and not from duty, lingered in a secret niche in her thoughts. Now even that tiny unrecognized hope was extinguished.

Eleanor was arch. "I understand that Lord Wroxton stays longer than he planned at Beechknoll. It is apparent that the reason is a certain young miss!"

The sound that escaped Lady Gaunt's lips was inelegant and fortunately inarticulate. If she intended to add anything to the conversation, she was forestalled. Pardoe entered the room.

"Lord Wroxton," he announced. "And Mr. Sadler."

"Mr. Sadler? Who is he?" wondered Eleanor aloud. No one enlightened her.

Jervis paused in the doorway. His eyes locked for a brief moment with Celina's before a telltale flush crept up from her throat to her cheeks and she wrenched her gaze away.

Greetings over, Jervis introduced "my great friend Adrian Sadler, who has come to enliven Beechknoll for me."

Adrian was of lesser height than Jervis and broader in the shoulders. His features were open and honest, and his blue eyes gave an impression of straightforward steadiness. His manners were unexceptionable, and he acknowledged introductions pleasantly.

Lydia, having heard Wroxton's voice, quickly returned to the salon. Smiling kindly on her, Wroxton said, "Miss Lydia, I should like to make Adrian Sadler known to you."

Lydia's beauty had its effect on Adrian. In truth, he was bereft of speech. His stunned thoughts tumbled over themselves. Had there ever been such purity of complexion, such a deep violet of the eyes, such shining golden curls? He never recalled what he said then, but the fevered expression in his eyes caused her to look away, even as her trembling hand lingered in the clasp of his fingers.

Lady Gaunt's gaze fell arrestingly on Jervis. His expression was bland, but the intelligence in his eyes invited her to share his satisfaction. The wretch, she thought. I knew he was devious, but this is beyond everything! What does he expect to accomplish by introducing this very ordinary-appearing young man into this boiling kettle? Eleanor will never let Wroxton wriggle away like that!

"Mr. Sadler," explained Jervis to Eleanor and Edmund, "is quite one of my greatest friends."

Eleanor searched her memory. "I wonder that I have not met him before. In London, perhaps?"

Not subtle, thought Lady Gaunt. She might as well ask pointblank his breeding and his fortune.

Jervis murmured something vague about pressing family affairs keeping Adrian in Yorkshire.

"Yorkshire!" echoed Lady Forsyth, as one might speak contemptuously of the antipodes.

Lord Wroxton glanced again at Celina. She was watching her eldest niece, who was looking shyly at her slipper toes, just visible at the hem of her yellow muslin round gown.

Lady Gaunt informed the company in general, "Old Scarburn's third daughter married a Sadler—before your time, likely."

Adrian's claim to respectability thus established, Eleanor regained sight of her main quarry. Turning to Jervis, she gave him an intimate smile and said gaily, "We shall have to provide some kind of amusement for our neighbors. Wroxton, perhaps we should plan an outing or two for Mr. Sadler."

And, thought Eleanor, I shall make sure that someone keeps Mr. Sadler fully occupied. He is such an ordinary man. Celina can amuse him. She'll be grateful for something to do.

Jervis rose after the prescribed twenty minutes. He had not met Celina's eyes after the first moment, but he was well aware of her presence. Her flustered blushes gave him hope. If her affections were untouched, she would not be embarrassed at seeing him again. But this time he must move with the caution of an American Indian stalking wild game.

So far so good, Jervis thought, as he and Adrian sent their horses trotting down the drive. He had told Adrian nothing about the part he was to play in his grand scheme. But suddenly Adrian began to write his own role.

"The loveliest face I ever laid eyes on," he said, bemused.

Jervis turned, startled. "Miss Forsyth? You consider her a great beauty?"

"Miss Forsyth? Oh, the aunt. Of course not. I mean Miss Lydia, naturally." Catching sight of Jervis's frown, he added tactfully, "Although I admit Miss Forsyth has a pair of speaking eyes."

Jervis suggested smoothly, watching his friend, "Quite struck with Miss Lydia? An unexceptionable miss."

"Unexceptionable! You've had your taste ruined by those Turkish women!" After a moment he said with a shamefaced grin, "I hope you will allow me to stay on at Beechknoll, for I am loth to leave now."

"As long as you like," said Jervis. He reflected a moment. Adrian was in danger of sending his scheme awry.

Jervis wished to immobilize, as it were, both young ladies. Lydia provided little danger to him, but if Nelly were to give full rein to her talent for mischief-making with the aim of marrying off her sister, her snares would of necessity entangle both himself and Celina. Jervis wished a free hand for his courtship, and Adrian was to be the means of accomplishing at least part of the plan.

"I suggest," he said at last, "that if you are determined to pursue Lydia, you make sure that Nelly goes along. You don't want to be embroiled beyond your depth." Adrian looked puzzled. "I mean," explained Jervis kindly, "that Forsyth is looking out for a husband for the girl. And his methods bear watching."

Adrian fell silent. Marriage was far from his thoughts at the moment. Only Lydia's incomparable beauty lured him. He needed to see her again. He dared not ask whether Jervis had a *tendre* for the girl, for if the answer was yes, he would be left to worship from afar. Strange how the expressions in old romances came easily to the lips. Sir Thomas Malory's Knights of the Round Table—he could understand them now. Struck all of a heap at the sight of Lydia, he gave himself up willingly to contemplation without ambition.

Jervis, after a few attempts at conversation with his friend, gave up, and they reached Beechknoll in silence. All was going according to his plan. With Adrian here to draw off the Forsyth ladies, he could get on with his pursuit of Celina.

But there were other obstacles in his path.

If Coleraine had made his offer already, it did not appear evident in the family gathering. He was quite certain that if Celina were now betrothed to the curate after her years of rural retirement, the assembled Forsyths would have so informed him. He had time, then, to deal with Coleraine.

But the lady had a high sense of honor, he suspected. He dared not let her become betrothed to Coleraine, for once committed, she would remain loyal, no matter how unsuitable such a match might be.

Jervis bent his formidable wits toward the successful disposal of the resident clergyman. The sooner, his instinct told him, the better!

Chapter XV

Celina did not know how much she had counted on Jervis's renewal of his offer of marriage until she was faced with the real reason she could never accept him.

Lydia was in love with Wroxton. And therefore Celina could not dash the child's hopes. It was useless to say that Lydia would get over her disappointment. Already she seemed to view Beaumont with a certain remoteness. But it was not necessarily how Lydia might feel or recover or go on into the future that bothered Celina.

She knew she wanted Wroxton. But could she live with herself, knowing that Lydia's heart was set on the same man and that she had stepped between them?

The reasons for her rejection of Jervis were few and cogent, at least to her. But the one reason that lay at the foundation of her increasing tumult of mind was by far the simplest. She was, to put it as bluntly as she saw it, afraid.

Afraid of Jervis? In a way, yes, but on a deeper level she feared her own emotions. Locked in his embrace there in the spinney, she had caught a glimpse of a brightly colored kaleidoscope of delights, ever changing, ever new. She longed with all her heart to reach out and grasp with both eager hands the joys just out of reach.

But Jervis, urged on now only by duty, was bound to

tire of her, and that she could not endure. Better never to know the joys than to have them snatched untimely away.

A cloud of dreariness descended on her that was not entirely due to the weather. In truth, the stormy weather began to abate, and she hardly noticed the pale rays of sun that fought their way through the dissolving clouds.

However, others were aware of the change in the weather and set plans afoot to take advantage of the bright October days that were at hand.

Lady Gaunt, not privy to Jervis's plans, despaired of him. If he would not move in his own interest, then she must take a hand. Stir up the pot, as it were. She was aware of the effect Lydia had on Mr. Sadler. The pair might serve her well as pawns.

"It's only a day's outing," explained Lydia, sent to the Dower House to tender the invitation. "Over to Finsgrove to see the old priory. Mr. Sadler has not visited this part of the country before, and it is Mama's wish to entertain him. Of course, Nelly and I shall go. The priory belongs to Lord Wroxton, you know."

Celina was able to translate easily. Under the guise of entertaining a visitor in the neighborhood, Eleanor was once again throwing her daughter into the company of Wroxton. If he were unavoidably detained and could not make one of the company, Celina was quite sure that the outing would be postponed.

"I do not think I will go," she said. "Don't look so stricken, child. You will hardly know I'm not there."

"But Aunt, Mama particularly insists that you come. The outing is entirely unexceptionable, you know. Aunt Tibby was to go as chaperone, and then you wouldn't have needed to, but now she feels pains in her foot, and the ride even in the landau must make her more uncomfortable. Please, Aunt Celina, otherwise we cannot go."

Celina's lips tightened. It had come to this! She was not only a spinster but also a woman in great demand by her family. Not as a delightful dinner companion or a popular and witty asset to any gathering, but only as a chaperone to fulfill the requirements of any occasion, much like a bundled-up mummy set in a niche in a temple.

She marshaled her words of refusal carefully. It was not Lydia's fault that her mother was so callous, so insensitive. She would turn this insulting invitation down and make immediate plans to flee the neighborhood. She had said once before that she was about to leave to take up residence in Bath. Temporary might well become permanent, at least as long as she could remember the scalding resentment that filled her at this very moment. She took a long breath before she spoke.

"I'll be glad to come," she said, to her own astonishment. "Will I ride in your mama's landau? Or shall I drive myself?"

"Oh, thank you, Aunt!" Lydia rushed to kiss her. "I'll let you know. We'll be off early in the morning, so to see everything. I do hope it is warm enough for my new sapphire cloak. I shall die if I must wear that old drab one with the squirrel lining."

The appointed day was warm with that special soft air that begged forgiveness for the week of raw, inclement winds and rain. From the broad front steps of Forsyth Hall, where she waited, Celina looked out across the green lawns sloping down toward a shallow valley. Forsyth land was gently rolling, as far as the eye could see, with no sharp, picturesque contrasts.

The copper beeches in the parkland had not begun to turn color, but far across the valley she could see the yellow smudge of the oaks against the dark mauve of the hill behind them. Farther down, toward the floor of the valley, touches of scarlet maples lit up the view like a bright thread in a tapestry.

A familiar voice spoke in her ear. "A lovely panorama, is it not? I believe we shall be traveling in that direction."

Startled, she turned. "I did not hear you approach, Lord Wroxton."

Her usually ready tongue failed her. Her companion,

however, did not seem to notice her silence. Indeed, the whole world seemed to be holding its breath. From far away came birdsong, and nearer at hand the sudden stamping of horses' hoofs, followed by the rumble of carriage wheels on gravel, heralded the approach of the picnic party.

"Perhaps," she said at last, "we shall make an early start after all."

In this hope she was disappointed. There was the endless business of getting the luncheon hampers stowed and room found for appurtenances, folding tables, dishes, oddly shaped baskets.

"Brewer," said Jervis into the middle of the scurrying servants, "put the food hampers at the back of my curricle."

The groom looked dismayed. "But there's no room, my lord."

"Find a place for yourself in the second carriage," directed his master unfeelingly, indicating the vehicle already aswarm with Forsyth servants. He added for Celina's ears alone, smiling down at her, "If we leave our picnic in the possession of the children, there will be naught left of it for ourselves. Adrian's appetite is formidable."

Her eyes traveled over the rest of the party. Lydia and Nelly stood beside Eleanor's landau, its top closed for protection against the wind.

Suddenly her spirits soared. This was only a day, after all, and not the rest of her life. The sun was warm, the air gentle with the spicy scent of the dying year, and Jervis was near. She would refuse to look ahead. A word of Scripture came to her. "The sun rises and the sun goes down; back it returns to its place and rises there again." She would enjoy this one day, no matter if tomorrow was the time for weeping.

Celina took a step toward the landau, the proper place for the chaperone to ride, but Jervis held her back. "You would not be comfortable," he told her. "Four passengers make a sad crush."

As he spoke, Lady Gaunt emerged from the door of the

Hall. "Celina," she instructed, "you are to ride with Jervis. You know the way. I can barely tolerate the idea of spending the day looking at ruins. I certainly do not wish to pass hours wandering without direction through all the lanes in Wiltshire."

So Celina was not needed, after all! She had been sought after as a chaperone, but no one had thought to tell her that Lady Gaunt had recovered sufficiently to provide the necessary presence of respectability.

Celina felt betrayed by them all, but there was no graceful way to bow out of the expedition, not when Aunt Tibby was throwing her into the company of Lord Wroxton, and he, ready to help her into his curricle, was smiling down at her in such a way!

At last the cavalcade appeared ready for departure. Jervis moved his vehicle smoothly to the point and looked back. He said in that intimate murmur that seemed designed for her alone, "Buckingham and I set out from Aleppo on our way across the desert to Baghdad with less gear."

"I should like to hear about your travels," she said in a demure voice. "That is, if you are not weary of the telling."

"An interested listener makes the telling a delight."

Lydia, she thought, hanging on his arm, listening to tales of wonder dropping from the traveler's lips. Just so had Nausicaa listened while Odysseus told her father King Alcinous of his ten-year ordeal.

Jervis interrupted himself from the need to deal with directions. Once well on the proper road, he resumed, "Perhaps this is the time for you to inform me just what this famous priory is that we are to view. I collect its name is Finsgrove."

"That is the name of the nearby village. The ruin is called Old Crimley Priory. Only the walls of the chapel still stand. The roof fell in long ago. There was much destruction in this region by Henry's men, and since the villagers defied them, they dealt harshly with men and with buildings."

"In Henry the Eighth's time my family did not hold land here."

"The Forsyths did," she informed him. "Later they lost much in the Civil War."

"Chose the wrong side?"

"They chose both sides. At the same time."

"A disaster," Jervis agreed, thinking that the family failing had reappeared in the current head of the family. Lord Forsyth wished to marry Lydia well, and if Jervis had been intimidated by bluster, Lord Forsyth would have carried the day. But he also wished his daughter to be happy, and that desire stayed his hand.

Jervis considered that he had to deal with sufficient in the way of obstacles between him and winning Celina, without worrying about Edmund's faults. He would at the proper time inform Celina's brother of his intentions. But until that time he would pursue his lovely girl in private ways.

They rode in silence for some time. Jervis frequently stole a glance at his companion's pure profile, content for this hour simply to admire.

Celina, riding against her wish in Lord Wroxton's curricle, began insensibly to relax under the benison of the sun. Her spirits continued to rise until they reached a plateau of content. It was a fine day indeed, one of the last, no doubt, before the grayness of winter set in.

Suddenly a flight of birds exploded far ahead of them, dark shapes against the sky as though someone had taken a handful of leaves and tossed them into the wind. She gasped in delight.

"Yes," he said. "A wonderful sight."

Conversation languished. The recollection of the last time they had been alone together, in the privacy of her salon, hung almost tangibly between them. At last he broke the lengthening silence. "I perceive we have come to a crossroads. Which way shall we turn?"

She gestured to the left. They waited past the fork to be sure the others did not miss their direction. Suddenly she could see the truth of Lydia's remark. She too felt comfortable with him. But for Celina, letting down her defenses could betray her.

The walls of the priory were still standing. It was not so much ruined as neglected. The heart of it had been destroyed by the great Henry's ruthless sweeping away of the privileges of the churchmen, and the fabric of the priory, like so many other stone and mortar evidences of faith, had gently moved toward dissolution.

"It's shrunk!" exclaimed Celina involuntarily at her first sight of the crumbling ruin. All but Lady Gaunt stood now a short distance from the edifice.

Jervis was at her elbow. "I imagine you saw this last when you were a child." At her nod, he went on, "A sad mistake to return to the days of one's youth. Not an original thought, Adrian, No need to frown at me."

Lydia shuddered. "I don't like old things like this."

"Everything's old," pronounced Nelly. "It doesn't make sense not to like them. Our own house is as old as this, at least one wing of it is."

"That's different. This is ugly."

Adrian looked down at the lovely face, a fond smile on his lips. "How pleasant this place must have seemed to the monks who lived here! I suppose down the slopes we can still make out the carp ponds. And there would be orchards and vineyards and perhaps a kitchen garden, although I doubt there are any traces left." He tugged gently at Lydia's sapphire cloak. "There's nothing to fear. No ghosts. Or if one does linger here, he must be friendly."

The sun slanted along one interior wall of the unroofed chapel through what may once have been a rose window. It took a giant leap of the imagination to see lines of gray monks filing in for compline, shadows cast by tapers leaping against the dark night framed by the lancet windows, and to hear rough voices chanting the ancient Latin words.

It was even beyond fancy to picture the hooded figures as being men at all, dealing with the small commerce of daily living but underneath it all resting on an abounding religious faith.

The chapel ruins were haunted, but not by long-ago monks. Celina had brought her unsettling anxieties with her.

"Come, Lydia, let me show it to you." Adrian put his hand under Lydia's elbow and urged her toward a gaping hole in one wall.

Celina remembered her duenna role. "We shall all go," she said, picking up her skirts to avoid the uncut grass. "Come, Nelly."

Not much remained of the ancient glories of the structure. But what was left was charming. Adrian seemed to be knowledgeable.

"This of course is not to be compared with Malvern Priory," he told them. "But just the same it could be restored to advantage, Jervis. It belongs to you?"

"I suppose it does."

"Look there. You can see the remains of decoration that I believe must be Norman. See the detail there? The small beasts' heads? This is a sure indication that the Hertfordshire school of carvers was at work here. And there's a centaur—you see the horse with the man's head, Lydia?"

Adrian's enthusiasm bubbled. He moved along the side wall, Lydia clinging to his arm, Nelly a few steps behind. Jervis remained with Celina just inside the entrance .

"Where is Lady Gaunt?" she asked.

"She stayed in the carriage, as befits an elderly chaperone. Lydia is perfectly safe with Adrian. Besides, is not Nelly's presence sufficient to dampen any man's ardor?"

"Lord Wroxton—"

"Never mind. I am sure that if we pay close attention, our lecturer may drop a word or two of some interest."

She suppressed a giggle. "Truly I doubt it. I agree with Lydia. All these old things are better left as they are."

"I am gratified to hear you say that, Miss Forsyth. For a moment I feared Adrian would insist that I hire an entire army of restorers and architects to rescue this pile of stones. But if the priory doesn't interest you, then I am spared such an undertaking."

"I—I have nothing to say about it. It is yours, Lord Wroxton, to do with as you please."

She caught the expression in his eyes and felt a queer disturbance in the region of her stomach. Surely she was mistaken. He had offered from duty, from a sense of honor, from the conviction that he had compromised her. But the amused intimacy with which he conversed with her spoke another language.

"Lydia—" she said in a strangled voice.

"Is in good hands," said Jervis. "And Nelly is standing by. If Adrian so far forgets himself as to require our intervention, I am sure she will inform us." Gratified by her small snort of suppressed laughter, he took her arm. "I am persuaded this place is damp. You are shivering. Come out into the sun."

Shivering she was, but she knew it was from his touch on her and not from the air rising from the damp and mossy stones. She had been wrong to come on this jaunt. She had felt it her duty to chaperone, as Eleanor had informed her through Lydia, but Lady Gaunt was here, and Nelly as well.

After a little he said, "You are lost in thought, Celina. Too deep to share?"

They had moved around the building to catch the sun. Here the wind did not reach them, and she could feel on her back the warmth reflected from the outer wall of the building.

The priory was built of course on a hill, not only to command a view of the valley but also to draw the eyes of the villagers constantly upward. The air was freighted with the scents of autumn. The spicy fragrance of fall flowers growing somewhere down the hill came to her in little waves on the gently moving air, and the tang of beechwood smoke drifted up from the village at their feet.

Finally she answered his question. "Not thoughts, Lord

Wroxton. In truth, I am not sure there is a thought in my head."

To her surprise, he nodded approvingly. "As it should be."

She was impelled to argue. "You feel that no woman should think?"

"I did not say so. Indeed, I should not for a moment find delight in talking to a vacuous mind." Involuntarily his glance slid toward the window not far away, through which they could hear Adrian's voice, still instructing.

"But I gathered—"

"I merely meant, my disputatious lady, that a day's outing is not the time for serious contemplation. Nor," he added in a wry tone, glancing toward the window, "for instructing unwilling maidens, although I do not think one at least was particularly unwilling."

He was speaking of Lydia, of course. Had the Moor, so to speak, found that his exotic tales were losing their power to charm? Lydia had not so much as glanced back at Jervis when she moved off, hanging on Adrian's arm. Did she take Jervis so much for granted that she knew he would not mind her absence?

She gazed at him, seeking to detect some hint of his emotions in his impassive features, in the hooded eyes, but she could not. Nonetheless, she believed she sensed great vulnerability in him. Even the strongest man, the most disciplined character, must have somewhere a weakness in his defensive walls.

Or *her* walls—for Celina was learning a bit about herself in these latter days.

"Let us go back to Aunt Tibby," she said in a flat voice.

He regarded her anxiously. "I've said something that displeased you. Will you tell me what it is?"

"Nothing," she said. "But I feel the chill a little."

He had thought the air particularly warm where they stood, but without a word he turned with her and helped her back down the rough slope to the carriage where Lady Gaunt sat.

Rioting through her head, and inspired by the heady nearness of him, the pleasant aroma of his shaving soap, the sight of his strong sensitive hands clasped on his knee, were thoughts she wished for her own peace of mind to keep hidden. He seemed at times almost to read her mind.

"I think I left my shawl in the curricle," she said, needing privacy for a moment. "Never mind, Lord Wroxton, I shall fetch it."

Lady Gaunt watched her out of earshot. She leaned forward urgently and said in a low voice, "Jervis, what are you doing? You've got that family in an uproar. Lydia's taken a liking to young Sadler, and her mother is furious."

"Why? He's entirely eligible."

"Not entirely. No title, you know."

Jervis shrugged. "But he's got estates, and an income at least as large as Forsyth's. He's highly eligible, Aunt. And I should think they would leap at the first man that offered. After all, Nelly's really vulgar determination to get married must of necessity make living in her vicinity immensely uncomfortable."

"Will he offer?" demanded Lady Gaunt.

"I don't know. He says nothing to me. In truth," he continued reflectively, "he has hardly spoken to me the last three days. But, of course in confidence, Aunt Tibby, I don't care what he does. He is here merely to keep those young women busy while I mend my fences with Celina."

"I don't know why," complained his aunt on a querulous note, "you don't press your suit at once in that direction. Perhaps she has changed her mind. You're an exceptionably desirable *parti*, you know."

"So I had thought," he confessed.

"You'll come up to the mark too late," she resumed, after a small silence. "You know Coleraine's spoken to Edmund."

"But that does not a betrothal make."

She ignored him. "Now I myself would not be tempted by that fanatic churchman. But he is persistent, give him that."

"Like a hornet."

"She glanced slyly at her nephew. "And he has Forsyth's encouragement. Fool!"

Jervis assumed she meant Forsyth. But on reflection he conceded she might refer to himself.

"And you haven't even spoken to Edmund yet. I thought you had more enterprise than that, Jervis. Have you changed your mind about the girl?"

"Not for a minute. Not ever. But I do not quite see myself lining up in the queue, do you?"

Lady Gaunt, with deliberation, thrust a needle-sharp remark at him. "She's already refused you. Perhaps she really favors young Coleraine. Had you thought of that?"

"She will be Lady Wroxton before spring." His voice sounded confident, but the furrow between his eyes said otherwise.

The picnic party was shortly augmented by Mr. Coleraine, who made a late entrance, not precisely declaring that he had been about his Master's bidding, but allowing the idle picnickers to think so.

"We had almost started without you," said Lady Gaunt, not unwilling to chide the latecomer.

"I am not," said the curate, "always able to follow my own wishes, you know. A clergyman must expect urgent calls at any time."

Jervis glanced at Celina. Her expression, under rigid control, told him nothing. Was it possible that she could tolerate such pomposity, such complete self-centeredness, even admire it?

He began immediately to frame a letter to his cousin the bishop, who held him in some affection. ". . . a curate, well bred, apparently devoted to his calling . . ." Jervis reflected, then in his mind's eye deleted "apparently." His thoughts ran on. "Many talents . . . wasted in a country parish . . . perhaps a position in a far diocese . . . he is not married, and"—here Jervis gave full rein to his devious mind—"I should judge celibacy to be most beneficial to his advancement at least for the moment. . . ." He would send Pollard with the letter no later than first light tomorrow.

In a hollow on the sunny side of the slope, sheltered from the wind by the remains of a foundation that anciently supported the ordinary offices of the cloister, the Hall servants brought chairs, spread cloths and rugs, and served the chicken, fruit, and little cakes that Mrs. Pardoe had sent along. There was wine in supply, and the party grew merrier.

The only untoward incident, according to Jervis's way of thinking, occurred when at the end of the afternoon Coleraine, under the pretext of escorting Celina to Jervis's curricle, spoke earnestly in her ear, holding her arm entirely too tightly.

Aunt Tibby cast a wary glance at her nephew. Good, she concluded, he was getting worried. He had taken Celina entirely too much for granted, presenting her with an offer of marriage as though awarding her a prize—Jervis, of course, had not seen this aspect of his behavior, but she knew him well enough to perceive his mistake.

Now, gratified, she watched Jervis's features cloud over as he watched the two in deep conversation. If it had not been so important to achieve the match she desired for dear Celina, she would have been able to enjoy the spectacle better. As it was, she was forced to stifle her strong impulse to prod Jervis into some action she could see. Or as an alternative to shake some sense into Celina.

Thought Lady Gaunt, the outing she had carefully planned was already bearing fruit. She would wait a bit to see how the harvest would set.

Chapter XVI

Jervis was ordinarily a man unhurried. Feeling little urgency in his days, for one seemed much like another, and impelled by little more than his own penchant, he moved without haste from one enterprise to another.

Stirred by a wish to see Constantinople some years before, he had calmly made arrangements to travel across a quarter of the world and had gone. Later, intrigued by the contagiously exotic tales of a traveled gentleman named James Silk Buckingham, he joined him on an excursion to Aleppo and beyond, journeying by way of Mosul and arriving in Baghdad in the heat of mid-July.

In Baghdad he was a guest of Claudius Rich at the Residency, where for the first time in months he had a bath, food worth the eating, and a comfortable bed. The temperature even at midnight often stood at 114 degrees, a condition that lent itself to slow and deliberate movement. He had been at the Residency still in mid-August, when he had been recalled by the death of his grandfather, the elevation of his father to the dukedom, and his own accession to his new title and estates.

But he was back in England now, and for the first time in his memory he was seized by a sense of the utmost urgency. He wanted Celina. This was the goal of his days and the dream of his nights. And he had thought—the biggest mistake he had made since he misjudged the temper of a certain bedouin somewhere near Ctesiphon—that she was willing, even eager, to embrace marriage with him. He had a magnificent title, he had enormous wealth, and he was considered a personable young man. But all these had not been enough to capture the lady. Now, to cap it all, his arrival turned out to be something of a spur to dormant intentions. Lawrence Coleraine, having as Jervis learned been at hand for two years, only now sought out Edmund to ask his permission as head of the Forsyth family to pay court to Celina.

At the moment, a few days later, when Jervis was awaiting a response from his clerical cousin, Celina was perusing a letter that had just arrived. Mary, her companion and dear friend, had been gone a month. Quite long enough, Celina considered, to visit a family of whom Mary was not overfond and to see a cousin safely married.

A few years ago, when Celina had first come to terms with her belief that since her two Seasons in London had not brought her the happy prospect of a marriage of minds as well as incomes, she would live out her days quietly in the Dower House, Mary had come to live with her.

Mary had come to stand in the place of the sister she never had, and Celina felt her absence sorely.

This had been quite the most trying month since Mary had joined her. So many things had happened, and she was denied the pleasure of talking them over with her dear friend. But, she realized as she unfolded the missive, there was much she would not be able to bring herself even to mention let alone to discuss exhaustively and exhaustingly.

In more than one way Celina was relieved not to have to suffer Mary's bright, inquisitive glance after a sleepless night. But soon Mary would be back, she reflected, and life would pick up its even tenor again.

An inarticulate cry escaped her lips as she scanned the first pages of Mary's letter. Then, with an air of disbelief, as though she must have mistaken the words, she began again at the beginning.

"Dearest Celina: This letter will come no doubt as a surprise to you, much as the burden of it has come with astounding swiftness to me. I believe I have never mentioned my distant cousin Geoffrey, from the other branch of the Remington family. He has been with the Company in India for several years and is now home on leave. He will be sailing for Calcutta within the month and he has asked me to go with him. I had never forgotten him from when we were children . . ."

At last Celina let the letter drop into her lap. Edmund had warned her of this very development. "What will you do if Mary finds a husband?" he had said. "She's likely to, you know. Will you find another companion?"

The fact that Edmund's prophetic words had come true even sooner than he expected did nothing to endear him to her. Mary had deserted her, but she could not blame her for grasping happiness as it came by.

She did not stir for a long time. She sat in her elegant satin-striped bergère chair in her fashionably appointed and luxurious drawing room, four servants within call, and felt as though she sat on rubble-strewn ground in the ruins of Carthage.

It was not Mary's defection alone that caused such devastation. This news only capped weeks of family strife and the upheaval in herself caused by the mere existence of Jervis Blaine, so near across the fields, so far removed from her.

She became aware of an urgent need to escape. Her first impulse was to order her affairs and flee to Bath for a year. Or buy a small house somewhere, anywhere, away from her brother's family, for whom she had recently developed a strong dislike. There were many things she could do.

But it came down to one thing: living, wherever she chose, alone. She could find another companion, not like Mary, of course, but satisfactory. And if that companion failed, then another could be secured. But the truth of it was that Jervis had opened up a small vista of what could be a great happiness. She herself had closed the door, and it would not be opened again.

For the first time she was beginning to recognize in herself the existence of passion that could in the end either scorch her into shriveled aridity or sweep her into a bliss only dreamed of till now.

Well, next time she received an offer of marriage, she would take it!

Celina had not long to wait. And yet, as marriage proposals go, it did not quite suit. In fact, as Lawrence Coleraine entered her small drawing room, he seemed not in the least like a man on the verge of hazarding his life's happiness within the hour.

After tea was brought and she had offered him one of Mrs. Elkins's tasty little macaroons, he settled back in the chair that best fitted his length and smiled benignly.

"I trust you took no harm from Lord Wroxton's outing," he began. "I thought it quite a blustery day, and certainly not one fit for a picnic when ladies were included in the party." He added after a moment, "But of course there could be no picnic without ladies. I cannot even contemplate a group of gentlemen sitting down on the ground to eat a cold collation in the open air. Quite like harvest hands."

He smiled again tolerantly, as though encompassing an acceptance of the wayward whims of young ladies and at the same time denying any snobbish intentions toward farm laborers.

"I quite enjoyed the weather," she protested. "I am a countrywoman at heart."

"I feared you would take cold. Indeed, I said as much to Wroxton. I know him hardly at all, you know, for he has been out of England this long time. But I have recently had the opportunity of becoming acquainted through correspondence with his cousin." To her inquiring glance, he answered, "The bishop. A prominent churchman. Of course, having the family interest of the Blaines is no deterrent to advancement. He's next in line for Canterbury, I believe. Or if not that post, then surely York or Durham. A very influential man."

Seeing that a response was expected, she murmured, "I have not met the bishop."

He reached for another macaroon. "Of course, most affairs of the Church would not be of interest to you. But when you realize that preference must wait upon interest, you will see that it behooves even the lowliest curate to have, as I think the sailors say, a weather eye out. Not that we would have to scrape and bow—oh, no. The Coleraines have some interests in the Church, and I fancy we will do quite well."

His manner puzzled her. He had adopted an odd fashion of speaking in the plural: *We will do quite well.*

"I fear your conversation has left me behind, Mr. Coleraine."

He lifted an aristocratic eyebrow. Not for the first time she wondered what strange forces had directed him to seek a career in the narrow paths of the Church. Younger sons of wealthy and well-born families often found themselves at loose ends, finding their amusement in gambling or the pursuit of other vices, but rarely did they take orders. Especially were they not content to remain in a rural parish for long.

Nor was Mr. Coleraine satisfied. His long, thin face had recently developed lines of thwarted ambition, and his manner, rather than accommodating itself to the ways of his parishioners, had become more reserved than ever.

"Do not fear I shall ever leave you behind, as you say," he said, gently reprimanding. "I am sure you recall my telling you about my wish for a charge where the rewards would be greater. I must confess I was misguided when I hoped for a transfer to the less fortunate areas of London. I admit that your kind encouragement to me at that time gave me much hope for the future."

Celina searched her memory frantically. What had she

said? The curate obligingly continued, fortunately giving her a reprise, "When you told me that any worthy woman would be glad to serve her husband and through him serve the Lord."

She bit her lip. Serving a husband and the Lord were not the same thing at all in her mind.

"Mr. Coleraine, I fear you are laboring under a misapprehension—"

He favored her with an indulgent glance. "I was much heartened," he emphasized. "But I shall not require you to share such straitened circumstances."

Celina listened, appalled. It was borne in upon her with some force that the Honorable Lawrence Coleraine had taken leave of his wits. At last she recalled Edmund's information, flung out at her in the heat of that encounter with Lydia and Nelly and Lord Wroxton in the spinney.

She had been recently thinking so strongly about certain other aspects of that meeting that she had tucked away the knowledge that the curate had asked Edmund for permission to pay court to her. But although she had remembered it at odd moments at first, she had dismissed any such eventuality from her mind, since Mr. Coleraine had been all that was proper—and to be truthful, even a little remote—since that day.

But now she remembered that Edmund had used the word "fiancé." So perhaps there was more to it than a simple request for permission to pay court. Could it be—Edmund would never *dare*, would he?—surely he could not have given her hand to Coleraine, without so much as a word to her! He could not have done so—but the question lingered, had he?

For Mr. Coleraine was speaking indeed as though the question were settled. As though, she thought, with sinking heart, she were all but packed to travel with him on their wedding trip.

This misunderstanding must be straightened out. She sat up straighter in her chair and addressed him firmly. "Mr. Coleraine, I fear you have made a mistake."

He smiled gently. "I should have expected you to demur. But the three years will pass quickly, buoyed up as we will be by the hope of our eventual union."

She blinked. She had surely missed a few words, and important ones, at that. "I don't believe—"

"I too was surprised that the bishop insists on celibacy for three years. I cannot find precedent for such a stipulation. But he surely knows best."

She was shocked into desperately plain speech. "Do I gather, Mr. Coleraine, that you are proposing to me a three-year betrothal? Because of some idiotic bishop's ruling that has nothing to do with me, for I am not planning to marry you."

He was wounded. "It is none of my doing," he told her, more truthfully than he knew, "but you must agree that the post at Ely Cathedral is greatly to be desired."

She swallowed the scalding words that rose, clamoring for expression, to her lips. Instead, feeling her cheeks warm with indignation, she began, hoping for a temperate tone, "I do not believe—"

He interrupted. "I know what you are going to say. Your sweet modesty is one of the attributes, even virtues, that I find most attractive about you. Do not fear that Bishop Blaine will find you lacking in the ways of the Cathedral Close. With due attention to learning the customs and the habits of your new position—you will have three years, you know, to prepare yourself—I am quite persuaded that you will win all hearts."

"Mr. Coleraine, I beg you to listen to me," she said, unhappily aware that her voice was strangled by anger. If she could manage to keep her temper, she would count it a great victory.

"Of course, Celina," he said, speaking her given name for the first time.

"I am pleased, as anyone would be, that you have attained at least one of your ambitions. But," she added, abandoning without guilt her recent promise to take the first proposal of marriage that came along, "you are much mistaken if you think that I shall be required to learn the ways, as you say, of the Cathedral Close."

His eyes narrowed. "Of course, my dear, I had no intention of speaking adversely in any way of your breeding or indeed of your behavior. It is only that—"

"I do not know what right you have to believe that I shall have any part in your future. Without even *asking!*" Her speech was getting hopelessly muddled.

"But your brother assured me that my suit would be welcome, indeed that you were eager to receive my offer."

Gathering the scattered fragments of her wits, she said, "But my dear Mr. Coleraine, I have not received your offer. It seems to me that you are taking my acceptance very much for granted."

He sat up, bewildered. "But—but he said—"

"My brother does not speak for me!"

"But you have received me here, *alone*."

"I am past the age for needing a chaperone," she told him icily, remembering that Wroxton had scoffed gently at this idea when he heard it. "And I cannot believe it improper to receive one's spiritual counselor in private. Although you will realize that you no longer hold that position with me."

Two unattractive red spots appeared in his cheeks. "I see," he said, rising, "that I have gone about this the wrong way. I lay the blame for this misunderstanding on your brother. He surely gave me to understand—"

She stood up to speed his departure. "I fear the misunderstanding is entirely yours, Mr. Coleraine."

At the door he paused. "I had not thought you the sort of woman who must be wooed like the veriest schoolgirl. But if I must, I must. I shall call upon you tomorrow afternoon."

"Pray do not," she said in some distress. "Truly, I shall not change my mind."

He smiled gently, sadly, skeptically, and went through the door Elkins, obviously lurking near at hand, opened for him.

The door was scarcely closed behind her misguided suitor when she turned to the butler. "Hot tea," she ordered, "and strong."

Even with the beverage steaming in her cup, she could not sit down. She moved restlessly from chair to window to chair. How dared he come in and calmly take over her life without so much as a by-your-leave? He had not had the decency even to state his offer, instead expecting that her brother had rushed to inform her of her great good fortune. She was to be grateful that Mr. Coleraine, the youngest son of the Earl of Rommillies, had weighed her in the balance and liked what he saw!

Little fragments of his speech fell through her mind like leaves falling in autumn. She would have no trouble learning the ways of the Cathedral Close. She would give satisfaction, if she put her mind to it.

Did he think—could he really believe—that marriage to such a self-satisfied noddy would be preferable to living in her own house with her own ample income and nobody to order her about?

If today was an example of his future behavior, she pitied any woman who accepted him. Whatever his wife might say, she could be sure that Mr. Coleraine would pay it no heed.

She at last gained a victory over her angry distress and finished the last of the tea, now cold in the pot.

By this time she had concluded that the curate was simply as ignorant as it was possible for a well-brought-up man to be and had decided merely to instruct Elkins that she was not at home to him. In fact, for the rest of the day she would be at home to no one.

By ill luck, before she had an opportunity to give directions to her butler, Eleanor came in. In spite of the calm demeanor she wore, she gave the impression of bursting in with disaster just behind her.

"Celina, I must talk to you. Yes, Elkins, you may take my cloak. No tea, please, Celina, I do not have the time."

Finally settled, the door closed behind Elkins, Eleanor

said, "What happened between you and Mr. Coleraine? I saw him leaving. Did he offer?"

"I hardly know what to say," said Celina, proceeding to say it. "Yes, he did, and no, he didn't. He seemed to have the mistaken idea that Edmund had handed me over to him like a roast pheasant on a Wedgwood platter. He didn't even have the grace to ask me to marry him. He simply told me what my life would be like, and—can you imagine this, Eleanor?—he told me that if I truly endeavored to succeed, the bishop might not throw me out of the Close."

"I can't believe it. Surely he's teasing you."

"Did you ever know him to see the slightest joke?"

"No." Eleanor added, struck by the workings of fortune, "But this works out so well, Celina!"

"Yes," said her sister-in-law dryly, "it does."

"But what I came to ask you, Celina, you might not have wanted to do, especially if you were formally betrothed. Now all is most satisfactory."

Celina, her heart sinking, ventured, "What is?"

"I have had," began Eleanor, "some very distressing reports about that outing of yours. That havey-cavey scheme of going to look at an old pile of stones. I should have known there'd be trouble."

"Did Lady Gaunt fall ill from the exertion?"

"Not at all. But I understand from Lydia and from Nelly that Mr. Sadler was very much in evidence."

"I thought the picnic was in his honor. Of course he was in evidence."

"But to take Lydia aside into that ruin without either you or Aunt Tibby, well, I must say I am gravely disappointed in Lydia's lack of decorum."

Eleanor's gaze was fixed on Celina, and it was clear that Lydia was not the sole source of her disappointment. Celina inquired gently, "Have you seen the priory lately?"

"Not since Edmund took me when we were first married. Why?"

"It has no roof. Only a portion of the walls still stand.

There are windows along the walls, without glazing of course. Eleanor, Mr. Sadler, and Lydia were not, as you put it, in private. Besides, didn't Nelly tell you she was with them?"

Eleanor's confidence slipped. "No, no, she didn't. That wretch! But still, I want you to do something for us. Don't say no before you hear me out."

Celina nodded, expecting some small chore along the lines of helping with entertainment or talking to Nelly. She was wrong.

"It distresses me to see Lydia spending so much time with Mr. Sadler. Not that he isn't a pleasant young man with excellent manners. I believe him to be quite unexceptionable in that direction."

"Hardly sufficient reason to forbid him the house," observed Celina lightly.

"Oh, no!" exclaimed Eleanor, horrified. "Lord Wroxton would be most irritated."

Celina pursued her own train of thought. "But if Lydia likes Mr. Sadler—"

"That has nothing to do with it!" Eleanor pursed her thin lips. "Of course she likes him. I do myself. But as her mother, I must take pains to guide her properly at this crisis in her life." Celina hoped her skepticism was not displayed on her face. Apparently not, for Eleanor forged ahead. "Nothing can be allowed to divert us from our goal."

"Which is?" murmured Celina.

"Lydia is deeply in love with Wroxton, as anyone with an eye can see."

Celina wondered what her sister-in-law would say if she told her Wroxton had proposed marriage to *her* and not Lydia. A small part of her mind gaped at the wonder of it: two marriage proposals, such as they were, within a fortnight. How ill-timed the events of her life were!

"And naturally, I do not wish her behavior to lead to any misunderstanding with him. He is of course more mature, and one can only hope that he understands the waywardness of young ladies. I had hoped that by now he would have come up to the mark, but I confess that I share Nelly's fears that he will delay too long. He must be made to understand that he must fix his interest at once with Lydia."

"You are sure," murmured Celina, "that Lydia's feelings are definite?"

"Oh, yes. You should see the way she looks at him."

"I have," said Celina, the memory sharp as a knife. That very look of adoration swam before her mind's eye, blurring any prospects she might entertain of Jervis's renewing his proposal. There were moments when she doubted her own belief that Jervis had offered for his honor's sake, having, it must be admitted, compromised her with his intimate kiss. Always at this point in her arguments with herself logic deserted her, leaving her to wander rosily in pleasing fancies.

"Well, then," Eleanor was saying when Celina came back to the present with a jolt, "we must give him a clear field, Edmund says. I had not thought him—that is, Edmund—to be particularly perceptive, but even he sees that Mr. Sadler is too much in the way. And that is where you can help us all, Celina."

Celina did not answer for a bit. "Has it occurred to you, Eleanor, that Wroxton may be sufficiently adept to provide his own opportunities to be alone with Lydia?"

"But Mr. Sadler is his great friend, I am told."

"If he gives way to Mr. Sadler, then he cannot be too enmeshed himself by Lydia, can he?"

Eleanor stared at her. "But he has to marry someone, now that he is the duke's heir. And it may as well be our Lydia."

Why not? Celina thought. Not every man wants a plain wife. Even though Wroxton himself had disclaimed interest in a vacuous woman—his own words—yet such ineffable beauty as was Lydia's had its own claims.

Besides, the generation of handsome children did not require conversation, vacuous or not. Wroxton could well have an eye to the production of beautiful progeny and still amuse himself with other, more intellectual, ladies.

She wished with all her heart she had never even heard his name!

"If you can just keep Mr. Sadler occupied, Celina, I shall take care of Wroxton."

Celina was amazed to hear her own answer. "No. I cannot."

"A mere matter of seeking him out for conversation. I know it will be dull for you, Celina, but surely he is better than Henry's old father. I shall probably give a dinner, suggesting, don't you know, that it is a farewell entertainment for Mr. Sadler. You can be quite determined in requiring his company, and I promise you he will think nothing of it. After all, he will have to be kind to you . . ."

Still talking, Eleanor rose to leave. Celina made another desperate attempt to communicate her wishes. "Eleanor, I cannot interfere in this. You or Edmund must deal with Mr. Sadler, although it seems to me there's no need. Edmund can always, if he must, forbid Lydia to see him."

"But not if he's Wroxton's friend." She received her cloak from the hands of Elkins and turned to say a last word to Celina. "You'll know just what to say to him, Celina."

I say no, said Celina silently. She wondered whimsically whether she had lost her voice or alternatively her hearing. She was positive she had said no, firmly and without equivocation, to Eleanor. But Eleanor had continued as though she had not spoken.

Nor, she recalled, had the curate seemed to hear her earlier that afternoon. She had told him under no circumstances would she marry him, and he simply said he would begin the courtship she demanded of him on the morrow.

What must she do to make her wishes known? She began to pace back and forth to relieve by physical action the anger sweeping her.

Wryly she remembered that she had given Wroxton a

small, even tentative, refusal. He had listened and had not approached her in that way again. She was surely making herself understood to the wrong persons!

Suddenly she saw that she held a Staffordshire vase in her hand. She stared at it as though she had never seen it before but with an effort she remembered that its usual place was on the mantel. Appalled, she was aware of a strong urge to throw it and listen to the satisfying crash and the tinkling of a hundred porcelain shards falling on the parquet floor.

She had not been seized by such a blind anger since she was in the nursery. Calm, sedate, poised, serene—all these words, she knew, described her, for she had heard them many times. But this blind lashing-out of fury, of stormy rage, all this was new. Where did such emotion come from?

Darkly, she knew. Jervis Blaine, Lord Wroxton, had opened a door for her onto the most delicious passion, but also he had unleashed the reverse side of the coin, the darker storms. And without his strong arms around her she knew it would be difficult indeed to master the unwelcome tempests of anger.

She took a deep breath. No one could force her to do what she did not wish to do. Anger would not help much. A simple, continuous, calm refusal must be the answer.

If she strove mightily, she might be able to forget the bliss she had glimpsed once. Likely as short a time as twenty years would suffice to restore her equipoise.

Chapter XVII

At this moment Beechknoll was the stage for another scene of some anger. Adrian Sadler, having come to visit his great friend Jervis for the pleasure of his company, had found his pearl of great price.

He had been numbed at first by the outstanding beauty of Miss Lydia. Hardly daring to breathe, he had approached her as a devotee might draw near to a goddess, with reverence and awe. Astoundingly, the lady had smiled on him, a smile, he considered, dulcet as the taste of the fabled nectar of the gods on Mount Olympus.

The sweetness of Lydia's disposition was genuine. He marveled at the way she had come through her life to this point, with her overly ambitious parents and her obsessed sister, and yet been untouched by the vicissitudes of life at Forsyth Hall. A Season in London, and miraculously no one had carried her off. He was relieved that he had not been forced to watch the hordes of suitors she must have had in these last months.

Jervis, watching him with his own senses unusually keen, recognized the clear signs of infatuation on the part of his friend. Not ordinarily one to interfere in another's affairs, yet he felt a kind of responsibility, since it was by his invitation that Adrian had ventured this far from Yorkshire.

He turned over in his mind a number of ways to broach the subject of Lydia, but in the end he did not need to resort to a devious approach. Adrian, usually silent at breakfast, at length spoke his mind, a week after the outing to the old priory. It was a measure of his mental confusion that he lacked his usual coherence.

He bore the look of one beleaguered, back against a wall, and forced against his nature to turn aggressive. "Jervis," he said in an odd tone that caused his host to glance at him, surprised, "I never thought you would trifle with a girl's feelings."

"Nor," said Jervis calmly, "did I. Pray tell me what causes this remarkable assessment of my character."

"Everyone expects that you will marry Miss Lydia," Adrian said, well launched and unable to retreat.

"Not everyone," corrected Jervis dryly. "I, for one, do not expect such an event."

Adrian swept on. "Lady Forsyth talks of little else. I believe she must already have planned the wedding dress."

Jervis wore an arrested look. Surely he was the one setting traps, devising snares. Had he been too deeply engrossed to detect a pitfall designed for himself? Swiftly he reviewed his recent actions and found no fault in them.

"Surely you exaggerate, Adrian. I have paid the girl no particular attentions."

Adrian summed up the communal state of mind at Forsyth Hall. "Biding your time, so they say. Letting Lydia become better acquainted with you."

"Fustian!"

"But if you do not linger here to fix your interest with Miss Lydia, then I am at a loss to understand you. Beechknoll, while it is comfortable, is far from being the kind of manor house you are accustomed to. And I must say the neighbors are an odd lot."

Jervis permitted himself a smile. "They are indeed. But I do have a reason for staying. My aunt wishes it."

Adrian looked at him with open disbelief on his frank features. "Lady Gaunt? I don't understand you, Jervis."

"You do not surprise me. But if you hesitate to cut me out with Lydia, pray do not give me another thought. I only suggest, Adrian, with the most delicate feelings in the world, that you consider what marriage with her would be."

Adrian's features took on what Jervis, to his great astonishment, recognized as an expression of beatitude.

"I give you her spectacular beauty, Adrian. In truth, I do not recollect ever seeing a more perfect face. But do reflect. It is of all things the most idiotic custom to deprive females of any learning beyond the execution of futile embroidery and playing a simple tune on the pianoforte." He spoke with some heat.

Adrian watched him curiously. Bound by his concentration on fair Lydia, he now saw that his great friend labored under a powerful, if undefined, emotion.

"You and I are such opposites, Jervis," he said ingenuously, "that it is a wonder that we can be such great friends. I am not very powerful in the intellect, you know, not in the way that you are. I know much about my lands and my stock, and I can conceive of no greater comfort than to sit by my fire in the evenings with a lady who thinks the world of me and who has the sweetest disposition ever. This would not suit you, Jervis."

His friend suppressed a shudder. "How cleverly the world is arranged," he said lightly, "so that we don't all want the same thing. What a muddle it would be if we came to blows over the same lady!" He poured two fresh cups of coffee to give himself time for thought.

Adrian burst out, "Then you're not going to offer for Lydia?"

"I believe I said as much."

"Is this your final word?"

"Adrian, be assured that at least as far as I am concerned, the young lady is all yours. What her family may decide is beyond my conjecture." It occurred to him that perhaps the circumstance that Adrian owned a substantial portion of Yorkshire and in consequence was nearly as wealthy as a nabob was not known to the Forsyths. Striving for a light note, he suggested, "Shall I put in a word for you with Forsyth?"

Adrian, surprisingly, laughed. "Good God, no! He's so bumble-headed he'd mix it all up, and *you'd* be betrothed to my girl before nightfall!"

Relieved, Jervis turned the conversation into other channels. His invitation to Adrian to visit at Beechknoll, self-serving as it had been, had borne unexpected fruit. Simply designed as an unobtrusive false trail to draw the Forsyth hue and cry away from himself, Adrian had fallen in love with Lydia of the beautiful face and the peahen wit.

Jervis had believed his way clear to remove Celina's suitor and substitute himself. Now Adrian bade fair to muddy the waters by his untimely pursuit of Lydia.

Ah, well, these things happen, as Adrian's own tenants might say.

It was toward the end of breakfast that Adrian dropped a bit of news into the conversation that caught Jervis's interest.

"The curate fellow, Coleraine. You've heard about him?"

"Nothing of moment, except that he is a fatuous idiot and a crashing bore in the pulpit. What of him?"

"He's being moved across the country all the way to Ely Cathedral. He's quite high-flown about his new position. Lydia says he's been at the Manor twice this week talking about it."

A chill touched Jervis. The removal of Lawrence Coleraine from Celina's vicinity was no surprise to him. Indeed, he blessed his cousin's prompt response to his letter. Jervis was now struck by strong doubts. What was the infernal nuisance doing at the Manor? It was quite within the bounds of probability that Coleraine might follow through on his wish to offer for Celina, even though Jervis could not believe that Celina would accept him.

He had thought to begin with that all that was needed was to remove the curate from the arena. Now, judging from Coleraine's visits to the Manor, it was possible that family matters—the betrothal of Celina, for example—were afoot.

The look he turned on his companion was cold. "Why?"

Adrian raised his eyebrows. "Why not? He's making no secret of his preferment. I must admit, though, there are some odd elements in this matter. I know very little about how the Church manages its affairs, you know. If there's a vacancy in one of my livings, the archbishop suggests a man, and I approve him. What do I know, after all, about preaching and the rest of it?"

"What indeed?" murmured Jervis. "No more than I do. You did say . . . odd?"

"The bishop apparently prefers a celibate priest, at least so Coleraine has informed us all. More than once. No marriage for three years."

Jervis's sigh of relief was soundless. His cousin had not failed him. "Three years? But why is he prancing up to the Manor?" He did not realize he had spoken the last words aloud until he caught Adrian's curious eyes.

Adrian answered casually, "To boast about his preferment, I suppose. He does go on a bit about his unique qualities that caused his bishop to take notice of him. Nelly says he thinks the Archbishop of Canterbury has him marked down to be his successor."

Then, thought Jervis, perhaps my ploy worked. Surely my dear Celina could not be taken in by such a fool!

"He did make something of a point," said Adrian, deceptively casual, "that to wait three years for marriage was not an intolerable burden. Especially when the lady can apply herself usefully to studying how she should go on."

Jervis's stunned reaction told Adrian all he wished to know. "Good God! She hasn't agreed!"

"No," grinned Adrian, "at least that hasn't been announced. But there's a smug look about Coleraine—"

Jervis lifted a hand. "Pray tell me no more. The man's affairs are of no interest to me."

Adrian was in the highest degree skeptical. But after all, Jervis was his great friend and was excessively kind to let him stay here and worship Lydia, and he forbore to express his opinions.

Jervis lapsed into a brown study. It did not occur to him to wonder why, after Celina's six years of unmarried living in the Dower House, suddenly there should be two suitors, himself and the curate, clamoring to pay court to the lady. Jervis knew that the Forsyths believed his arrival to herald his interest in their eldest daughter. He did not recognize that his appearance had caused a ripple of unease in various directions to move through the unattached men of the neighborhood. Jervis only knew that he must prevent Celina from an ill-advised and overhasty capitulation to any besieger save himself.

Now his rival was, so to speak, removed from the arena, the way appeared clear to him. He would this very day ride over to the Dower House and put his fate again to the hazard. He had not been this nervous since, five miles from the gates of Baghdad, Buckingham, irritated by the arrogant demeanor of the Turkish guards, had suddenly drawn his pistols and demanded entrance to the city. That had been touch and go. But then only his life had been at stake.

Now, to Adrian, he said only, "Forsyth recommends the traveling fair today at Ludgershall."

"You? On the roundabout?"

Jervis eyed him gravely. "Your wit suffers a decline. I shall not attempt to ascertain the cause, although I suspect Lydia has much to do with it. Forsyth is putting some of his livestock up for sale. You may find it desirable to take an interest in his success."

Jervis, riding a little later down the long avenue away from Beechknoll, allowed himself a smile. If Adrian expected him at the fair, he must brace himself for disappointment.

Jervis was on his way to the Dower House and Celina. He was, fortunately for his present state of optimism, not to know he was too late.

Chapter XVIII

The village of Ludgershall was rarely entertained by such a diversion as a traveling fair. But, wonder of wonders, Richardson himself, through a series of misfortunes, found himself with his troupe at loose ends in Wiltshire.

He had packed up his booths at the end of August, when Bartholomew Fair was over, expecting to make his usual circuit through the provinces and emerge at Greenwich at Eastertide.

What was primarily ill fortune for Mr. Richardson was a windfall for Ludgershall. Popping up overnight like mushrooms, stalls and tents and cages sprouted in a field just north of the town, a profusion of sights, one more exciting than the next.

It was quite the most spectacular sight to come to the village within the memory of the oldest gaffer. There were stalls selling toys or trinkets for souvenirs of the wonderful occasion. One could eat to repletion from the various delicacies offered: oysters, gingerbread, brandy balls, roast pig. There were whelks offered, fresh from the sea, it was said, although anyone with any learning knew that the sea was nigh a hundred miles away. And, unfortunately for the continued equilibrium of many of the attending folk, a good supply of gin. A magnificent menagerie caught the lively curiosity of the local inhabitants, most of whom had never traveled a greater distance than the twenty-five miles to Salisbury, and what with the marvelous wonders of dwarfs and giants, it was all too magical to take in at once. In addition, the livestock sales captured a certain element in the region.

Such an opportunity of expanding one's experience did not go unnoticed by the residents of Forsyth Hall.

Adrian had conceived a mistaken idea of the journey to the fair. He had believed himself to be in sole charge of Lydia, and of course Nelly as chaperone, to ride at leisure to the fair. The hours ahead stretched out in a pleasurable haze, hours spent in Lydia's undemanding company. He could deal, he believed, with Nelly, and the anticipation of Lydia's violet eyes gazing into his, the two of them as alone as one could be in the midst of jostling throngs, nearly overcame him. But such bliss was not to be.

Lord Forsyth and his factor, Lady Forsyth and Lady Gaunt, Miss Lydia and Miss Nelly, it was at first expected, made up the party from the Hall. Word of the wonders to be encountered in the field by Ludgershall trickled down to the younger levels of the family, and Lady Forsyth found it impossible to refuse the combined pleas of Sophie, Catherine, and Amelia. The five girls, in the smaller of the Forsyth carriages, were put in Adrian's charge.

Mr. Coleraine, pursuant to his fixed idea that Celina sentimentally required to be wooed, arrived unheralded at the Dower House. He was driving a smart black horse, one of his own, set to a curricle.

"I should not wish you to be compromised by riding in the tilbury that the church had given me for my use. I know you are no longer a giddy schoolgirl," he said, bowing handsomely, "but no female of whatever age can be too careful of her reputation."

Celina did not speak. Indeed, she could not, for to make a choice among the scalding words that came to her tongue was beyond her. She well knew she was long out of the schoolroom, but it was still hurtful to be reminded of the fact, as Lawrence Coleraine seemed to do with unwelcome frequency.

A day spent in his company would be intolerable. "I have no wish to go to the fair," she said, adding silently, particularly with you.

"I must apologize for not sending ahead to inform you of our plans, but a man of the cloth never knows when he may be called to a deathbed or some other tragedy," he said with no trace of gloom. "I am prepared to wait while you ready yourself for the outing."

The fleeting thought came to her that a month or so ago she would simply have swallowed her irritation and responded kindly to him. Now, since Jervis had introduced her to the existence of passion of all kinds, she seethed.

"I have no need to ready myself." Then a wayward thought struck her. She really wished to see the fair. "I shall fetch my bonnet," she told him.

The day was unusually fine, as autumn days after rain usually are. Handed up into the curricle, Celina determinedly set about enjoying herself. A vital element in her pleasure was to turn a deaf ear toward her companion. The curate did not appear to notice.

"I have ordered a nuncheon at the Bull," he informed her. "We may retire from the entertainment whenever we wish."

"But the point of going to the fair," Celina protested, "is to attend it, not retire from it."

"You are right, of course. I thought by one o'clock you would be ready for refreshment."

"Perhaps you did not properly hear me," she said distinctly. "I do not wish to retire to an ordinary lunch in an ordinary inn. I recall Bartholomew Fair very well indeed and I look forward to enjoying every minute of this one."

He was wounded. His eyes looked anxious for a moment. Then a happy thought came to him. "Of course. It is my pleasure to accede to your wishes. I had forgotten that is one of the customs of courtship. Pray forgive my lack of *savoir faire*. I have never before approached a female for the purpose of marriage."

Or, she thought unkindly, probably for any other purpose.

Celina mentally threw up her hands in dismay. He did not listen to her. She shuddered again at the thought of spending the entire day in the company of the Honorable and Boring Lawrence Coleraine. But she was already too late for the party from the Hall and in fact she had been reluctant to join what would be a great squeeze.

Imagine traveling even a short distance with Edmund, Eleanor, Lady Gaunt, and likely a maid or two. Or alternatively, according to information received only that morning, in the second coach with five overexcited giggling girls and Adrian Sadler. There was not much to choose from.

At least in the curricle the air was fresh on her face, and the sun lay warm across her shoulders. And if she paid her escort a return compliment—not listening to him—she could go on tolerably well.

She had made, over recent days, some progress in forgetting Jervis—not forgetting, precisely, but to some degree banishing him from her thoughts for an hour or two at a time. She had a strong suspicion that he was purposely avoiding her, a circumstance that gave weight to her belief that he had offered marriage only out of his sense of honor and was marvelously relieved when she refused him.

She told herself, not convincingly, that she too was satisfied that the ordinary course of social intermingling in the neighborhood did not bring him to her frequent notice.

Riding along in a dreamy state of mind—aware only of sun and air, of the faint aroma of wood smoke and the sharp smell of fallen leaves—Celina scarcely knew where they were. They passed the corner where the road leading to Beechknoll turned off, and she did not notice it.

If she had noticed it and looked a little way down it, she might have recognized the solitary horseman, a tall, erect figure, riding his mettlesome Arab Babil. Jervis, however, had no difficulty in recognizing the two occupants of the curricle and drew up sharply. So Coleraine considered himself still in the running!

Jervis sat, not moving, for a long time. Babil at length expressed his opinion of such unseemly behavior—were they out for a gallop or not?—by a loud whicker.

"All right, old man," said Jervis, leaning forward to pat the arched neck. "Subtlety didn't suffice. Plain speaking will have to do."

To Celina's satisfaction, Mr. Coleraine's conversation along the road to Ludgershall was unexceptionable. He rambled on in a monologue that reached her in unheeded fragments. A word or two of uncommitted response now and then sufficed.

She could hear and smell the fair long before she could see the gay awnings of the booths and the milling, happy crowds. There was the pungent, earthy smell of animals mingling with an enticing fragrance of roast meat and cakes hot from the oven. She realized suddenly that she was hungry, and it was only mid-morning!

It seemed as though all of Wiltshire was here, and perhaps it was, for a fair of this size was a rare treat. But it was a good-natured crowd, tolerant, ready to be entertained. Mr. Coleraine stabled his horse at the Bull, and they walked through the small village to the field beyond. The high hum of laughter and the monotonous roar of many voices greeted them as soon as they moved away from the inn.

"Your family will doubtless be here," suggested Mr. Coleraine. "We shall seek them out first."

She had learned the futility of speaking her mind on any subject, even one as trivial as that which he had just broached. She merely nodded and let him propel her through the throngs.

She caught sight of Nelly on the other side of the gingerbread booth, but before Celina could catch her eye she was gone. Celina and her escort watched the clownish antics of the Merry-Andrews for a long time, enjoying the high-pitched squeals of delighted children. Surely the buffoons would enliven many a dream this night.

She herself, she decided somewhat later, would be fortunate indeed if the Man-Monkey did not stalk through her own nightmare. At length she began to grow weary of the heat and the noise. She knew Mr. Coleraine would take her home at once if she complained—and if he heard her—but she was unwilling to leave the entertainment, at least until she had eaten something. Even luncheon was designed to remove her from the attractions before her, for her escort expected to eat in the drab surroundings of the inn.

Suddenly his fingers tightened on her elbow. "Ranny! There's Ranny Ford. He looks—There's something wrong. Ranny!"

The boy, the son of a Forsyth tenant, looked around, hearing the voice of authority. His face clouded, and he made as if to dive into the shelter of the crowd. Mr. Coleraine was too quick for him.

"What's amiss, Ranny?" he said, keeping tight hold of the boy's arm.

Resigned, the boy ceased to twist in the curate's grip. With happy invention, he announced, "Me mum's sick."

"Oh, dear," said Celina with sympathy. "Is she at home?"

"No, miss. Just on the other side of the Talking Pig. She liked him a treat!"

"I must go to her," said the curate. "I must not neglect my duties at the last."

"Of course you must," said Celina warmly. "I shall come too, Ranny."

"Oh, no, miss! She's got my aunty with her." He thought a moment. "She didn't rightly say she wanted preacher either."

"Do you think I am needed?" she asked Mr. Coleraine.

"I think not," said Mr. Coleraine. "I hardly know what to do, for I cannot leave you here in this dangerous situation, but of course I must see to Ranny's mother."

She looked around her. "The crowd seems well behaved to me," she told him, adding untruthfully, "I see Edmund over there. I shall join him."

"Where? I do not see him." Ranny pulled away from the curate then and vanished in the crowd. Mr. Coleraine hesitated, then plunged after him.

Celina soothed her conscience. Edmund was surely in the throng somewhere. She did not expect to seek him out.

She moved slowly, obstructed by the crowds. She had no fixed goal, but she was increasingly hungry, and the smell of hot meat pies lured her like the Sirens' song. No lady eats in public, she told herself, biting into the delicious treat, but today I am simply a villager. What would Mr. Coleraine's bishop say? If he were an agreeable man, I should give him half my pie.

She stood a little removed from the crowd, in the shade of a mammoth oak tree at the edge of the field. She thought she had never eaten anything so delicious as the pie as she licked her fingers to obtain the last crumb. Somewhere behind the curtain at the back of the meat-pie booth existed an incomparable cook possessing a masterful hand with pastry.

Suddenly she felt she was not alone. She glanced up quickly and met hooded eyes filled with mirth at her discomfiture.

"Lord Wroxton!" she exclaimed. How dreadful of him to come upon her when she was engaged in such common behavior! She felt heat invading her cheeks .

"What have you found that is good?" asked Jervis, his manner merely friendly and not in the least critical. Abruptly her embarrassment left her, and she was no longer surprised to see him. In truth, she knew now, this was why she had come to the fair at all; just the hope of catching a glimpse of him made the hours with Coleraine tolerable.

"Those little pies there," she said, gesturing toward the booth.

"I'll take your recommendation. May I get you another?"

She was still hungry. This fresh air—"Yes, if you please."

They stood, a little later, eating their pies in silence. She did not notice that he had maneuvered her so that the trunk of the tree stood between them and any casual observer.

When they finished, he offered her a handkerchief to wipe her fingers clean. "You did not come alone?"

"No," she said, bristling. "I came with Mr. Coleraine."

"You need not explain yourself to me," he told her gravely, "now or ever." Then on a lighter note he added, "I simply wondered if you were free for an hour to see the sights with me."

It occurred to her that suddenly the day had taken on a burnished hue, an air of richness and warmth. The spectators at the fair were quite the most charming people she had ever seen, the very flower of England.

She tucked her hand through his elbow, and they moved among the milling crowds. Caught up in the nearness of him, of the touch of his muscular arm beneath her fingertips, she entirely forgot the curate. Such pleasure could not last, but at least she might have today.

They paused for a moment at the Punch and Judy and markedly longer before the Talking Pig. Ranny's mother had thought the porker a rare treat. And so he was. He could, so his human companion boasted, spell, read, cast accounts, and tell the age of anyone who asked him.

The character of the fair altered as they approached a growing knot of rustics clustered around a spectacle Celina couldn't see.

"The Bully," murmured Jervis, "offering to fight anyone who has a notion to have his few brains knocked out. And for only a round of cheese!"

Celina expected him to drag her away, protecting her from such a scene of violence. Jervis did not. Obscurely she was flattered; at least he gave her credit for her own judgment.

Anxious to understand the fascination the boxing match exerted, she lingered on the outskirts of the crowd.

The Bully lived up to his name. A brutish hulk, he

towered over the challenger by a head. Celina decided the cheese had not yet been made that could induce her to take even one step closer, to say naught of striving for it.

Jervis, beside her, ejaculated, "Good God!"

The challenger, stripped to the waist, bared impressive shoulder muscles and a strong chest. But the Bully's long arms already reached out, ready to mangle. She turned away, unwilling to see the slaughter.

"He'll be killed!" said Jervis, under his breath.

She looked again, startled. "It cannot be!" she cried. "It's Mr. Sadler!"

"The young fool!" said Jervis, angry. "I suppose he has to impress that—" He recollected in time that the nitwit he was speaking of was niece to Celina.

He moved as though to rescue Adrian from the ring, but changed his mind. Adrian would have to fight his own battles. Jervis would simply stay to scrape him off the floor of the ring and call the surgeon to deal with him.

"I should take you away from here," said Jervis somewhat absently, "but I really cannot leave."

"Of course not," she said heartily. "But I am not sure why he is fighting. Surely not for the cheese."

He didn't answer at once. To her surprise, she found herself spellbound by the action, hardly aware that she winced with every blow that landed on either man, an occasion which was far more frequent than Adrian could wish.

At one moment she screwed up her eyes to avoid seeing the battle, but in spite of herself opened them again, intent on the contest. The challenger, Adrian, was at least temporarily a worthy opponent. He was a fine physical specimen. What was the phrase the beaux used in London? He stripped to advantage, that was it.

Adrian landed a good blow. The Bully rocked back on his heels. Jervis murmured, "He only slipped," and her heart sank again. Adrian could not follow up his advantage. Even from here she could see that his chest heaved like a blacksmith's bellows, and she believed the fight could not last much longer.

The crowd moved in and out like smoke. In one of the small openings, she caught sight of Adrian's reason for fighting: Lydia, her hands hiding her face, and, Celina was willing to wager, tears streaming down her flawless cheeks. Nelly, her face distorted with a combination of disgust and anger and perhaps despair, had one arm around Lydia's shoulders, but her eyes were fixed gravely on the fighters.

Suddenly the impropriety of the situation of the Forsyth young ladies, including herself, struck her. She had thought much better of Adrian's good sense. She closed her eyes momentarily, the better to contemplate the depths to which Lydia and Nelly had sunk. She herself was past redemption, being six and twenty years old. Since the girls' parents were not at hand, the occasion called for a strong hand from whoever was nearest. She touched Jervis's sleeve.

"I agree," said Jervis. "But the damage has been done. They are quite safe, at least till the fight is over." He looked over Celina's head to where the girls stood. What could have possessed Adrian to abandon them thus and hazard his own health, even his life, on this schoolboy prank? He had not a chance in the world to escape unscathed from the fists of the fair's champion, to say nothing of carrying off that immense round of cheese.

The onlookers, aware that the challenger was not known to them, in truth was one of the nobs, pressed closely around the ring. Jeers and cheers rose from the crowd, composed entirely save for Celina and her nieces of men, most of them stocky farmhands on a rare holiday.

Celina took a step toward her nieces, who were standing a little apart from the crowd. Jervis smiled down at his distraught lady. "Do you think you have the slightest hope of removing them now?"

She managed a wry smile in return. "Perhaps not." She cast a quick glance about her. She recognized no one. So far, so good.

But she kept an eye on her relations. Nelly now shook

Lydia's arm, forcing her to raise a woebegone face from her hands. They were engrossed in an argument—at least, Nelly was talking briskly and intently, but Lydia only shook her head and turned away.

Celina's impulse was to hurry to them, to comfort Lydia and quite possibly shake some sense into her sister. Now, above all times, was not the moment to point out shortcomings to Lydia, either her own or, as was more likely, those of the hero in the ring.

A loud, animal-like cheer rose from the throats of the male spectators, followed by a short muffled scream, doubtless from Lydia's lips. Celina looked quickly at the ring. Only one man still stood, hands clasped high above his head in triumph, and, predictably, it was the Bully. Adrian must be lying supine on the canvas, for she could not see him.

"Oh, dear," she said to Jervis. "Do you think he is badly hurt?"

Jervis answered dryly, "I imagine he will be uncomfortable for a few days. Don't worry, I shall not scold him. I fancy his own bruises will provide sufficient chastisement."

"I cannot help but feel that he merits the most cogent indictments," she countered, "and certain phrases suggest themselves to me. But first I must see to the girls."

His gaze had strayed beyond her in the direction of the two girls. Seeing his eyes widen, she looked at them also, and the sight of Lydia, straining in Nelly's grasp, obviously intending to rush to the fallen warrior, tore a short but pithy exclamation from her lips.

Jervis murmured, "Pray excuse me, while I rescue my reckless friend." He did not seem to be in any hurry. "We each have our chores to do. I hope yours will not be overly difficult, although, from first glance, I do not envy you. Would you like me to come too? Adrian can wait a bit longer. Indeed, I doubt he is conscious yet, and I do not feel it quite the thing to drag him away by the heels."

"How kind you are! But I think, under the circumstances,

that it would be best if you do not appear in the matter. I may hope that neither has seen you here with me."

He lifted an eyebrow. "But why should the sight of me bring disaster upon you all?"

She was back on the instant into the oddly constituted slough of delicious memories and despair for the future. "If you cannot understand me, Lord Wroxton," she said, finding relief in irritation, "you might at least step out of my way."

He inclined his head. She hurried toward the girls, angry with herself for her inexcusable rudeness with him. The day was spoiled. But she could not dwell on her disappointment. Jervis was right not to envy her the task of subduing her niece. It took some forcible and angry remarks and much calming on Celina's part to render Lydia ready, if not to agree, at least to listen.

"You must know that the entire shire is here watching you," scolded Celina. "Lydia, pray calm yourself. What can have possessed Mr. Sadler to expose himself to such an outcome I wish you can tell me."

"Lyddy, for heaven's sake!" added Nelly in a fierce undertone. Her tone indicated that she had been saying much the same thing for some time now. "Stop that blubbering! It's nothing to you that Mr. Sadler has, from his own wish to show off, a bump or two on his head. Aunt Celina's right, you know. We're disgraced. Everybody's looking at us, Lyddy!"

Celina glanced, surprised, at Nelly. Not for the first time she regarded her second niece with some alarm. It was not in the least characteristic of Nelly to range herself on the side of propriety. But she must defer consideration of Nelly's motives to a later time.

She looked quickly toward the ring. Small fistfights had broken out along the edges of the crowd, and at least one seemed likely to move in their direction. She gripped Lydia's arm tightly. They must leave at once!

By chance, Celina found the right note to resolve this

idiotic exhibition. What Eleanor would say when she heard of this was past imagining.

"Lydia," said Celina with intensity sufficient to overcome the lingering gulping sobs, "Lord Wroxton has gone to take care of Mr. Sadler. There is nothing for us to do but to go home. And what your father will say to this afternoon's work I dare not think."

"Lord Wroxton?" echoed Lydia. These were the first coherent words she had spoken. She smiled through her tears, warmly, like sun after rain, and added, "Now all will be well. Lord Wroxton will manage everything."

With Nelly's help Celina managed to drag Lydia, who persisted in many a languishing backward glance, in the direction of the Forsyth coach.

"Where are your sisters?" Celina asked Nelly. "You surely didn't leave them alone."

"Of course not. Molly came along to take care of them."

So she could take Lydia and Nelly home with a clear conscience. That was one blessing, if at the moment the only one she could see. Suddenly she had remembered Mr. Coleraine. She thrust Lydia into the interior of the coach, and gave instructions to the groom who was holding the door.

She climbed in after Lydia. "Come, Nelly, the fair is no place for us. We must get Lydia home out of all this before the entire county has time to wonder at her want of conduct."

Nelly pouted, but when her aunt added honestly, "I did think I saw the general looking at the fatstock," she climbed in with alacrity. Henry's father was a person to avoid.

"I just hope Lyddy hasn't done for us all," she muttered darkly. She turned to Celina. "We were just strolling along, and all at once Mr. Sadler hurried us along to that tree where you saw us and then he disappeared. The next thing I knew he was up there in the ring, bare as a baby—"

"Not quite," Celina pointed out soothingly. "Do not

fret, Nelly. I do not hold you responsible for Mr. Sadler's sad want of conduct."

Fortunately neither Edmund nor Eleanor was at home to receive their daughters. Pardoe merely blinked when Lydia and Nelly entered the Hall, the one showing signs of recent tears, the other brittle with irritation.

He caught Celina's eye and murmured, "I shall send for Nanny, Miss Celina."

"At once, if you please, Pardoe," said Celina pleasantly. "I recommend, pray tell her, a hot drink and a fire in Miss Lydia's room. Even a hot brick in her bed," she added for Lydia's benefit, "and an hour's rest would be most beneficial."

Pardoe left to discharge his instructions, and Celina turned to Nelly. "I know you are bursting with all kinds of reasons for your behavior. In truth, I do not wish to know why you and Lydia were standing in the public gaze, unescorted, in such a state of misery, even though Mr. Sadler had placed you there. I am persuaded that neither of you is incapable of movement. Certainly you could have moved away from such a display of violence."

She was struck by the recollection that she herself had stood watching the contest and had not even thought of leaving. She hurried on.

"I suggest that you both bend your wits to concoct a concise tale for your parents."

Nanny bustled in, arms reaching out for Lydia. "My poor pet," she crooned, emitting a faint aroma of malt into the air, "something nasty happened? Never mind. Nanny will make it all well. Come along, there's a dear."

She put a fat arm around her favorite and drew her toward the stairs. Over her shoulder she addressed Nelly. "I don't know what mischief you've been up to, miss. It's always something with you, and the Lord knows the end of it. Come away up, now. You didn't ought to have gone to the fair, and I said so all the time. A nasty place to go and not fit for a young lady. I can't think what your mother was about to let you go. Now look at you . . ."

Her voice died away as she propelled Lydia up the broad stairs, Nelly dragging behind them. They were soon out of sight on the landing.

Celina lingered in the hall. "An unfortunate occurrence, Pardoe," she explained easily, "but no harm was done. By the way, if Mr. Coleraine should come to inquire for me, pray tell him I am safely at home but I do not wish visitors."

If the groom had been able to find Mr. Coleraine and give him her message, he might well come to the Manor to inquire about the young ladies. Celina pinned her hopes on Pardoe. The butler would make it clear to the curate that Celina wished to rest all afternoon.

Pardoe nodded wisely. He had his own opinion of the curate, and it was gratifying to be able to snub him upon instructions.

Celina started out for the Dower House. The exercise and fresh air might drive away the throbbing headache that had come as she dealt with her refractory niece.

She walked down the driveway. The wind here in the park was strong, making it much chillier than the flat, protected field where the fair was pitched. She turned up her collar.

Now that she had leisure to think about the untoward incident at the fair—imagine a well-bred young man engaging in a boxing match in full sight of two young ladies!—she spared no time to contemplate the strong representations that Edmund would be impelled to make to his family.

And rightly so. But even worse than Mr. Sadler's lapse was the sight of Lydia so far lost to propriety as to stand in a public place, witnessed by all who cared to look, in unbridled distress. Nelly's behavior as well, while not totally outrageous as Lydia's was, nevertheless gave signs of a sad want of self-control.

The Dower House, as she went in, had the unmistakable air of being unoccupied. She had, upon receiving Mr. Coleraine's invitation to accompany him to the fair, given her servants leave for the afternoon, and she had no doubt they were all at the festivities.

All of them; and she was certain, with a sinking feeling, that the story of Lydia's breakdown at the sight of Mr. Sadler's bare chest being pummeled was already current among the Forsyth servants both here and at the Manor.

She dropped her bonnet and her cloak on a chair in the foyer and wandered into the parlor. She would give much for a cup of hot, strong tea, but there was little hope of Mrs. Elkins or Carrie returning for another hour.

She leaned back in her chair and closed her eyes. She was simply too old, she thought, to sustain any prolonged high emotional pitch. Twenty-six, after all.

Purposely she sent her thoughts plodding in certain directions. She had had a sufficiency of Mr. Sadler and his odd effect upon her nieces. She wondered whether Mr. Coleraine had received her message and if so what conclusions he had leaped to.

But central to all, and no matter how she sent her thoughts in all directions, like the spokes of a wheel they all came back to the hub.

Jervis Blaine.

She thought with a lowering feeling that the high spot of the day, of the entire week, in fact, was the few moments of standing with him, eating little meat pies in pleasant, undemanding companionship. It was not so much contentment, she realized, as it was—how should she say it?—contentment laid against an unspoken background of passion recalled in tranquillity.

Passion recalled—and not passion to come.

Chapter IX

Time passed in a sort of dream, and still she sat. She felt weary to her bones, and her fatigue was no more than half the result of physical exertion. True, she had walked farther than ordinarily at the fairground and again from the Manor to the Dower House.

The weariness that descended on her, no matter what its cause, oppressed her. She felt a slight draft on her feet from the direction of the foyer and knew she had not properly closed the outside door. She did not move. She could close the door later. Just now she must think.

Why had she gone to the fair in the first place? She had no wish to countenance Mr. Coleraine's attentions to her, although to tell the truth he did not seem to need much encouragement.

If she was to be perfectly honest with herself, she might as well confess the lurking hope that in such a crowd she might catch a glimpse of Lord Wroxton. As indeed she had.

But also she could now recall in excruciating detail the behavior of her niece Lydia. One might think her a delicate creature, overly sensitive to cruelty, to violence, to the sight of her friend engaging in fisticuffs. After this afternoon's unseemly display Celina could better understand the defection of Lord Beaumont. Lydia might think he did not offer because of her ugly green gown. Celina was convinced that the reported scene in the Tower over the poor beasts in the menagerie had not only turned Beaumont off but had fed the rumor mill to the effect that no one else wished to offer for her.

Lydia might well have soft feelings for all created animals. However, it was a question in Celina's mind—sign that her character was undergoing some unedifying changes—whether, if Adrian Sadler had managed to give the Bully a leveler, Lydia might not have cheered him on.

Skepticism, she finally decided, was not a becoming attribute in a lady, even one of mature years like herself.

However, beyond all was the haunting recollection of Lydia's beaming expression when she heard that Mr. Sadler would be cared for by his good friend. "Lord Wroxton," she had cried in accents of adoration, "will manage everything."

She was irritated with Lydia, not the least because she herself shared that blind confidence—surely Lord Wroxton would manage everything. She could have cursed that impulse in him that had led him away from England at the time that she had made her own debut in Society. Surely in two Seasons, had he been moving in the social whirl at that time, she might have fallen under his spell at an appropriate time. Now, even though she realized that he was the one man in the world she wanted, he had come too late.

She heard a tentative footstep in the foyer. Elkins home early? She opened her eyes. Elkins could bring her tea.

The visitor who now stood in the doorway was the precise vision that stirred in her mind: Lord Wroxton himself, his eyes filled with concern.

"I am sorry to intrude," he said, "but the door was ajar. I did knock, but apparently no one heard me." Then in an altered tone he said, "Are you alone here?"

"The servants have gone to the fair."

"I cannot think it wise to leave the door open. No, my

dear, I do not mean to scold. Merely, I am glad it was I who discovered the open door."

"So am I," she said wryly. "My visitor might have been Mr. Coleraine."

"I am sorry to disappoint you."

"Believe me, I am relieved."

"I came to inform you," he continued after a long moment, "of the outcome of today's small contretemps."

"We have not seen," she pointed out, "the outcome yet."

He raised an eyebrow. "Perhaps I spoke in too sanguine a manner. I meant merely the present state of Mr. Sadler's health."

"A subject in which I have very little interest. I am much displeased with the way he discharged his duties as escort to two impressionable young ladies."

Jervis did not try to hide his amusement. "I collect you are speaking of Miss Nelly as well as Miss Lydia?"

Suddenly she laughed. "How pompous I am!" she admitted. "Lydia's behavior is in no way my responsibility."

"I should think not!" he agreed. "But I confess Adrian's is mine, for I introduced him into the neighborhood."

Restored miraculously, and merely by Jervis's presence, to her usual good humor, she relented. "I truly hope he has not suffered unduly."

"No more than one might expect, except perhaps in his self-esteem."

She smiled. "I cannot think it any way healthful to sustain such a beating. Pray sit down, Lord Wroxton. I must apologize for my abrupt greeting. I cannot offer you any refreshment, since everyone has gone to Ludgershall. Unless you would find a glass of sherry appealing."

"If you will join me," he said. "I do not mean to be impertinent, but I should imagine that your interview with your sister-in-law must have been somewhat harrowing."

"The sherry," she said, "is in the dining room."

"Let me find it," he offered.

"As it happened," she said, when they were settled

again, "I did not see Eleanor. Nor Edmund, for that matter."

"I can inform you about your brother. He was engrossed in livestock. I noticed him and his factor speaking very intimately over a half-dozen particularly handsome dark-red cows."

She smiled. "How like him! Edmund, I must tell you, has a great interest in his farms. A great virtue in a landowner."

"And you think I am derelict in this? I object to your view of me as a dilettante. I have had, in fact, several fruitful interviews with the staff at Hohenheim, a new farmers' training school in Germany." He noticed her eyes bright and intelligent on him. "I had the surgeon call at Beechknoll to look at Adrian," he continued. "He will be confined to his bed for a few days, but eventually he will be right as rain."

"Did you by any chance, I wonder, learn from him his reason for trying to win a cheese? Surely Beechknoll has sufficient provender for its residents."

"You have not heard from your nieces as to how this occurred? No, I see you have not. I do not know all the right of it, but I believe that his feat was much on the order of a small boy standing on his head in hope of impressing females of his acquaintance."

"Adrian? Oh, no, not Adrian! He seems so steady, so, so unemotional."

"I assure you you have not plumbed the depths of Adrian Sadler. The conversation, so he tells me, had turned on the feats of strength exhibited by a certain strong man at a booth near the entrance to the fair. When the Bully's manager taunted the spectators nearby as having—the very words, I believe—no bottom, Adrian was in no way minded to dismiss him."

"And only for this reason he challenged the Bully? I should think this could easily have repelled Lydia."

Gently he suggested, "It occurs to me that Adrian rightly estimated Lydia's quite juvenile reaction." Seeing assent in her face, he went on, "And you heard nothing of this from the young ladies? Then perhaps we should air this no further than your very attractive salon."

Her thoughts slithered away from Adrian's character. Lydia was entirely right. Lord Wroxton not only had removed his friend from his supine position on the canvas, conveyed him home, procured medical attention, come to inform her of the outcome, but now was taking pains to see that Lydia and Nelly did not suffer through him.

Lord Wroxton had managed it all.

Perhaps it was the wine. Perhaps it was Jervis sitting not far away. But more probably it was simply that her thoughts were in such a tangle that she did not know precisely how she felt or how she would go on.

It was clear enough, at most times, that is, that Jervis would in the long run marry Lydia. It was clear, at other times to be sure, that he had more than an ordinary feeling for Celina herself. She felt so comfortable with him, such a relaxed intimacy that surely meant something. And besides, he always made her laugh.

As he did now. "I must confess myself greatly relieved that Adrian saw fit to match himself with a mere prize-fighter. Suppose he had been moved to emulate the jester with his pet goose. Did you see them? She was purported to be the only dancing goose west of London."

She chuckled, vastly entertained. It was thus that the curate found them by virtue of the door that Jervis too had failed to close behind him.

Mr. Coleraine's features were mottled with ugly red spots. Celina's heart sank. She recognized the signs. Mr. Coleraine was in a very unchurchly high temper.

But to her relief he was tolerably civil to Jervis. "After all," he said after a few sentences of greeting, "your cousin and I shall be in close collaboration, you know." He peered at Jervis with suspicion. "Perhaps she told you as you escorted her home."

"He didn't—" Celina began, and then lapsed into silence. She was persuaded that Coleraine would not heed anything she said. And besides, whether Lord Wroxton drove her home or not or whether he took her dancing at midnight in the village square did not concern the curate.

"I have been offered a very handsome post in connection with the cathedral at Ely. Where your cousin the bishop presides, if I am not mistaken. Indeed, it was he who wrote offering me the position."

Jervis bowed in agreement. "I shall give myself the pleasure of writing to him at once," he said solemnly. But his gravity received a blow when he caught sight of Celina's magnificent gray eyes fixed on him in a speculative gaze. Surely the lady could not read his thoughts, could she?

He hastened to take his leave. Mr. Coleraine stayed in the parlor, looking around him vaguely. Celina escorted Jervis to the door.

Under his breath he muttered, "Good God!"

She smiled mischievously. Then, in a voice intended for her visitor in the parlor to hear, she said, "Thank you, Lord Wroxton, for coming so promptly to reassure me about Mr. Sadler's health. It was most kind of you."

In a low voice he inquired, "I do not quite like to abandon you. Shall I stay?"

Lord Wroxton was prepared, she could see, to manage all!

She smiled sweetly. "No, thank you. I believe I can go on satisfactorily."

Her departing guest once gone, she glanced around the foyer as if to see what candles must have gone out. The day was perceptibly darker. With a suppressed sigh, she returned to her parlor and her guest.

"I rather wonder," the curate said, "that you did not send for me when you believed it best to take your nieces home from the fair. I should have come at once. I am persuaded that you would have welcomed the company of a gentleman to take charge of the affair."

Stung, she retorted, "I was perfectly capable, Mr. Coleraine, of managing, as you say, to put my nieces into the Forsyth carriage and of giving instructions to our old family coachman to drive us the few miles to Forsyth Hall."

He bowed. "As you say. But my thought was particularly intended to express my wish that I could have spared you much agony of mind under the circumstances."

Startled, she exclaimed, "Circumstances? Whatever do you mean?"

"I must say I do not understand you, Celina. You seem to be of the persuasion that a young lady of quality in hysterics and another young lady pushing her way through a crowd of men and shaking her parasol at a most common pugilist is quite the ordinary thing. I cannot quite accept that position." In a more playful manner he continued, "And I am sure that, if this kind of contretemps happens again, the bishop may give you the slightest scold, don't you know."

"The bishop would not dare," she said deliberately.

He smiled ruefully. "Let us hope there is not a great scandal about this. I do regret that you did not think it advisable to send for me. Surely my presence must have mitigated any gossip, for I fancy not a few know of our understanding."

Celina was very near hysterics herself. "There is no understanding between us!" It was a statement that held truth in more than one way.

Mr. Coleraine caught sight of the sherry glasses. "Perhaps tea," he said, "might have been more appropriate to serve Lord Wroxton." Without waiting for a reply, he went on. "I cannot persuade myself that Sadler is aught but a foolish country fellow. I myself have never met him in company."

"He has," said Celina, anger making her voice ominously steady, "excellent manners. I understand he comes from a fime Yorkshire family."

"Yorkshire!" exclaimed Mr. Coleraine, in much the same tone that Eleanor had used on another occasion.

"At any rate," continued Celina as though he had not

spoken, "I fancy that Lord Wroxton's guest need not explain himself to anyone."

"Except his confessor, my dear. You must remember in the future not to underestimate the privileged position of the clergy."

Involuntarily she echoed Jervis's last words to her. "Good God!"

Chapter XX

As Celina might have expected, Edmund arrived early on the doorstep of the Dower House. He seemed to have aged overnight, and although many of his woes were of his own making, yet she felt a sisterly compassion stir in her.

Such a tolerant affection was soon to be tried sorely. Edmund was querulous. "I can't think whatever got into you, Celina!"

"Into me?" she echoed blankly. "I am not aware of any fault in me that should come to your attention. Perhaps you will enlighten me."

"You cannot think it was the thing to watch a display of violence at the fair yesterday."

She had known at the time that she should have removed herself from the vicinity of the Bully and his challenger. But how could she, when her nieces were present and quite obviously in great distress over the spectacle? She remembered that Lord Wroxton had allowed her to make her own decisions as to her own deportment.

"Come now, Edmund," she said, "surely you cannot consider yourself responsible for your spinster sister."

"Not your behavior, Celina, although that, I understand, was sufficiently indecorous as to cause comment. But I cannot think why you got Lyddy and Nelly home in such a ramshackle way."

"What can you mean? I took them home in your own coach!"

He waved that fact aside. "But if you had sent for Coleraine, he could have helped you, and perhaps his presence would have lent some respectability to the affair."

She was aghast and made no secret of her shock. "You've lost your wits, Edmund. Why on earth would I need his permission, as you seem to indicate, to put my nieces into their father's coach and bring them home? John Coachman drove, and I think a footman was up behind. What, pray tell me, could Mr. Coleraine have done more?"

Edmund felt in the wrong in a way he did not understand, except that his sister's blazing gray eyes informed him so. But he was most disgruntled over his wayward daughters, and Celina, being at hand, was easy to blame.

"Coleraine agrees with me that his presence—"

"Oh, this is outside of enough! The day I need a man to tell me how to go on, especially a witless promposity like him . . ." She subsided into silence. Indeed, she could think of no words strong enough to express her flaming indignation.

At length, somewhat calmed, she said, "I promise you, Edmund, had I been in charge of your daughters from the beginning, nothing untoward would have taken place. And if I had been assigned the duty of chaperone, I would admit to whatever blame you wished to place on me. But I do hope you will remember, dear brother, that I happened upon the scene quite by chance. Surely you would not have wished me to play the Samaritan."

"Samaritan?" he echoed blankly.

"Walking by on the other side," she explained impatiently.

"But couldn't you see what a scandal can do to us all?"

"Certainly I am as conversant with the possibilities as you are. What I entirely fail to understand is what you suppose I had to do with it."

Grumbling, Edmund conceded that while he did not precisely blame her for Lydia's waywardness he was not content with the way it had all come to pass. Surely someone, if not Celina, should have done better with the entire episode.

"I could forbid Sadler the house," he said at last.

"But he is Wroxton's great friend!"

"He's been at the house too much, and never with Wroxton. I think Lyddy's too kind to send him away. He's likely to get much the wrong idea about—well, about things. I've seen it coming on, but Eleanor has some maggot in her head about not upsetting Wroxton. It seems she would rather upset me."

He got to his feet heavily, like an old man, and she felt a pang of pity. Poor Edmund! He was no match for his lady.

"I think," he said slowly, "that Wroxton will never come up to the mark. In truth, I can't say I put much blame on him. Every time I see the girl these days she's bawling her eyes out. What man wants to marry a dashed fountain?"

The next days passed quietly. Word came to Celina that Mr. Sadler took no great harm from his encounter with the Bully.

She did not make any overtures toward the family at the Manor. She had indeed seen quite enough of them all. Perhaps they too wished to forget that entire debacle at the fair.

More probably they were engaged in such an uproar over Adrian Sadler, over Wroxton's failure to offer for Lydia, over Lydia's own emotional storms, that they had forgotten her entirely. There was a certain relief in the prospect.

But she was wrong. To see Nelly standing in her salon, her eyes tempestuous, her very posture in the highest degree a sign of distress, brought her quite back to normal. Celina felt a strong pang of regret that this was so.

"Henry's going to India!" Nelly wailed. "I've got to go

with him and I don't see in the least how it can be arranged. I may have to turn stowaway or even take a job as nurse to a sniveling baby, but I'm going to be on that ship when Henry goes!"

Celina made a soothing gesture. "But I see no obstacle. Lydia is soon to be betrothed, and surely your mama will allow you to wed, since Henry is leaving England."

"It's not like that!" cried Nelly, wringing her hands in despair. "He's leaving in a month! And Lydia's *not* betrothed! And I cannot even follow Henry to India and marry him there. Papa would not permit it. I simply must marry him before he goes, and there's no time to waste! Aunt Celina, what shall I do?" She paced back and forth across the small salon.

"You are wearing out my rug," pointed out Celina, no sympathy in her voice. "Besides, you're giving me a headache with all your pacing."

"But Aunt Celina," wailed Nelly, "Lydia cries all the time. Mr. Sadler can't come to the house."

"Why not?" Celina had apparently missed an incident of some magnitude, for Eleanor had been much opposed to such drastic action lest Lord Wroxton take offense. Edmund must have prevailed, but Celina would wager the victory had not been easy or without its moments of high drama.

"Because of that idiotic fight at the fair. Papa sent word to Mr. Sadler not to come again to the Hall. And Lord Wroxton came flying up the drive, all agitated."

"Did he really?" Celina was fascinated.

"Mama saw him coming and thought he looked like a man tormented by love. Don't blame me for such high-flown nonsense. It's what Mama said."

"Tormented?" echoed Celina faintly. "I cannot believe—"

"Pray try to do so," urged Nelly earnestly. "He demanded to see Papa, and Mama thought he was going to offer at last for Lydia and she got Lydia down into the drawing room in her best morning muslin, and he didn't."

"He didn't?"

"Aunt, please don't echo everything I say. He didn't. Offer. For Lydia."

"So?"

"So then he wanted to know if Papa blamed you for that dreadful mess Lydia got herself and me into."

"Blamed me?"

"You're repeating again! And Papa told Lord Wroxton that he had no business to ask about you, because you were betrothed to Mr. Coleraine. You really aren't, are you, Auntie, because he is the dreariest man! And Lord Wroxton told him to go to the devil."

"Lord Wroxton did?"

"I'm telling you, Aunt Celina. I wish you'd pay more attention to me. So Mr. Sadler can't come to the house anymore. Nor will Lord Wroxton, you may be sure." With a quick flash of wisdom, she added, "I am not sure that if I were you I would hurry to visit at the Manor."

"I," retorted Celina with bitterness, "had nothing to do with any of this. I should simply have left you two to your well-deserved fate."

"Well, I wish you would put your mind to *my* fate."

After Nelly had gone, leaving behind her wisps of dramatic despair and threats of coming disaster, Celina lost herself in thought. She had, in truth, much to think about. Allowing for Nelly's normal amount of exaggeration, Lord Wroxton did seem to have behaved in an untoward manner. Telling Edmund to go to the devil! She had often, she realized, wished she could have done as much herself.

She moved back over Nelly's narrative, testing every scrap for its truth and its relation to the next scrap. When she had finished, the tapestry she had put together bore a startling pattern.

If Lord Wroxton was so exercised at the thought she might have suffered unwarranted censure, then he must not be indifferent to her. Edmund had nearly spoiled everything by insisting that she was betrothed to the curate.

How could she ever make Edmund believe she would never in this wide world marry such a pompous fool?

Nelly was not Celina's only visitor that morning. She had allowed her thoughts, weary of trying to make sense out of Nelly's plaint, to travel with Mary and her new husband to London, thence across the oceans to India, land of romance and exotic experiences.

And Celina sat alone in her elegant salon and watched Lydia enter, handkerchief at her eyes, which were swollen from recent tears. She had the strangest feeling that she had lived through this very moment before, many times before. Not long ago Lydia had come in just this same way, complaining that her parents were going to marry her to that horrible old man Lord Wroxton. Now, of course, that match was probably what she longed for above all. Celina, remembering the charming way Lydia sent adoring glances in Jervis's direction, had no doubts at all.

"Dear Aunt," Lydia began, "you don't look the thing. Have you another headache?" Without waiting for an answer, she went on, "I am so miserable. You may not know it, but I long to be married."

Celina said drily, "I believe you."

"But it seems that everything has gone wrong."

It occurred to her that Nelly's version of events as they transpired might well be distorted. If anyone would know whether Lydia was planning to marry, it should be Lydia herself. "Has he offered?" She waited with dry mouth for her answer.

"Oh, no. And I am wretched."

"Has he spoken to you about it?"

A smile broke through Lydia's flawless beauty, lighting it up from within. "Oh, yes. He is so gallant, so interesting to listen to. He has the most entertaining stories to tell. And he loves me."

Her voice dropped on the last words, so that Celina had to strain to hear her. Well, Celina told herself sharply, so much for Lord Wroxton. He had not sought permission from Lydia's father to woo her and he had even told him to go to the devil. But yet he was so lost to propriety as to make advances to the girl herself, aware as he was of her extreme youth and inexperience. No wonder she was beside herself.

A jealous imp prodded her. What kind of advances had he made to Lydia? Had he drawn her into the privacy of a spinney and tilted her face up to his and claimed her lips as his own to do with as he would?

Had he?

"Has he what, Aunt?" Lydia's puzzled expression told Celina that she had spoken aloud.

"Mentioned marriage," said Celina hastily.

"To me?"

"Of course to you, silly. Or perhaps he spoke to your father."

"Oh, no, Aunt Celina. How could he?"

How could he indeed? thought Celina, although for different reasons altogether.

"It would not be proper!" Lydia's violet eyes brimmed over. "Besides, how can Papa—?"

Celina was mystified. She had always made allowances, sometimes past the limit of her patience, for Lydia's slow understanding. But she could not, in spite of long practice, thread the maze of her niece's thoughts, such as they were, to find a coherent core. Later she would wish she had made more of an effort to clarify Lydia's meaning.

She remembered suddenly that she had made a decision or two during her recent solitude. She would no longer be at the mercy of the family at the Manor to plan their entertaining, to do their chores, or, as in the present circumstance, as a stage for their all too frequent emotional dramas. They must all—Lydia, Nelly, even Eleanor—study to overcome a want of conduct. Celina would no longer serve as a receiver of unwanted confidences.

It had been borne in on her that the two elder girls were

only the beginning. She had a vivid mental picture of herself growing grayer, more desiccated, sitting forever in her salon while a succession of nieces burst in with loud complaints and unreasoning demands for help: Sophie, Catherine, Amelia. It was a future not to be contemplated.

But just now Lydia was in her salon, weeping in the most affecting manner, and Celina was hard put to keep her resolve. At length Lydia resorted to a subject on which her opinions were unequivocal.

"And Nelly is such a bore, Aunt, you will not believe it. I am sure that she has already come to tell you all about it."

"All about what?" ventured Celina, fearing there was another aspect of Nelly's predicament that had not been explained.

"I can't think why she wants to go to India, of all places. I think that it must be a very dirty place. Lord Wroxton has told me that it is a very picturesque country, but then," she said shrewdly, "he has not been there himself."

"Nelly," said Celina wisely, "is not going to *India*. She is simply going *with Henry*."

"I don't know what you mean, Aunt. It's Henry's regiment, of course," said Lydia, under the impression that she was explaining everything. "But Mama says no."

"Mama," observed Celina with some tartness, "may find a scandal on her doorstep." Eleanor had never quite probed the depths of Nelly's determination even on smaller things. It was quite possible that she was blind to Nelly's real desperation on this head as well.

After a few moments Lydia obviously steeled herself to a grave confidence. She leaned forward and said in a low voice, "I shall try to be all that Mama wishes me to be. I could not bear it if she turned against me. But I know I could not bear it either if . . ." Her voice died away.

"If what?" prompted her aunt.

"I do not feel very strong. I do want . . ." Then she burst, not surprisingly, into tears again. "But Mama does not care what I want."

Celina tried, though not vigorously, to extract from her niece the meaning of her half-sentences. In the end she gave up. No doubt she would learn soon enough and she had a dark suspicion that she would be happier if she remained ignorant.

After Lydia had gone, Celina ordered tea. "Strong," she told Carrie, "and hot." She was drinking entirely too much tea, she knew, but the alternative was to take to the sherry bottle, and she had not quite reached that state of mind. Although, reflecting upon the morning's events, she thought it likely that turning to drink might become attractive fairly soon.

In a calmer mood she sipped her second cup of Bohea and leaned back comfortably in her chair. So Lord Wroxton had been in a taking about her! How ridiculous! No, how delicious!

Could she deduce anything to her comfort from the report of Lord Wroxton's interview with Edmund? Common sense told her that the narration could well be exaggerated and likely was.

More to the present point, Nelly's captain was forcing the pace. She wondered how much of the urgency of Nelly's wedding was due to Henry. Celina gave a moment to consideration of Henry: a stolid, untalkative man, built on a large physical scale, and competent, from all she had heard, in his chosen career. Did he have as strong a feeling for Nelly as she had for him? With a sigh of relief, Celina realized that this too was none of her affair.

She wished in a way that she had made good on her threat to travel. She could easily have gone to Bath or to London or to any place in the country she chose. She could even, now that the Bourbons sat on the throne again, have gone to Paris. There was a lively English colony resident in the French capital, and surely there would be diverting entertainment.

Any present journey, however, would be only a temporary expedient. A more permanent plan was required against the day when Lord Wroxton came into the Forsyth family by way of Lydia. Any slight hope that might arise in her, based on what garbled word came to her from the Manor, must be stifled. Disappointment she had already experienced and, she believed, overcome. But she dared not risk another blow.

It would have been better to have taken a house in Bath, even for a month or two, thus removing herself from the vicinity of Forsyth Hall, than to hear Lydia's adulation of Lord Wroxton and Nelly's interminable wish to get her older sister married.

Why all the turmoil? Why didn't Jervis simply say, "I wish to wed Lydia," and have done with it? Lydia was more than willing, and Jervis gave every indication of remaining in the region for a purpose—and that purpose must be Lydia.

All that was needed to encompass her complete misery, Celina thought morosely, was to have Mr. Coleraine renew his attentions. An unwelcome thought, triggered, she realized at once, by the sound of carriage wheels on the drive.

A quick glance through the window confirmed her fears. She could not endure Mr. Coleraine this morning.

"Elkins! I do not wish to see any more visitors today. At least—" Suppose Jervis were to come?

"Very good, miss," said Elkins, more knowledgeable than she expected. "I shall deal with the present visitor and then come to take your further instructions."

"Thank you, Elkins," she said, relieved, and moved swiftly to take refuge upstairs.

In the meantime Nelly was brooding. The last few days had gone by far too swiftly, each of them leaving her with a colder feeling at the pit of her stomach. Henry's regiment would leave in a month, and she was determined that nothing would keep her from going with him—nothing!

Even though Henry might not be everyone's beau ideal,

he was Nelly's and had been since they were children together. The five years' difference in their ages had not separated them. Instead, Nelly, whose temperament was volatile in the extreme, found in solid, square Henry the stability she needed. She did not of course lay out these reasons even to herself, but her instinct was sure. She needed Henry. And she would not entertain even the thought of being separated from him by half the world and for who knew how long a time.

Her only hope of achieving her goal respectably was to get Lydia at least betrothed. She considered that her parents might relent sufficiently to deem a betrothal as good as a wedding. And while Nelly would not like to miss her sister's wedding, she had not the least intention in the world of missing her own.

Wroxton must be brought up to the mark.

Nelly was above the average in intelligence, but still her experience of the world was limited. It had not occurred to her that Lord Wroxton might not be susceptible to the manipulations of a young miss not long out of the schoolroom. She knew how these things were achieved in the novels that she read unknown to her father, and she set herself to plotting.

She had planned one episode designed to get her sister betrothed, but it had failed signally. She had not gone far enough, she believed, nor had her plan contained more than half measures.

Half measures would not get the job done.

This time she would not rely upon Lydia, who was incapable of following the most elementary directions, especially if they required invention on the spot. She knew that her sister did very well, provided that she was not set down in a situation that was outside the ordinary.

Nelly's conscience, though rudimentary, was sometimes insistent. She found her sister at her window, looking morosely out across the lawn but seeing nothing. "Lydia, what's the matter?" she asked. "Has—anyone—left the country?"

Lydia turned a tear-stained face to her. "No, but he might as well have gone to Baghdad!"

Nelly, touched by her sister's misery, went to sit by her. "Dear Lyddy, it can't be that bad," she coaxed. "I know you've been wretched. You've not talked to me for such a long time, but I know."

"I've talked."

"Not really talked. But don't give up. You'll be betrothed before—before you know it," finished Nelly cautiously.

"It's impossible," Lydia told her. "I shall never marry if I can't marry him, and Mama will scold, and Papa will look at me in such a sad way. Oh, Nelly, what shall I ever do?"

Nelly was stirred. Besides her own need, she was suddenly aware of a strong urge to arrange Lyddy's life before she herself left for India. Spinster Lyddy, without Nelly's support, might well fade away under their parents' combined disapproval.

"Leave it all to me," said Nelly with enormous confidence. "I'll take care of it."

She left the room. Lydia gazed after her, dimly aware of the beginnings of uneasy suspicion.

It was the moment, Nelly knew, for action. But there was not enough time to set out a plan, examine it from all angles, and allow certain elements to mature. Less than a month left to announce her own betrothal to Captain Gordon, to assemble a trousseau, to plan the festivities attendant upon a marriage—her scheme must be put *en train* at once.

It was as well for Celina's peace of mind that she was ignorant of the entire affair. She would, if made privy to Nelly's plot, have pointed out several flaws, any one of which could bring the entire plan collapsing in ruins about her ears. Nelly, however inexperienced she might be, yet was not naive enough to bring anyone else into her machinations, so Celina was spared.

Lady Gaunt, however, was of a suspicious nature at best. Ordinarily she would have left Forsyth Hall some weeks ago and continued on her usual round of country house visits. But she had a strong wish to see Celina removed from the manipulations of her family and into the safe hands of Jervis. The boy (even though he was past thirty years, she still considered him a mere lad in need of guidance) had made a mull of it at the start. She intended to stay until she had seen him back on the right road.

Having little to occupy her mind, and having no obligations except those she wished to entertain, she was particularly curious about Nelly's odd behavior.

The girl had sustained blow after blow in the last weeks, she knew, and Nelly was not one to suffer disappointment lightly. It was foolhardy in the highest degree for Eleanor to believe that Nelly could be dismissed with no more than a maternal fiat. No wedding for Lydia meant no wedding for Nelly; so thought Eleanor.

Lady Gaunt surreptitiously eyed Nelly with misgivings. The girl was too silent, too brooding, to give any intelligent spectator any sense of ease. The girl, to put it plainly, as Aunt Tibby did to herself, looked about to explode like one of the larger examples of fireworks.

It might be more comfortable to take her departure from Forsyth Hall, to remove herself from whatever disaster might result from Nelly's shattered hopes. But if she were not badly mistaken, the girl had not given up hope of leaving, respectably married, for India at the end of the month. Lady Gaunt was above all things curious. Besides her concern for Jervis and Celina, wild horses could not have dragged her away from the Manor until she learned what mischief Nelly was brewing.

Lady Gaunt had not the slightest doubt that Nelly was concocting some sort of scheme.

The two days moved slowly as snails. Only Lady Gaunt seemed aware of Nelly's state of mind, and Nelly took pains not to be alone with her. Nelly was poised on a knife-edge of anxiety. If the plan did not work, then her life was ruined. At eighteen, it is a sobering thing to contemplate years and years of barren wretchedness. Nelly, true to her nature, refused to consider failure.

Chapter XXI

The notes were sent, the arrangements were made, the day had arrived.

It was mid-morning. Rain continued to drizzle down, as it had for two days. The clouds, still heavy and gray with moisture, descended until the tops of the trees in the park were hidden, and even the chimneys of the Hall ascended into mist.

The grounds were sodden. In the rare intervals between downpours the silence was broken by the monotonous drip of water from every branch and twig. Nelly dismissed the thought of wet feet as of no importance whatever.

She had enlisted the aid of one of the upstairs maids, Molly, whose admiration of Nelly's sprightly and sometimes kindly actions bound her to Nelly as though with fetters.

Nelly took one last look in the glass. Lydia's sapphire cloak looked quite well on her, and she toyed with the thought that perhaps Lydia, overcome by gratitude at the outcome of today's events, might be persuaded to give it to her. She fancied it would serve admirably to wear on shipboard, at least until the ship reached warmer waters.

Molly, speechless with admiration, could only sigh, "It fits you a treat, Miss Nelly." Molly's part in the prank, for as such it had been explained to her, was important. She had been required to steal into Miss Lydia's room, taking care that no one observed her, and remove the sapphire cloak from the wardrobe. It was the one article of clothing that would proclaim Lydia's presence to any member of the family. Molly did not know exactly why the borrowing of the cloak was to be such a secret, but she dared not ask. It was sufficient for her to believe that her vivacious idol trusted her.

Molly placed the cloak around Nelly's shoulders. Lydia was two inches the taller, so the hem touched the floor. Too bad, but it could not be helped. Nelly would simply have to remember to hold her skirts above the wet grass.

Nelly, not ordinarily prone to doubt, abruptly fell into a thought that for the moment paralyzed her. What if she failed? What if the entire scheme fell through? What if her note to Mr. Sadler miscarried? What if . . . What if . . .

This was no time for faint hearts.

With one last look into the glass, and a minor but necessary adjustment of the hood of the sapphire cloak to conceal her features more effectively, Nelly left her room and moved stealthily down the hall toward the back stairs. Lady Gaunt was fortunately lodged in a room on the floor below, along the same corridor as Edmund and Eleanor. There was little chance of running into her.

Nelly reached the back stairs without incident. She paused on the third step from the bottom, listening. The door ahead of her was kept closed, and sounds filtered through in distorted fragments.

She reached another moment when her heart failed her. If she stepped out of the house onto the lawn, she could still turn back with some kind of excuse ready to her lips if she were discovered. A taste for fresh air or a desire for exercise, either would be a plausible explanation, even though the sapphire cloak would not be as easy to account for.

But once across the lawn, through the rose pergola and the belt of shrubbery, and onto the path that led through the woodland to a field beyond and nowhere else, she would be committed to an action not susceptible to any innocent construction. How could she maintain that she was merely strolling, on a day of drizzle and raw wind, wearing her sister's best cloak, through the dripping, leafless woods?

It took only a moment to banish these last few doubts. She hurried across the lawn, her too-long skirts catching on the wet grass. By the time she had reached the edge of the woods, her clothing was soaked above the hem and swirled uncomfortably clammy around her ankles.

She spared a thought for Lydia's best cloak. The damp would stain it indelibly, and she knew that already the garment was ruined. She would not ask Lydia for it even if the scheme turned out profitably, as she expected, for both of them.

"If" was a word she did not care to use. "When" was better.

The path through the woods, trodden frequently when she was a child and now kept open by the younger children, was covered with fallen leaves. The small ribbed beech leaves had been defeated by the constant assault of the rain and now formed a slippery, treacherous covering on the old path. Nelly's foot slid more than once, frightening her.

Ordinarily a complacent young woman, usually obtaining whatever she wished without too much opposition, she had run up against barriers that had foiled her in the gaining of her dearest wish. Mama had been quite gothic in refusing to allow her to marry until Lydia was well launched. In truth, Mama had given signs that she might in the long run be induced to concede that Lydia's betrothal was sufficient evidence of a coming marriage and therefore allow Nelly to wed her captain.

But circumstances, as she had found out, altered cases.

First, there was the unaccountable delay in Lord Wroxton's coming up to the mark. Lydia was smitten with him, it was clear to Nelly. She had said only two days ago that if she did not wed him, she would wed no one. Even though in the last few weeks Lydia had seemed to confide in her much less, yet Nelly never questioned that she knew her sister's mind. Her memory held fast to the occasion when Lydia, past her first dread of the visiting Lord Wroxton, had told her in the talkative interval before falling asleep that she had come to like him, indeed to like him very much.

Therefore there was nothing to keep Lydia from marrying him. Lord Wroxton was not such a fool as to pass up the greatest beauty in England, thought Lydia's loyal sister.

A branch slapped her face wetly.

If it had not been for Nelly's conviction that she was doing what was best for Lydia, the second changed circumstance would have been enough. Henry was posted to India. Nelly wanted to marry him and go along. She believed, as she had decided not long before, that Mama would in the end indulge her. However, a month goes by faster than anyone can conceive, and only four weeks from now would see Henry aboard ship.

But not, she vowed again, without her.

Her victim, even Nelly considered him such, must be now waiting at the far gate of the field beyond the woods, at the edge of Forsyth land. If she could be sure he understood her message!

She had had to disguise her handwriting to make it as much like Lydia's as she could. She did not know whether her sister had exchanged letters with the gentleman or not, but it was foolish to take undue chances.

The note to Lord Wroxton, sent quite an hour ago, should have led him to summon his curricle. He must be doing it this very minute. The note was cunningly devised, she thought complacently, to indicate to the dilatory suitor that he was in danger of being forestalled by his great friend.

If this scheme, whose simplicity guaranteed its success, did not work, then . . . Nelly quite firmly banished the notion of failure. It *had* to work! She would rest a bit longer—Adrian would come to no harm by waiting—and then she would continue across the field to the gate.

Her thoughts moved ahead. There would be a satisfactory confrontation between herself, head down and face concealed by her hood, and Adrian, who without question expected to meet Lydia. This, of course, was the reason for the readily identifiable cloak.

And then, before she was forced into too many awkward explanations, Lord Wroxton would arrive on the scene, breathing fire and furious with Adrian for cutting him out with Lydia.

Suddenly she was dismayed. Suppose Wroxton called Adrian out? Duels, she knew, were forbidden in London; this was the country, but perhaps the same rules applied. Well, she would just have to meet that question when it arose.

She was early. She had feared to meet obstacles on her flight from the Manor and had allowed more time than, as it turned out, she needed. In a few moments she would leave her comfortable seat and begin the long walk across to the gate, putting her great scheme to the hazard.

It was well that she was not privy to certain actions now *en train* at the Hall. The scheme was in its essence simplicity itself. Lydia (at least her sapphire cloak) would be seen to be eloping with Adrian Sadler, and Lord Wroxton would pursue them and hurl mighty threats at Sadler and clasp Lydia to his bosom and swear he would speak to her father at once.

It would not matter to Nelly if Wroxton in his wrath rang a fine peal over her. All that mattered was sailing with Henry, married, of course.

But as a novice in spinning fine plots, she did not take sufficiently into consideration the human tools with which she had to work. Molly, delighted with her new position of confidante to the dashing Miss Nelly, could not arrange her features into the noncommittal mask required to avoid discovery by the sharp-eyed Mrs. Pardoe.

Molly sauntered into the kitchen. "I'll just die if I don't have a cup of tea."

"A cup of tea, is it? And what'd you do all morning that earned it?"

Mrs. Pardoe believed in a strong and oppressive way with the maids in most circumstances. This practice came easily to her with Molly, a witless wench if she ever saw one. Head full of airs, fancying herself a lady's maid to Miss Nelly, when all she was was apprentice to Lady Forsyth's Emma.

"I been upstairs with one of the young ladies," said Molly. Mrs. P. didn't need to think she was going to find anything out. Miss Nelly's instructions was what she was doing, never mind anybody else. She was proud of her discretion.

"There's your tea," said Mrs. Pardoe. She cast another look at Molly. The girl was up to something, she'd be bound. There was no mistaking that *shiny* look to her. A cat after catching a bird, that's what she looked like. The cook was not one to be put off by the likes of Molly.

"And," said Mrs. Pardoe, advancing ominously, "What was you doing?"

Long habit dies hard. Mrs. Pardoe's frown had reduced Molly many times to stammering apology. And this time was no different. Miss Nelly, after all, was not standing over her, and Mrs. Pardoe certainly was. Molly made what was for her a valiant stand.

Even though she shrank back, she blustered, "Just doing what Miss Nelly said I should." She clapped a hand over her mouth in dismay. "I wasn't supposed to say Miss Nelly," she whispered guiltily. It was all over then for Molly.

Mrs. Pardoe was as well as a skilled cook an accomplished questioner. Years of practice on Pardoe himself and on the serving girls had honed her technique to a razor's edge.

A very short time later she stood back, hands on hips, and surveyed the wretched Molly, head down and sobbing on the table. "So that's it. And you're party to it, you silly. Think on it. What's going to happen when Miss Lydia hears about it, stealing her fine blue cloak and all? To say naught of sending the footmen here and there to a fine gentleman's house! And when the mistress finds out, glory alone knows what's to do. If I have my way, you'll be sent packing and without a character!"

After several more satisfying minutes of haranguing the derelict maid, and after finding Pardoe and giving him certain instructions, Mrs. Pardoe bustled up the back stairs, panting with the unaccustomed exercise. Two flights up, she moved in the stately fashion befitting her position down the hall to Miss Lydia's door.

Pardoe would already be making Lord Forsyth privy to the actions, if not the intentions, of his second daughter. From now on the problem was his lordship's. But she could not let Lydia, her favorite among the girls, pass the rest of the day in ignorance of what could be a scandal to shake the rafters. The least she could do was to warn her. She rapped on the door and was invited to enter.

At the last minute Mrs. Pardoe suffered an access of caution. She had only that foolish Molly's word for what had gone on, and it was not past Nelly's mischief-making guile to tell the maid a Banbury tale simply for her own amusement.

"Yes, Mrs. Pardoe. What is it?" asked Lydia, surprised to see her. There were not many occasions for the cook to visit any of the daughters of the house. In fact, Lydia could not remember one.

Closing the door behind her in a portentous manner, Mrs. Pardoe asked, "Did you—that is, was you wanting me to brush down your pretty blue cloak, miss?"

"My blue cloak? Whyever for? That's Molly's work." Then, beginning to be suspicious, Lydia continued, "I haven't seen Molly this morning. Is she not well?"

That provided the proof that Mrs. Pardoe needed for her own satisfaction. "Miss, I know it's a funny thing to ask. But, not to put too fine a point on it, where is your blue cloak?"

"In the wardrobe, of course. Mrs. Pardoe, I don't understand."

"Neither do I, miss." Her expression had turned grim. "But if you don't mind, I'd like to see it."

Lydia, while slow of understanding as a rule, was not stupid, particularly along lines with which she was familiar. Molly's absence and Mrs. Pardoe's presence both rang alarm bells in Lydia's mind. The sapphire cloak was in the wardrobe, where else?

Where else, indeed?

It was not in the wardrobe. Mrs. Pardoe looked through the many garments hanging in the enormous double-doored closet and could not find it. Lydia, unbelieving, searched more frantically.

"My favorite cloak! Where is it?"

She turned, wide-eyed, to Mrs. Pardoe. "You know where it is. I know it!"

Solemnly Mrs. Pardoe nodded. "Yes, miss. I have a good notion where it's gone to. Out in the woods."

In a short time Lydia was informed about the morning's events. The cloak borrowed, notes sent to his lordship, and to Mr. Sadler . . .

"Adrian! Surely not! What can it mean?"

"I'm sure I don't know, miss. But Pardoe will inform your father, and he'll sort it all out, I know."

Her duty done, Mrs. Pardoe returned in an aura of satisfaction to the kitchen. She had nothing to do now but wait upon developments.

Lydia on her part was in a less calm frame of mind. Knowing her sister very well indeed, she shrank from contemplating the depths of her perfidy. Stealing her favorite cloak was bad enough, although nothing to alarm. But, as Mrs. Pardoe had informed her, a footman had been sent to Beechknoll twice, once with a missive to Mr. Sadler—if she understood Mrs. Pardoe, that was yesterday, and once this very morning with a note addressed to Lord Wroxton.

What could it all mean? she thought again. Her powers of imagination were not strong. She could not explain Nelly's actions, but it was clear even to her that some scheme was afoot. And if the scheme involved the gentlemen at Beechknoll, then quite simply it must needs involve herself.

She had moved again to the window, where Mrs. Pardoe had found her, while her thoughts churned. Thus it was that she caught a glimpse of the most dreadful sight she could imagine: Papa crossing the lawn toward the outbuildings and carrying a gun!

Lydia shrieked faintly. And suddenly she was in the grip of the most powerful emotion she had ever experienced. Papa, hearing about Nelly from Pardoe and starting out to deal with the situation—with a gun!

Lydia threw on her squirrel-lined cloak and sped down the stairs. She hoped she would meet nobody on her way, for she had not time to make up a story that would suit. She ran across the foyer and out the door, and one pair of eyes watched her as she flew down the driveway on her way to the Dower House.

Chapter XXII

The constant downpour of recent days had had its effect upon Celina's mood. No longer able to deny that she had a strong feeling for Lord Wroxton, cursing herself daily for refusing his offer, and alternating between contemplation of her foolishness and the very unwelcome conviction that he was destined to marry Lydia, she was in a dangerous frame of mind.

She was determined to leave the neighborhood before the idea of Jervis's marriage became fact. She turned over various plans in her mind and rejected them all. Added to her restlessness was the knowledge that for the first time in her life she had lost control of her emotions. She believed she was sacrificing her own wishes for the anticipated happiness of her niece. She did not go willingly to the block.

The appearance of Lydia pushing past Elkins and bursting into the salon, sobbing for breath and bearing every evidence of great distress, did nothing to lighten her aunt's mood.

"Aunt! You must come! Nelly—it's dreadful!"

Aware of the butler's avid eyes, Celina said calmly, "Pray close the door. Lydia, I shall not listen to a word until you can calm yourself."

Indeed, had she been willing to listen, Lydia could not have made coherent sense. Her flight down the driveway had been accompanied by pictures that struck horror to her heart.

At length Lydia was able to relate to Celina all that she knew of Nelly's machinations. Celina's heart sank. She should have realized that Nelly was desperate, and done something. But what could she have done?

"Papa will shoot him!" Lydia wailed. "We cannot let him! He's done nothing! He's the kindest, most wonderful man in the world, and Papa's going to kill him!"

Celina was startled out of her gloomy thoughts. Edmund a killer? Nonsense. Especially would Edmund not kill Jervis, even if there was cause. The kindest most wonderful man in the world had surely not alienated his future father-in-law to the point of murder, had he?

Spurred to drastic measures, Celina took her niece by the shoulders and shook her vigorously. The golden hair slid out of its pins, and curls cascaded riotously. Lydia lifted drowned violet eyes to Celina and said miserably, "What shall I do if he's killed? Aunt Celina, we've got to stop him!"

For once Celina did not object to the Forsyth's habit of demanding assistance from her. If Edmund indeed had set out with a gun, then there was no time to lose. Steps must be taken, and at once. Celina bit her lip. There was something about Lydia's narration that did not ring true. Not that Celina doubted the girl, not at all. But experience argued that Lydia might be wrong. It was under the circumstances not an unreasonable conclusion.

"Lydia, I am sure you must be mistaken. Now, child, don't look at me in such a way. We'll just drive over to Beechknoll, and you can see that no harm has come to him."

The girl's eyes brightened. Celina hoped Lydia would never know what it cost to be made once again privy to her adoration of Lord Wroxton. When this was all straightened out, Celina promised herself while ordering her phaeton and donning cloak and bonnet, she would indeed leave the Dower House. France was not sufficiently distant. She had heard that winters in Florence were exceptionally pleasant.

Celina drove well and swiftly. What seemed to Lydia a stretch of some hours was in reality only a matter of less than thirty minutes. Lights, required by the gloom of the lowering clouds, streamed from the windows of Beechknoll.

"You see, Lydia," said Celina bracingly, "all is in order here. There's no sign of your father. You've made a tragedy out of a simple misunderstanding, and how I will explain this visit to Lord Wroxton is more than I know."

Lydia was somewhat heartened at the absence of bodies lying around before the entrance to Beechknoll. But she had been too frightened to lay aside her fears yet. "Please, Aunt, inquire. I'll hold the reins."

Celina, alighting from the vehicle, hesitated. Lydia was frightened to death of horses, so her distress was genuine. Celina dared not leave her with the reins. Her dilemma was resolved when a stableboy appeared suddenly, and with relief she turned the horse over to him.

"Wait for me here," she ordered. "I shall not be long."

She squared her shoulders and started up the steps. The door opened before she reached it. She hesitated, seeking words for the servant, but it was Jervis himself who stood in the doorway, and light from the hall behind making him loom larger than life and to Celina equally formidable.

"Where have you been? What is the meaning of this?" he roared. "I can't believe that you've entirely lost your wits! I hope you have some kind of explanation!"

Unused to being roared at, Celina took a step backward. Then her fading courage turned into rising anger. "I have indeed, Lord Wroxton, and if you were to cease imitating the Bull of Bashan, you may care to hear it."

He seemed to shrink as he recognized her. "My—my abject apologies," he stammered, hot with embarrassment.

"I did not see . . . I did not think it was . . . I believed you to be Adrian."

"He is not with you?"

Once more master of himself, Jervis said, "He is not, or I would not be standing on my own doorstep roaring, as you rightly put it, like a bull, would I?"

"I daresay," she rejoined. "I think, Lord Wroxton, that we have a matter of mutual concern. And your doorstep is not be the appropriate place for a discussion."

He looked beyond her to the curricle. "Is that—"

"Lydia," said Celina, pleased to note that her voice remained steady "She is, as a matter of fact, my present concern. She, that is, and the news she brought to me."

"We had best go inside," he agreed, becoming grave in his manner. He stepped to the curricle and handed Lydia down. Celina walked into the hall.

"Now then, my dear," he said to Celina when they were seated in his drawing room, which bore the signs of some years of neglect. "Some refreshment, perhaps?"

"Oh, no," cried Lydia. "There is no time. Papa will be here and then—"

"Papa?" echoed Jervis. "Lord Forsyth is always welcome, as I am sure he knows, but I do not quite see why his arrival should spell doom."

Celina, however, pursuing her own line of thought, found herself facing a puzzle. If Lydia was so concerned about Jervis, why, seeing him whole before her, was she still nearly hysterical?

The answer came to her as a wild surmise, but she dared not risk another disappointment and refused to contemplate what logic was bringing her to.

"Where is he?" demanded Lydia.

Celina said sharply, "Lydia, have you lost your wits? Can't you see . . ." Her voice trailed away. She caught Jervis's eyes on her, amusement lurking in them, and she fell silent, struck with wonder. Not—*not Jervis?*

"I see you and I have reached an identical conclusion," he said quietly to her. "Now perhaps, if you can enlighten me, we may proceed to the crux of the current crisis." He smiled warmly at her, and she began to feel quite odd. "Then, if you please, we may return to our own concerns."

"Why don't you do something, Lord Wroxton?" fumed Lydia. "He may be lying dead—bleeding—" She broke off in a sob.

"Lydia," said Celina. "Pray let me explain." She turned to Jervis. She suddenly was breathless, so aware of his nearness that she was unable to think.

He leaned forward and touched her hand. "Later, my dearest, we shall have all the time in the world. At the moment I think you must tell me what so exercises your niece."

"Of—of course. Your note must be part of that wretched Nelly's scheme. I am persuaded of all girls, she must be—but as you say, that must wait."

"I trust we will never be required to discuss the girl," he murmured.

She shot what she considered a quelling glance in his direction, but he seemed unaffected by it. "Nelly's captain, you know, is posted to India, and it seems Eleanor remains adamant. . . ."

Under the circumstances Celina managed a creditable narration. It was, she thought later, something of a feat, since beneath the prosaic words detailing Nelly's sordid schemes, or as much as was presently known to her, she was aware of a strong thrumming of happiness and wonder just under the surface of her thoughts. But there would be time hereafter, so Jervis said, as soon as this foolish business of Lydia and Nelly and, surprisingly, Adrian was settled.

"Adrian must have received a letter, one that drew him out to a rendezvous," summed up Jervis. "Purportedly signed, do you think, by Lydia?"

"I do not doubt it. But your own letter, sir?"

Glancing at Lydia, who was engrossed in her own unhappy reflections, he murmured, "Let me rephrase your question. *But your own letter, Jervis darling?* Does that suit?" Vastly gratified by the rosy flush that crept up her cheeks, he continued, "But we must deal with the matter at hand first. And then . . ."

The expression in his eyes left no room for doubt as to his subsequent intentions. But she could not easily capitulate, for she had dwelt too long in the twilight of uncertainty. "She seems to prefer Adrian," she said tentatively. "Does this make you unhappy?"

He realized that he held in his hand the thread to the maze that had surrounded Celina and kept her from him. Some day he might understand all the storms that had driven her here and there. Sometime in the future, when he felt so sure of her that nothing could trouble the tranquil waters, he might ask her. But just now he contented himself with a simple question. "How can you be so foolish, my dear love?"

Lydia brought them back to the point. "I cannot think why—you must not have listened to me. Papa was so angry about dear Adrian at the fair and he said such things to him! I couldn't even see him, not even for a minute in company—And, oh, Lord Wroxton! Do something! Papa had a *gun!*"

"Quite right," said Jervis in a brisk manner. "We must prevent your papa from doing anything rash. I myself hold little hope that he will come to his senses unaided."

Jervis took the reins. Celina sat beside him, with Lydia next to her. "I think this arrangement more expeditious than getting out my own carriage," he told Celina. "Besides, the fewer servants in our confidence the better."

"I agree entirely," said Celina, pleasurably aware of his hard-muscled thigh pressing against hers because of the crowded seat.

Following Celina's directions, Jervis turned the last bend before the rendezvous appointed by Nelly. The rain had lessened during the past hours, and visibility was unimpaired.

Ahead of them in the road opposite the gate stood a phaeton and horse. At the side, almost on the grassy verge, they saw Lydia's sapphire cloak, its occupant clearly irate, and the subject of Nelly's diatribe, Adrian Sadler.

Jervis pulled up. "At least we need not follow them to Gretna Green."

"As if there was any question of that," retorted Celina. "If Nelly does not go to India, she will not go anywhere."

"Do you, my love, hold the reins, while I go to rescue Adrian." His laughing eyes held hers for a long moment before he put the reins into her hands.

Their bemusement with each other shut out much of what was happening around them. She was dimly aware of Lydia's jumping down from the seat and screaming at Nelly. Nelly, expecting Wroxton to arrive in high dudgeon at the idea of his prospective bride running away with Adrian Sadler, was startled to see him strolling calmly toward them in great good humor.

"What is this nonsense, Adrian?" he said. "If you wanted Nelly, all you had to do was ask her father."

"But," sputtered Adrian, clearly going over ground he had already covered at length with Nelly, "I do not want her."

"Well, of all things!" exclaimed Nelly, indignant. "I am not such an antidote as that!"

"I would have put in a word for you, you know," continued Jervis, enjoying himself hugely. "You will remember I offered."

Lydia joined the trio. "Nelly, I shall never speak to you again! Papa is coming! He's got a gun! How could you do this to me?"

"I have done nothing to you," retorted her sister with spirit. "I just wanted to make Wroxton jealous, to make him think you were going to elope with Adrian."

"Ah, but, Miss Nelly," said Wroxton, "I do not wish to marry Miss Lydia."

Nelly stared at him. "You don't? Then why are you still at Beechknoll? Why did you believe my note? How can you not want to marry Lydia?" she exploded with sad inattention to grammar.

Celina, regarding the scene before her as merely a necessary prelude to a highly satisfying conversation, and more, with Jervis—*Jervis darling?*—hardly heeded it. Suddenly the sound of carriage wheels in the road clutched at her attention, and she turned to look behind her.

Eleanor's landau, Edmund holding the reins, was approaching at speed. Celina had time only to think that at least Edmund couldn't shoot while he was holding the pair before Jervis heard the carriage and turned sharply.

"Forsyth," he called. "At last. Now perhaps we can sort all this out."

Edmund secured the reins and climbed stiffly down. "I have a few things to say to you, Wroxton. Trying to meet Lyddy in the spinney wasn't enough for you. You've got to commit an abominable outrage like this—dragging me out in the rain and the mud, and the servants in an uproar, and I don't even want to think what Eleanor will say."

He was brought up short by a spectacle that stretched his credulity to the utmost. His beautiful daughter Lydia, hair streaming like a schoolgirl's over her shoulders, stood, arms extended, in front of that fellow Sadler, screaming at him—at her own father, "Don't shoot, Papa! I love him, Papa! Don't shoot him!"

Bewildered, Edmund said, "Why should I shoot? I don't even have my gun. Besides, I wouldn't trouble myself with that ninny. I'd shoot Wroxton!"

Jervis managed to preserve his calm. "Is it possible, Forsyth, that you still have no grasp of the situation?"

"I understand well enough," retorted Edmund. "A mishmash, that's all. I admit I don't understand why Lyddy is screaming about shooting and Nelly—that's not your cloak, Nelly—and Aunt Tibby dragged me here to bring Wroxton up to the mark. I'll tell you the truth, Wroxton, I'm tired of all this business. If you want Lyddy, just tell me. You can have her. If you want Nelly, well, there I don't know." With one hand he wiped the expression of befuddlement from his face. "I'll tell you one thing, though.

It'll be a cold day before I get chased out to another of these junkets in the rain."

Lady Gaunt, having descended from the carriage, took a decisive hand in the affair. "Edmund," she said vigorously, "you do not listen to what anyone tells you. You never did, even when I told you at the start that Eleanor would not make you a good wife."

She was suddenly the center of fascinated attention.

"Did you really?" murmured Celina. "I did too." She felt Jervis's gaze lingering on her and fell silent.

Edmund succeeded in blustering, "Women don't ever get things straight, anyway. There's Nelly set on that army fellow, and here's Lydia with her arms around that ruffian boxer Sadler—" Edmund's eyes bulged. "Good God, Lyddy! Get your hands off him!"

Lady Gaunt stepped into the middle of the group. "Now, Edmund, hold your tongue!" She emphasized her recommendation with a firm push on his chest. She quelled Nelly, whose lips were open to speak, by a fierce glance. She regarded Lydia without favor, but decided against possibly, by ill-timed chiding, setting off a hysterical outburst.

"Now then, Edmund, listen to me. I shall speak extremely clearly, so that even you cannot make a muddle of it. Nelly is to be married at once. I shall give her her trousseau for a marriage gift, since India's climate will require an array of new gowns."

"Aunt Tibby!" breathed Nelly. "Can you manage it?"

"Of course," said Aunt Tibby grandly. "Now, Edmund, you are to allow Lydia to be wed. You're glancing at Wroxton, but you couldn't be more addlepated if you think they would suit."

"But you sent for him to marry Lydia," said Edmund quite humbly.

"Disabuse yourself of that notion, Edmund. Not for a moment did I contemplate such an event. Never mind what I expected."

She glanced at Jervis, seeking information. His slight

smile told her what she wanted to know. Her initial plan, to make a match between him and Celina, was accomplished.

"And," she resumed, "I shall wish to see Lydia married to Mr. Sadler."

Edmund looked up quickly. "I don't know, Aunt Tibby. Eleanor is going to kick up a fuss about that."

"That shows only Eleanor's ignorance. I am sure Mr. Sadler will be able to satisfy you as to his means and his breeding. At any rate, you may tell Eleanor that I do not wish to abuse her hospitality, which has already been extended for a longer time than I expected to stay. My departure will follow directly on the weddings."

"Weddings?"

"Lydia first, since the priority seems to signify to Eleanor, and then Nelly. Both in the next fortnight. Edmund, I am persuaded that obtaining special licenses will present no obstacle. I confess I am quite anxious to move on, I think this time to Bath."

Aunt Tibby had performed something of a miracle, Celina decided, observing the swift dissolution of the group, knotted, before Lady Gaunt took charge, in a tangle of misunderstandings and faulty apprehensions.

Edmund's landau, holding Lady Gaunt and Nelly, turned in the narrow road. Facing the road toward Forsyth Hall, he pulled up his pair and called to Adrian, "I agreed to let Lyddy ride with you in your phaeton. Engaged couple, after all. But"—he swung his arm in a wide gesture—"you go ahead of us. And mind you don't get out of our sight!"

If Celina believed Lydia was excessively happy before, when speaking of Lord Wroxton, she had been mistaken. Here and now was bliss that blinded the onlooker, and not only on Lydia's features but on Adrian Sadler's as well.

After the others had left, Celina looked down at Jervis, standing beside the phaeton. He was watching her intently. "My love?" he said at last, tentatively, questioning.

For answer, forsaking all propriety, she put her free hand on his shoulder and bent down to kiss him. She felt his lips moving under hers, his arms encircling her. For a long time the only sound she heard was the dripping of water from the bare branches of the trees and her own heart pounding in her ears.

At length he let her go. "Give me the reins, dearest," he said, "while you straighten your bonnet. I wish you could take it off, but do you know, it's begun to rain again."

It had, in fact, begun some few minutes before, and now was coming down hard. So delightful had been that long kiss that she had not noticed the showers beginning.

Possessed of the reins, he turned the phaeton and started it, much more slowly than Edmund's carriage, toward the Dower House. He drew her to him to protect her as much as he was able against the weather. She laid her head on his shoulder and felt all the restlessness and the turmoil and the tension and the great unhappiness of recent weeks drain out of her, like the rain running off her heavy merino cloak.

He kissed her forehead and then, when she lifted her lips to his, kissed her more thoroughly. "A good thing," he chuckled quite a long time later, "that your horse knows the way to go."

She laughed shakily. "As," she said, "I do too. Now."

About the Author

Vanessa Gray grew up in Oak Park, Illinois, and graduated from the University of Chicago. She currently lives in the farm country of northeastern Indiana, where she pursues her interest in the history of Georgian England and the Middle Ages. She is the author of a number of bestselling Regencies—*The Masked Heiress*, *The Lonely Earl*, *The Wicked Guardian*, *The Wayward Governess*, *The Dutiful Daughter*, *The Innocent Deceiver*, *The Reckless Orphan* and *The Duke's Messenger*—available in Signet editions.